Return to Cheyne Spa

DAISY VIVIAN

ZEBRA BOOKS
KENSINGTON PUBLISHING CORP.

ZEBRA BOOKS

are published by

Kensington Publishing Corp.
475 Park Avenue South
New York, NY 10016

First Zebra Books printing: December, 1990

Printed in the United States of America

The new Zebra Regency Romance logo that you see on the cover is a photograph of an actual regency "tuzzy-muzzy." The fashionable regency lady often wore a tuzzy-muzzy tied with a satin or velvet riband around her wrist to carry a fragrant nosegay. Usually made of gold or silver, tuzzy-muzzies varied in design from the elegantly simple to the exquisitely ornate. The Zebra Regency Romance tuzzy-muzzy is made of alabaster with a silver filigree edging.

KING OF HEARTS

"I think even you must admit, sir, that a slightly tarnished reputation is a potent lure for any woman," Elinor challenged.

"A much overrated attraction," the Tyger protested. "Young women — even perfectly ordinary ones — are quite a bit more sophisticated in matters of that sort than you allow."

Lady Augusta bit her lip to keep from laughing. "What a rogue you are. I admit that you and your sort provide spice in society, but I would never trust the judgement of any young woman where her safety is concerned."

"Lady Augusta, I hardly know whether to feel set down or flattered," the Tyger said with a wry chuckle. "From the expression on the face of your pupil here, I have the impression that she too has absorbed a good deal of your prejudice toward impoverished, but high-minded gentlemen."

Elinor was quick to answer. "That is possibly because I have been acquainted with too many game-sters, sir. You forget my background. I am aware that the truly dedicated gambler will play with anything: spades, clubs, diamonds — even hearts."

Dobyn all but whooped at this sally and threw his hands up protectively. "Help, help, I concede. No man could ever hope to win a match against the two of you together, I fear."

THE BEST OF REGENCY ROMANCES

AN IMPROPER COMPANION   (2691, $3.95)
by Karla Hocker
At the closing of Miss Venable's Seminary for Young
Ladies school, mistress Kate Elliott welcomed the invita-
tion to be Liza Ashcroft's chaperone for the Season at
Bath. Little did she know that Miss Ashcroft's father, the
handsome widower Damien Ashcroft would also enter her
life. And not as a passive bystander or dutiful dad.

WAGER ON LOVE   (2693, $2.95)
by Prudence Martin
Only a rogue like Nicholas Ruxart would choose a bride on
the basis of a careless wager. And only a rakehell like Nicholas would then fall in love with his betrothed's grey-eyed
sister! The cynical viscount had always thought one blushing miss would suit as well as another, but the unattainable
Jane Sommers soon proved him wrong.

LOVE AND FOLLY   (2715, $3.95)
by Sheila Simonson
To the dismay of her more sensible twin Margaret, Lady
Jean proceeded to fall hopelessly in love with the silver-
tongued, seditious poet, Owen Davies—and catapult her
entire family into social ruin . . . Margaret was used to
gentlemen falling in love with vivacious Jean rather than
with her—even the handsome Johnny Dyott whom she se-
cretly adored. And when Jean's foolishness led her into the
arms of the notorious Owen Davies, Margaret knew she
could count on Dyott to avert scandal. What she didn't
know, however was that her sweet sensibility was exerting a
charm all its own.

for Judith Kneitel
. . . . at last!

=1=

"Either I have my money in full tonight, my girl, or you'll sleep in the street and that is final!"

Elinor Hardy winced as the door of the roominghouse slammed firmly behind her. Mrs. Smeed had every right to be outraged, of course, because she had been paid nothing for more than a month. Elinor sighed and her lovely grey eyes took on a worried look. Perhaps tonight the luck would change: new surroundings, new employment, new associates. She re-collected herself and squared her shoulders proudly. She might go down, but it would not be without a strong try. Resolutely, she stepped out along the pavement, oblivious to the stares of the Londoners who rarely saw a beautiful young woman in evening dress walking the streets at teatime.

Indeed, she was beautiful: small of stature but exquisitely fashioned with a kittenish face topped by a mass of chestnut hair. "A regular pocket Venus," she had overheard one elderly gentleman remark about her to a friend, and she had not been at all displeased. But her looks had told against her in her previous professions. No sensible gentlewoman wants to employ a companion or children's governess who will present a danger amongst the men of the household. Now it was to be seen whether she could charm gentlemen enough to make them careless at their games.

Never in her most droll expectations had she thought she would find herself employed in an establishment such as Lady Bassingbrook's gambling hell, but there it was. Even a friendless gentlewoman must eat; and, even if it meant becoming déclassé, dealing out cards and raking in coins was far better than starving.

Lady Bassingbrook's house was in Jermyn Square, an ideal location in that it was close to Piccadilly and the great houses there, yet discreetly removed from the ways of common traffic. Elinor set a pleasant smile upon her lips, lifted her chin and walked self-confidently up the steps. She rattled the door-knocker, a lion's head with a sneering expression; and the portal was grudgingly opened by a manservant whose look exactly matched that of the knocker.

"Yes, miss?" He asked in a superior tone. "We do not accept visitors until nine o'clock."

"My name is Elinor Hardy," she explained. "I have been employed by her ladyship as a hostess and dealer."

"Indeed?" he asked. His tone implied that, in his valuable opinion, her ladyship must have taken leave of her senses. "Then you must, in future, use the side entrance." He opened the door a further inch or two, leaving her just enough room to slide through. "However, since you are already here, you may as well enter this way."

He closed the door behind her and turned the key. "We discourage early visitors, you see. That is why you must use the other entrance. I expect you must have been here before when I was not on duty. The day-maid never knows what she's about. I have spoken to her of it more than once."

It seemed to Elinor that this imparting of privileged information to a complete stranger was quite unusual. She put it down to personal eccentricity on the gentleman's part and followed him silently through the elegantly appointed rooms while he kept up a running commentary as though he were a hired guide.

"Here are the lounges, nicely appointed, as you can see. Her ladyship likes to encourage the gentlemen to relax as if they were in their own homes.

"This is a smoking room," he said as they passed a parlour with an immensely long table standing upon legs of shining oak and many drawers and cupboards underneath. "That monstrosity you see is a shuffleboard. There is also a billiard table in the second floor smoking room. Very popular, both of 'em. Too popular, if you ask me. Cuts down on the house games, you see." It was evident that he took the possible profit and loss of the establishment very much to heart. "The gaming tables with which you will be working are situated in the old ballroom on the first floor." He turned into a narrow corridor and knocked upon a door.

"Yes?" asked an irritable voice.

The manservant raised his brows to Elinor and rolled his eyes. "There is a young person here, your ladyship, name of Miss Hardy."

"Miss Hardy? Who is Miss Hardy?"

The man's voice assumed a timbre of infinite patience not altogether appropriate in a servant, no matter how trusted. "I believe you employed her this morning, madam. When I was out," he added reproachfully as if this were somehow a breach of faith. "Will you see her, madam?"

The door was flung open, and Lady Bassingbrook stood there scowling. "I don't know why I put up with you, Jenks. Of course I will see her."

She turned a cold smile upon Elinor. "So happy to meet you again, my dear. I am not at all certain this isn't a great mistake, you know. I have never employed a female dealer before, and I cannot say what effect it will have on my clientele. If they don't like it, or if I don't like it, you are out. No questions asked."

"Yes, your ladyship, just as we agreed this morning," said Elinor smoothly. "I am sure I shall do my best."

"So long as the terms are understood." The proprietress surveyed her with a sharp eye. "So this is the costume you have selected? Turn around, please. Yes, I expect you will do so far as the look of you is concerned. Men always seem to be unduly impressed by that dark-haired, soft-eyed appearance, as though butter wouldn't melt in your mouth. You manage it well. I daresay you will cut quite a swathe. Just be certain your flirtations do not interfere with the gambling."

Her ladyship was a tall, rather angular woman, well into her second youth, with a large quantity of unconvincingly golden hair which she wore, against all fashion, tumbled atop her head higgledy-piggledy and skewered with long pins and gaudily bejewelled combs. Only a liberal application of "lead and red," white paint and rouge, alleviated the inroads the passage of time had made upon her countenance. However, she had a brash, somewhat horsey manner about her which Elinor suspected went down well with sporting men who would find her friendly and accommodating until the time came to settle scores. Then, whether winners or losers, the gentlemen would discover how little camaraderie counted in the final reckoning.

"I hope I shall know how to conduct myself as a lady should, madam," Elinor promised, only to be quite surprised by Lady Bassingbrook's reaction.

"Not too much of a lady, I hope, my dear. You are not a Cyprian, we know. Do bear in mind that a smile goes further in our game than an upturned nose. It is possible, I think, to be respectable without becoming a prude."

"I am sure it is," Elinor agreed but resolved that if that were not possible, her career with Lady Bassingbrook would be very short indeed.

Her ladyship tapped her closed lips with a forefinger and stared speculatively at the girl. "I believe we forgot to mention your family, my dear."

"I have none, if your ladyship pleases. My mother died in giving me birth, and my father was taken not above a year ago."

"I daresay it was he who taught you the cards? You have no other connexions in London?"

Elinor hesitated before answering, "Not in London nor anywhere, so far as I am aware, madam."

Without further comment, her ladyship yanked open the door of the office and leaned into the corridor. "Jenks!" she bellowed. "Come to me!"

The manservant appeared from around a corner. "Yes, madam?" Elinor heard him ask with suave equanimity. "Your ladyship called?"

"Tour the girl about the house. I want her to be completely familiar with all of the public rooms before this evening. Make sure she is introduced to the others, the house servants now and the dealers as they come in.

"You are to be friendly with all, Miss Hardy," she warned, "but intimate with none. Do I make myself clear?"

"Perfectly, your ladyship. I am not to allow any friendships I may make to interfere with my work."

Lady Bassingbrook chucked her under the chin with a thin smile. "What a delightful girl you are. I hope you find your footing. I rely on you to do your utmost straight from the start, of course. It is a principal belief of mine that we go on as we begin."

"I shall do my best, madam."

Her ladyship nodded without expression. "See that you do, my dear. Very well, then, Jenks, take her away."

Once he had begun to relax a bit, Jenks was a rum old fellow, Elinor discovered; and he proved to be a mine of information about the household. He introduced her to the servants individually and with great ceremony, then enlarged upon the weaknesses of each as they moved away.

"No better than she should be," he said of a fluttering parlourmaid; and, "I suspect she has a secret bottle," he observed of Cook when she had gone to fetch a bit of cake and Madeira for the newcomer. "You'll see what I mean. Her rum cake is a mite too rich for an abstainer, and her whiskey cake is sinful."

"Then you do not indulge in such things yourself, sir?" Elinor asked with a smile. Jenks pretended to horrification.

"I, miss? Certainly not. On my free days I am a preacher of the gospel. Sinful liquor never passes my lips."

"How inspiring in this day and age," murmured Elinor. "Not even a little wine for your stomach's sake?"

He gave her a sidelong glance. "I hear the subtle levity in your voice, miss. Yes, I do have a glass of wine from time to time, a canary or a bit of port; but only, as you say, for medicinal purposes. I feel it incumbent upon me to set an example to the household."

Cook returned with the wine and cake for Elinor and set the snack carefully upon a snowy napkin. "You are certain you'll have nothing yourself, Mr. Jenks?" Cook looked at him askance. "My cake come over you too rich all of a sudden? I never knew you to refuse it before."

She stood, arms akimbo, watching Elinor clean every crumb from the plate. "There now, that's what I likes to see, a young lady with an appetite. I'd offer you more, but I don't like to spoil you for supper. What? You didn't know? Oh, yes, we allus eats before the guests arrive. No time for it later on, you see. I'm too busy serving up little tidbits for the customers to be thinking about the likes of us as well."

"You had best come along with me, now, miss," Jenks urged. "We'll finish with the upper rooms of the house. I daresay you'll get your footing quickly enough and feel quite at home here in no time at all. Just you stay on the right side of her ladyship and you'll be right as rain."

Cook snorted derisively at that. "You'll not find *that* so easy, my dear. She's not so easy to please."

Elinor was not certain what footing she might find; but, she reminded herself, beggars cannot be choosers. It would be to begging she'd soon be reduced if this last chance went awry. She was determined to succeed. That first evening, however, was not to be an easy one for her.

The former ballroom, now filled with the bulk of the gaming tables, was as elegant as any Elinor had seen since childhood. High-ceilinged and beautifully proportioned, it was decorated with a series of paintings of the Judgement of Paris: that biased decision which brought in its wake the fall of Ilium. The goddesses, here depicted in all their physical glory, were actually, Jenks whispered after glancing about to be certain no one was near enough to overhear, the leading Cyprians of the previous generation. He identified them, one by one, rolling the names about his tongue with obvious relish. They still came to gamble at the tables beneath their likenesses, he continued, but the scandal meant little to Elinor who had no idea who the women were. It seemed, however, that the beauty of the goddesses must make it evident to any spectator just what a difficult time Prince Paris had had of it.

As for the gaming floor, there were tables for roly-poly or E.O., French hazard, faro, macao, chemin de fer and *rouge et noir*. The room was immaculate with brass, copper and glass aglow. The air was faintly scented by attar of roses which Elinor found a trifle cloying. Looking toward the ceiling and the great fans, now inactive, she guessed that this evening the moving air would soon dissipate the scent.

"We accommodate three hundred," Jenks informed her proudly. "More, if necessary, but the atmosphere becomes a bit frantic then."

"What time do we shut up shop? Dawn, I suppose?"

Jenks nodded and sighed disconsolately. "As near as makes any matter. Her ladyship is loath to surrender a sixpence while there is yet a pigeon upon the premises."

"You are saying her ladyship is greedy, sir?" Elinor thought of her own empty pockets. "I am sure that as a businesswoman, she sees it in quite a different fashion. We women, I fear, do not have the advantages inborn with the male of the species. We must make our way as best we can."

"Very touching, I am sure, Miss Hardy," said a chilly voice from behind them. It was Lady Bassingbrook, her mouth pursed up in annoyance. "I believe you have duties below-stairs, Jenks."

The manservant, who seemed to stand in very little awe of his mistress, bowed half ironically. "As you wish, milady. I was merely showing the young woman about as you instructed."

"And serving as the town gazette as well, I'll be bound," the proprietress snapped. "I will speak to *you* later."

"As you wish, milady," Jenks responded coolly and sauntered toward the service stair.

Lady Bassingbrook regarded Elinor with a mixture of reserve and contempt. "I fancy I can defend my own motive and actions, miss. Your requirements here are merely these: to look pretty and guileless, to dress well and to play the games with sufficient skill to keep our rather extreme expenses under control. You understand me?"

Elinor nodded, retaining her composure despite the biting tone her employer had elected to use. "I hope you will have no reason to complain of me, your ladyship. I shall certainly do my best."

Lady Bassingbrook snorted. "If I have reason to complain of you it will be once only. A second complaint will find you on the street again. I am bowing to fashion in employing you only in the hope that it will increase trade. If it does not—or if you are more trouble than you are worth—I shall not hesitate to wash my hands of you."

She then began a circuit of the room, head turning ceaselessly from side to side, examining every aspect, her sharp eyes missing not the slightest bit of dust or chair placed awry.

"One thing, milady . . ." the girl called after her hesitantly. Her ladyship did not turn around.

"Yes, I have not forgotten," she answered, as if she had been waiting. "I remember what you told me when I hired you this morning. You require a small sum before you return to your lodgings or you will be put into the street. Is that not correct? I cannot believe your landlady would be so unkind, but we shall see how best to deal with it. You may not find the work here to your liking, after all. You may not last out the evening, and I have an antipathy to paying good money to persons who do not meet my standards. You are on trial, you know. Your destiny depends only upon you."

She glided to a small service table which held an array of crystal wine goblets and held one of them up to the light, rotating the stem between her fingers as she searched for streaks or smudges.

"Yes," she repeated almost absently. "All depends on you."

= 2 =

ELINOR'S PROBATIONARY EVENING began well enough. The gamesters straggled in a few at a time and by ten of the clock the establishment had taken on an almost festive air. In the soft glow of candlelight the handsome rooms transcended themselves, becoming to Elinor's glamour-struck eyes a kind of wonderland populated with beautifully dressed women and distinguished gentlemen. She found that, by her employer's decree, she was not restricted to one table of play as were the male dealers. Instead, she was expected to mingle among the guests, accommodating herself to whatever game they might fancy, be it faro, basset, E.O. or chemin de fer.

Unfortunately for Lady Bassingbrook's expectations, the presence of a female dealer was not the novelty she had hoped, her ladyship being a bit behind the time. Other establishments had already taken the edge from the notion and, with it, the drawing power of notoriety. Consequently, Elinor found her role at first to be merely a utilitarian one. This suited her very well, but did nothing to enhance her position in the eyes of her employer who had hoped the girl would cause a stir. However, this relatively placid condition did not last for long.

Elinor had been dealing from the box at the faro table to a mixed set of dandies, Corinthians and young bucks. They were, in truth, a rowdy lot; but the girl was pretty and apt of tongue. She had been popular enough in her young life to have learned the control of young men. The truth was that, below their high spirits, they were in general gentlemanly and recognised Elinor as one of their own, temporarily down on her luck but capable of rising as easily as she had sunk. In the world of gaming, this circumstance could happen to any of them, and they thought none the less of her for it. She was a lady, after all. Nothing could alter that.

Once or twice when one among them flew a little close to the fire with a dubious suggestion, his fellows quieted him easily enough with the thrust of an elbow and the hint that bad behaviour was "not quite the thing, old fellow, don't you know?" For the most part, they were merely young and callow. Unfortunately, the exception to that rule was to prove something of a problem.

He was a man of about fifty, well enough turned out by his tailor, but with a head of glossy black hair so even in colour it hinted of the dye pot. He was long-jawed with a pasty and unhealthy complexion. Cold, gooseberry-coloured eyes flanked a great beak of a nose. Elinor did not recognise him, but she guessed from his condescending manner and the respectful way some of the bucks responded that he was known to them as a person of significance.

He played as any casual gambler might do, tossing his money down with a carelessness that bespoke a plentiful reserve. Winning or losing seemed all one to him. Because Elinor had enough challenge at hand in fending off the banter of the younger men, she contented herself with treating him fairly but with no special attention. She was, therefore, somewhat nonplussed to realise that, little by little, one place at a time, this man was edging closer and closer to where she stood. Eventually, he was at her left hand, and there he stayed.

The game went on. The coin was dispersed or raked in by the pretty dealer. The younger men came and went, but this older one remained. He said nothing to her beyond the ordinary cant of betting. Yet Elinor found his very presence beginning to unnerve her, almost as if he emanated some malign and stultifying influence. Her aversion grew all the greater as she came to recognise him embarked upon a pattern of either trying to catch her eye or brush against her. This latter assay was accomplished so unobtrusively that, had it happened less frequently or in some other circumstance, she would have passed it off as merely accidental. When, at length, his arm ventured so close it rubbed against her own, she drew back as if she had been burned but did not fail to notice the faint leer upon his coarse features.

"A bit touchy for a table-girl, eh? We shall have to work on that."

He spoke in an undertone. Still, his voice carried well enough to make some of the other players turn their heads. One of these, a tall, young fellow with dark hair cut à la Brutus about his attractive face, passed a quiet remark to the companion next to him; they both looked at the older man with contempt. Whether her accoster was essentially craven, or if he had some reason to preserve his composure, Elinor did not know. He scowled fiercely upon the pair of youths and, at his next loss, flung himself away from the table with a muttered oath. Elinor smiled at the two young men with a good deal of relief.

"You mustn't let that sort of blackguard put you out, miss," said the Brutus-cut. "That kind will take any advantage he can so long as you seem to allow it."

"You ought to watch out for his sort," the other chimed in. "I expect you are still quite new to this?"

"Very new," the girl admitted. "Only two hours of it so far." She straightened her shoulders self-confidently all the same. "I daresay I shall soon enough learn the pitfalls and how to avoid them, but your kindness is most gratifying."

"I expect most of the other chaps have been able to see that you ain't the sort he thought you were," said the first of them. "You cannot blame him in a way. One or two of the gels in the other houses are not above finding that sort of advantage. But it is evident you are a lady, no matter what circumstances have brought you here."

"I expect you are correct, young Marston," said a handsome woman of early middle years who had come up to the table. "In fact, I have the impression that this young lady and I have been introduced."

The young man she had so addressed drew back to make room at the table. "Your grace! What a pleasure it is to see you. I had no idea you had come up to town from Cheyne."

His companion's throat was cleared significantly, and Marston took the hint.

"I beg your pardon, old chap. Your grace, may I have the honour of introducing my friend, Mr. Acorn? John, Lady Augusta Trenarry, Duchess of Towans."

Young Acorn was visibly impressed and bowed deeply. "Is the duke with you tonight, madam? I have always held him in high regard."

Lady Augusta raised her eyebrows slightly. "Have you? I had fancied my lord kept himself rather out of the public eye." It was not said unkindly but might have served as a set-down to anyone less ebullient than John Acorn.

"As to that, madam, his Lordship's ward, Mr. Wetherbridge, is a friend of my older brother. They were in the same house at Oxford."

"Ah," said the duchess noncommittally, "dear Gerald," then turned to Elinor. "Speaking of school, I believe this is Miss Hardy whom I have known since she was a very small girl."

At Elinor's consternation Lady Augusta laughed merrily. "No, no, my dear. Do not rack your brain. I knew your dear father. He was a friend of my first husband; and you, if I mistake me not, were at school with my own nieces, Barbara and Lavinia. Is it not so?"

The other players at the table, who might justifiably have complained, simply drifted off when they discovered the play preempted by social precedence. One can hardly request a duchess to "play or pass." The only alternative was to pass on oneself and find a livelier game.

"Oh, I say," Acorn enthused. "You don't mean Lady Barbara Pentreath?" He nudged Marston with his elbow, which earned Acorn a cutting glance from the Brutus-cut's dark eyes.

"Acorn," he muttered, "try not to be more of an ass than you can help." To her grace he apologized. "He don't mean to be a goat, you know, madam, but Lady Barbara *did* rather take London by storm last season."

The duchess smiled and patted his arm. "I know it all too well, dear boy. I have had such a steady trail of suitors through my drawing room as you would not believe." She considered. "No, perhaps you *would* believe it, after all, since I remember having seen your own face there on one or two occasions."

Acorn looked at him with interest, and young Marston flushed.

"True, your grace, but I fear I was quite edged out by the crush. I believe Lady Barbara scarcely knows my name."

"Oh, I am certain she at least knows that. I have the impression she keeps a very close tally of the gentlemen who call. Rather like a shooting party list, you know. It helps her to remember who is who."

It occurred to Elinor Hardy that this might be considered a cold-blooded manner of dealing with the crowd of one's admirers, but she deemed that might be necessary under the circumstances. Even she was aware that Barbara Pentreath had last season burst upon the ton like a blazing star, quite sweeping all before her.

Elinor and Barbara had, at school, given each other rather a wide miss for the most part, mutually civil but instinctually aware that they were too radically different in nature for friendship. Elinor had always felt she might have made a friend of Barbara's sister, the more serious Lavinia; but the difference of a year or two in age precluded that as well. In fact, Elinor had few friends at school, she thought ruefully. Papa's fortunes being what they were, she had never stayed in one place very long at a time. When his finances failed altogether at last, they had rather been thrown upon their uppers. Elinor loved her father very much, but it was not hidden from her that like most gamblers he was a vastly improvident man.

Elinor saw with alarm that Lady Bassingbrook was heading in the direction of their table, and she had a determined light in her eye. "Please, your grace. Gentlemen," Elinor pleaded. "Would you not prefer to go on with the game?"

The duchess turned her head, following the direction of Elinor's eyes. "Why so alarmed, my poppet? It is only Bassingbrook. You are not afraid of *her* surely?"

"At the moment I fear she controls my future, madam," Elinor replied. "I cannot afford to fall in her estimation, or I may find myself on the street."

The duchess gave her another questioning glance, but led the young men back into the play. "Come, gentlemen, who will challenge me in this? What stakes shall we set for a side bet, Marston?"

"Whatever you like, your grace," he replied gallantly. "So long as it will not quite beggar my father. He has grudge enough against me as it is."

"I shall pledge you a guinea, madam, if I may," put in young Acorn boldly, watching to see how she would react to such a small sum.

The duchess took it well. "Then," she said, "let us see the colour of your money if we do not wish our pretty dealer to be put into the street."

Before the proprietress had time to make her way across the room, the play was rising and others were hurrying curiously in their direction, eager for a bit of fast play. Lady Bassingbrook prowled suspiciously about but, not being able to put finger on a precise complaint, was forced to move away again.

The game then, of a sudden, became fast and furious

with cards riffling out quickly on one or the other of the two piles. A palpable current of excitement coursed among the players. In a brief lull while a winner was being paid, a deep, masculine voice spoke into Lady Augusta's ear. "Good evening, your grace. What a pleasure to see you in London. Is the beautiful Lady Barbara with you?"

Her grace acknowledged the salutation of this handsome man with the hawkish features by the slightest inclination of her head, meanwhile, scarcely taking her eyes from the gaming table.

"Mr. Dobyn, I believe? No, my niece is not with me, and I fear I shall be going away again almost at once."

The man's amber eyes seemed to twinkle with humour as his full lips curved into an engaging smile. "Somehow, your grace, I guessed such would be your answer. How could that happen? Do you suppose I am psychic?"

The duchess laughed and tapped him on the forearm with her fan. "What a most transparent rogue you are, sir. I wonder that you have not caught your heiress long before now and made your peace with all the mothers of the world."

He spread his hands deprecatingly. "It has not been for lack of diligence on my part, madam. I do assure you. Yet I apprehend that a great many mothers see me as an ever-present danger. Now why should that be?"

Tyger Dobyn was well known in the sporting community. His handsome face showed no evidence of his several years as a gentleman pugilist, but his fine physique could have come from nothing but intensive training. Though that fact fluttered the heart of many a young woman, it was a danger in the eyes of London mamas.

The duchess retained an amused composure. "I am sure I cannot imagine, sir. Would you join the play? I am certain my young friends will allow you room."

"Oh, I say, Tyger, do!" crowed the young Mr. Acorn. "Come play here by me. It'll be a feather in my cap."

"Do you mean to say that losing money to me in side

bets will set you up, young sprout?" Dobyn asked with a chuckle. "If that be the case, let us play, by all means. I'll be pleased to take as much blunt as you have in your pocket. How about you, Marston?"

"No thank'ee, sir. I'll restrain my pride to wager against her grace alone."

As it happened, on this particular evening, the house took all and no one won: a pleasing circumstance for Lady Bassingbrook. Presently Lady Augusta was hailed by an acquaintance and flew across the room to greet her. A high roller made a stir at another table, and Acorn and Marston ran off to catch a piece of him. Only Tyger Dobyn was, for the moment, left with Miss Hardy. Now that they were alone, he looked her over carefully.

"You are new on the circuit, I think?" he asked. "I know I have not seen you before. Have you worked one of the houses outside of London?"

He said it so casually yet with such insolence that Elinor was quite stung and all but snapped back at him. "This is my first night and my first table, sir. So far as the circuit is concerned, I do not know what the term means, though I fear I can perhaps guess."

The Tyger clapped a hand to his forehead in mock abjection. "Egad! I have insulted you? Another lady fallen upon evil times, is it? Well, my gel, if there were as many destitute ladies manning tables in gambling hells as claim they are, I fear the aristocracy would be fair depleted."

His response startled her out of her pique, and she almost laughed. "You really do not believe me? I assure you, sir. I have indeed fallen on very hard times, whether you accept my antecedents or no."

He gave a little bow. "And this is your very first night of work?"

"Exactly."

He barked an incredulous laugh at that. "Well, then, dammee, the way you make the pasteboards jump about, I can only think you have a natural aptitude. If you are a mere tyro now, I shudder to think what you will be in a year."

"Come back in a twelvemonth then, sir, and we shall see if I have become a paragon. I daresay by then I shall be running my own game and not merely dealing. If I have the aptitude you say, best to employ it as I can. Would you not agree?"

Lady Bassingbrook, seeing that Elinor was no longer under powerful protection, moved toward them and spoke sharply to her. "I pay you to deal or circulate, Miss Hardy, not to waste your time chatting with people like the Tyger. You will forgive me, sir," she added, turning to the gambler. "I must remind you that I hold a fistful of markers from you. Will I be deriving any satisfaction from them soon, I wonder?"

"Bless you, Bassie, I hope you will." He favoured her with a broad wink. "Unless you wish to forego them for fancy?"

Her ladyship was not amused. "Any fancy you might have held for me was dissipated long ago," she said coldly. "If you cannot redeem them, I must find a less pleasant way of pressing you for them."

He sighed, not altogether in mock plaintiveness. "Oh, Bassie, you couldn't do that, could you? To me? Heaven forfend, you know I am good for my markers. You have never lost for holding them yet, have you? I have always redeemed them eventually."

The proprietress was at the point of responding, when there was a flurry of words and the sound of a hand striking against flesh. The gambler and her ladyship swung about to see Elinor shrinking from the abuse of the large-beaked man with the dyed hair. His mouth was spilling out a stream of invective as he clutched her wrist to prevent her escape and Elinor's cheek was a blazing red.

"You insolent trollop!" he screamed at her. "How dare you speak to me in that manner? You and your kind should be honoured that a man of substance even deigns to acknowledge your existence, let alone shows you a little kindness. I could have taken you out of this place to be treated like a queen; but, no, you think yourself too fine, too high-and-mighty for the likes of a mere member of Parliament, eh? Well, I shall soon have you out of here, like it or not!" He stared wildly about. "Where is the owner? You there, where is the owner? Find Lady Bassingbrook for me at once!"

The proprietress came scurrying across the room. "I am here, Mr. Gully. What in the world seems to be the trouble?"

"*Seems* to be, madam? Would I summon you on a mere whim?" He pointed contemptuously at Elinor. "It is this wench of yours. She is insolent and, I expect, a cheat as well, though I could scarcely expect you to be concerned about that."

"I am no such thing!" said Elinor stoutly, rubbing her wrist as she finally freed herself from him. "This—man made me the victim of an indecent proposal, and I had the good taste to reject it. He had not been cheated in the least. All that is smarting is his pride, and not his pocketbook."

"See here, Gully," said the Tyger, coming toward them. "Everyone knows that you operate on any new skirt you can get between your fingers. Why don't you leave this one alone? She seems too nice a lass to be treated so badly."

The M.P. sneered at him. "I expect you are in league with her, eh, Dobyn? Was that your scheme, to get me into her clutches and then try for a bit of blackmail? I know your sort, you'll stoop to anything."

Tyger Dobyn's lip curled. "What a sorry piece of offal you are, Gully. And to think you represent some benighted borough which trusts you. I'd call you out, but you're too slimy to dirty my hands with."

To Lady Bassingbrook he said, "The girl is perfectly innocent, you know. His honour is an old hand at this sort of thing. He uses his position to inflict himself on those who have no defence. I expect he didn't think to find this one so spirited."

But her ladyship's face was as hard as flint. "I am not interested in your opinion on the matter, Mr. Dobyn, and I would be very glad if you were to quit my establishment and to be so kind as to avoid it in the future. You have ever been a source of trouble to me, and it is time to bring that to a close.

"As for you," she sneered at Elinor, "I only know that you have insulted one of my patrons. I suspected from the first it was a mistake to hire you, and now I see that confirmed. You may leave my house at once, if you please. I have no use for the likes of you."

"I will be glad to leave you, madam," said Elinor calmly. "If you will be good enough to tender my pay for the evening, I will trouble you no longer."

"Your pay? Surely, you must jest at my expense? I do not pay for the privilege of losing custom to your wicked temper, miss. Get out at once. You are lucky that I do not summon the watch and have you carried out. What insolence!" She began to slap ineffectually at Elinor with her hands.

"Pay her no mind, Miss Hardy," said the calm voice of the Duchess of Towans. "I fear that, though Lady Bassingbrook is possessed of a title, she retains a tradesman's mind. Come along with me. There must be many pleasanter places of employment than this one."

The duchess held out an arm to the Tyger. "Will you be good enough to escort us to my carriage, sir? I find the present atmosphere rather fetid."

Lady Bassingbrook capitulated immediately. "Oh, but your grace, if I had known the girl was under your particular protection . . ."

"That hardly applies, does it?" asked Lady Augusta. "Has patronage now become a substitute for honesty? They say the revenue of your establishment is falling, madam, and that your fad has passed you by. I believe I can guess why your former patrons have chosen to divert themselves elsewhere. *I*, for one, shall certainly do so in the future and suggest to all of my acquaintance that they do the same."

Taking Elinor's hand protectively under her arm, while extending her own hand to the Tyger, the duchess made a stately progress through the gaming rooms toward the stair. For a moment a hush fell over the assembly, then, one by one, other players began to follow her grace's lead, falling in behind her—not all of the gamesters, of course, but a substantial portion of them.

Lady Bassingbrook was devastated to see them go. "Oh, wait. Please, wait. This is all an unfortunate mistake, a mere contretemps. Please, won't you stay and allow me to . . . Oh, please, sir. Please, your lordship. Please, madam. Don't go, I beg you. I'll keep the gel. I'll make it right with her. I'll even engage more females to deal if that is what my patrons want."

Gully moved to follow the others, knowing when to quit an unpopular scene, just as if he had not begun it all himself.

"And where are *you* going, sir? It was all for you, and now you are deserting me as well?"

The Parliamentarian stared her down. "You *are* a very fool, madam. Do you think I would stay with you now? I have a reputation to consider, and I must be careful in what company I am seen."

Jenks leapt to attention as he saw the company descending the stairs. His self-satisfied little smirk suggested that news of the debacle had already filtered down to him. He would enjoy Lady Bassingbrook's discomfiture.

"Shall I send a boy for your grace's carriage?" he asked eagerly.

Lady Augusta considered. "What do you think, Mr. Dobyn? It is such a fine night, and the Peverly so near. Mightn't we walk?

"You don't mind, do you dear?" she asked Elinor.

"Whatever your grace wishes."

"Tyger?"

The pugilist unconsciously flexed. "I daresay I can stand as protection for two ladies for a square or two," he said.

"Oh, but I . . ." Elinor began, then subsided into silence.

Truth to tell, she thought, she had no better way to spend her evening. She began to consider ways by which Mrs. Smeed might be persuaded to let her lodge only a few days more.

"Oh, you will be coming with us, child. Of course you will. This whole affair has had you as its centerpiece. You can scarcely elope and leave us with our curiosity unsatisfied."

"Curiosity, madam? Curiosity about what?"

The duchess enveloped the girl in the warmth of her personality. "About *you*, dear heart. Everything about you. Now come along to please me. Do."

3

"Do you mean to say that you literally have nowhere to sleep?" the duchess asked incredulously. "Then you will, of course, come to my hotel until we decide what is to be done with you." She surveyed the girl with a friendly regard. "You are hardly dressed for a night in St. James's Park."

"I would not presume to impose upon your generosity," said Elinor sincerely, then stopped.

Even if she could bring herself to beg mercy of Mrs. Smeed, the respite would be temporary at best. Elinor had nothing of any value left to sell or pawn and no prospect for employment, save tramping from gambling house to gambling house in hope of the same sort of position she had with Lady Bassingbrook. She would still do that, if necessary, but it could wait until tomorrow. In the meantime, through her grace's generosity, Elinor might enjoy some of the luxury of the old days when Papa was flushed with victory and they were able to afford the Peverly Hotel in Piccadilly or Grillon's in Albemarle Street.

She had always loved the Peverly best because the staff had taken pity on a lonely child and treated her like one of their own, allowing her to range throughout the hostelry without let. There was not a nook or cranny from attics to cellars that Elinor did not eventually explore. Unlike the more stately Grillon, returning to the Peverly, even for one night, would be like going home.

"Thank you, your grace," she said gratefully. "You are very kind."

The duchess, of course, noticed the hesitation and divined the ensuing process of thought. She pressed the girl's arm in a comforting way. "Perhaps, with a little thought we can settle your immediate future as well. There must be something in this world a well-bred young woman can find to do, eh, Tyger?"

"Oh, I am as certain of that as that the sun will rise," Dobyn answered, his amber eyes warm. "It remains only to determine in what arena Miss Hardy will choose to test her talents."

Their contemplation of this ambiguity was interrupted by a hallooing and thudding of boot heels as the Messrs. Acorn and Marston hurried after them.

"I say, Tyger, sir," Acorn accused. "It is hardly the act of a sporting man, is it, to abscond with the two handsomest ladies in the place?"

Young Marston was more circumspect. "I trust your grace will excuse us, but it seemed pointless to remain at Bassingbrook's when your departure has effectively extinguished the evening there. Is everything quite all right? Will Miss Hardy be secure?"

"You must say if there is anything we can do to help," Acorn insisted. "Perhaps we could all contribute to an annuity?"

"I believe that will not be necessary, Mr.—Acorn, is it?" answered the duchess kindly. "But what I do apprehend that we need, Miss Hardy and I, is the company of another gentleman or two at supper. Mr. Dobyn is considered a great hand with the ladies, but perhaps three and two will make the odds more equitable. You do not mind, Tyger, if they join us?"

"By no means. I expect the Peverly will be much honoured by just such a quintet as we shall present them. But," he warned the younger men, "we chaps must all be on our best behaviour so as not to compromise the duchess's position as a guest there."

The two youths gave their word eagerly. As they made their way out of Jermyn Square, young Acorn quite bubbled over at the prospect before them. "I've never supped there but once with my guardian, and he did the ordering, you know. I expect the score is steep, eh? Have you a yellow George or two to lend me, Marston? Lady Bassingbrook took my last. Good guineas they were, too," he added ruefully. "The last of my birthday *douceur*. I expect I shall be on strait-strect all term unless old Rowley softens his heart toward me."

"Oh, as to that," scoffed Marston, "he's not so bad as you make him out to be. He has always come through for you before, hasn't he? As guardians go, he ain't the worst, I believe. He's been a bit behind sometimes, but you've never starved."

"There is no question of starving tonight, in any case," said the Tyger. "I have a pocketful of blunt from Bassie and you shall all be my guests." He chuckled. "I don't expect she would have been so glad to see the back of me if she had known how much I had taken from her tables tonight."

"Well, sir, I don't know," Acorn protested. "I am glad you won this evening and all, but it is one thing to hit up old Marston and quite another to badger you. One doesn't like to drag the gods, as they say."

"Oh, I shall still respect you in the morning, if that's your worry," laughed Dobyn. "Besides, I daresay it will be your own coin you'll be getting back. It will merely have gone from pocket to stomach."

"No need to fuss, anyway, John," said Marston. "I have plenty. A whole pocketful of Georges, in fact."

"Now I do not see how that can be, since we played together all evening."

"Luck of the game, old fellow. I liked different numbers than you, that is all."

"I see that everyone was lucky tonight but me," John Acorn said mournfully. "Well, everyone but me and Miss Hardy. I daresay your state is worse than mine, miss. Or at least more worrisome."

"No, even Miss Hardy need have no worry at all," said the duchess. "Fate has brought us together tonight, of that I am sure. But let us hurry along. I suddenly find I am quite ravenously hungry."

Minor changes had been made in the entrance rooms of the Peverly since Elinor was last there, but not in the warmth of welcome.

"Why, Miss Elinor, is that you?" asked the hall porter as he flung open the door. We was speakin' of you only a day or two ago and wonderin' how you was gettin' on. I must say, you looks well, miss." Then he saw the company in which she was travelling. "Oh, yer grace, forgive me. And Mr. Tyger, sir. It is just that Miss Elinor is one of our own, you might say."

"So you know me, do you?" asked Dobyn with a small smile.

The porter seemed astonished at the suggestion that he might not have done. "What, not know such a sporting gentleman as yourself, sir? Why, you've made me many a penny, sir, and I thank 'ee for it."

"Well, I don't put up my fists anymore, you know," the Tyger said. "I leave that to the younger fellows. Perhaps one of these chaps will provide you with some entertainment one of these days."

"Aye, sir, they might," the porter acknowledged. "But they won't hold a candle to you, I *am* sure. One of the great gentlemen pugilists, you was, sir, and I am sorry that you gave it up. But good luck to you."

"And to you, my friend."

The party moved on into the lobby, and young Marston seized the opportunity to edge nearer Dobyn. "I say, sir, shouldn't you have slipped him something?"

"Oh, do you think so?" asked the Tyger.

"Well, he was awfully attentive, wasn't he?"

Tyger raised a cautionary finger. "Yes, but he was attentive as a man and a sportsman, my boy, not as a servant. A hall porter may, indeed, be given a little something; but I would hesitate to so insult a sporting man. It isn't the thing, you know. D'you follow me?"

Marston's brows wrinkled. "Yes, sir. I think I do. I shall certainly keep it in mind. I hope you don't think I was being forward, sir."

"Not at all, my boy."

The man at the desk flashed a friendly smile at Elinor and spoke a word to a boy who went running off immediately. Then the clerk came forward to bow to the duchess.

"Good evening, your grace. I hope everything is entirely to your satisfaction?"

Lady Augusta had been duchess a short enough time still to be amused at such extreme deference. Only a year or two ago she had been scrabbling to find husbands for her two virtually penniless nieces and, though never snubbed, was often accorded rather perfunctory service."

"Quite satisfactory," she acknowledged. "Are we still in time for a bit of supper?"

"Oh, certainly, your grace," he answered with an implication that the kitchens of heaven would have been opened had she wished. "Will you go in?"

"We will, but first I must speak to you privately about a matter." She waved the others casually on into the supper room and took the man aside, speaking to him urgently for a moment as he listened attentively, nodding his head all the while.

"Only a trifling matter," she explained as she joined the others. "I wonder what is on the bill of fare."

Elinor looked up from the menu card. "The quail is quite pleasant, I believe," she said, then suddenly stood up, holding out her hands to the man crossing the room. "My dear Mr. Johns, how very good to see you!"

The Peverly's manager wore a face wreathed in smiles. "My word, Miss Elinor, it has been a long time . . . too long."

The girl flushed, partly from pleasure but also from some slight chagrin. "You must know, sir, that the fortunes of the Hardy family have always been variable."

His penetrating grey eyes read her expression with concern. "But, my dear child, you should have come to me. Why, you are a part of the Peverly legend. Sometimes when I am in the upper corridors I fancy I can still hear you scudding along the hallways, screaming with high-spiritedness." Then his tone fell. "I was sorry to hear about your father."

"You were always a good friend to us, Mr. Johns. I know Papa always appreciated that. Everyone here was so kind. The other girls at school seemed to have aunts and uncles by the score, but they were all envious that mine were the staff of the finest hotel in London."

She turned back toward the table. "Your grace, may I present to you the manager of the Peverly?"

Lady Augusta nodded amiably. "We are already acquainted, my dear. Mr. Johns and the staff have been most hospitable."

"Mr. Acorn and Mr. Marston, my new friends," Elinor continued, "and—"

"Oh, Johns doesn't need an introduction to me, do you, Wyvern? We've run across each other at too many meets to be strangers."

"Quite right, Mr. Dobyn," the manager answered with a faint reserve in his voice that made Elinor glance quickly at the gentleman pugilist by her side.

The Tyger was certainly an arresting man. Still, she knew he had a distinctly raffish reputation. From her childhood, the manager had been her self-appointed protector.

She patted his hand reassuringly. "We all met this evening at Lady Bassingbrook's."

Johns seemed mollified by that and took his leave, enjoining the waiters to especial attention.

Unfortunately, as Johns quit the supper room, a less pleasant personage arrived. Jasper Gully made his appearance at the door. Upon his arm was the sort of woman no respectable establishment would have admitted under any circumstances. It was not that she was not beautiful. In her hard-faced way, she was very beautiful indeed; and her costume was in the very forefront of fashion. Yet, there was about her an inescapable air of the profession she followed.

"What do you mean we cannot be admitted, my good man?"

Gully's voice, trained for public speaking, carried easily throughout the supper room. In its wake, the civilised clatter of china and silver hushed.

Through the stillness came the question, "Do you know who I am, sir?"

After so many years at the Peverly, Mr. Johns took the challenge in stride. "Yes, Mr. Gully, I know who you are, but I fear I am unacquainted with your companion."

"She is my guest, sir. That should be enough." the M.P. thundered.

"I regret, however, sir, that *you* are not presently a guest of the Peverly and our supper room is not a public one."

Gully's glare swept the room, surveying the diners with scorn. "And, I suppose, all these are presently registered inhabitants of the Peverly?" His beaky nose seemed to quiver with outrage, and his thick forefinger stabbed the air as he pointed accusingly. "Including, I expect, that young piece sitting at the table in the corner? You are quite high-and-mighty, sir; but I happen to know she is no better than she should be and was discharged from her position in a gambling hell this very evening!"

Mr. Johns's gaze followed the pointing finger, and he only half stifled a smile. "I fear you are quite mistaken, sir," he said frostily. "The young lady to whom you seem to be referring is Miss Elinor Hardy, granddaughter of the

29

old Earl of Glastonia. I have had the honour of knowing her since she was a small girl. With her is the Duchess of Towans, whose husband, I believe, holds considerable property in the district for which you stand. Both ladies, sir, are presently guests of the Peverly. The gentleman is Mr. Tyger Dobyn, of whom, I daresay, you have heard. I should not wish him to believe I intended an insult if I were you, Mr. Gully, even though you are a member of the Commons."

Taking advantage of Gully's momentary stupification, Johns herded the pair toward the door. "I know you will understand and forgive, sir, but, even in these lax times, the Peverly must keep to its standards."

This shot did not pass Gully by. "See here, you are addressing a member of Parliament. Do you understand that?"

"Yes, sir. You have explained that already, sir." They were out of the supper room door by this time. "Now, if you will excuse me?"

Oh so smoothly—exhibiting well that Mr. Johns had a vast amount of experience in these matters—Jasper Gully and his guest were deposited with the hall porter, who, giving every appearance of deference, showed them out of the door.

"What possessed him to say I was presently a guest?" asked Elinor, looking worried. "I would not like to be a source of trouble if Mr. Gully should decide to take it further."

"Oh, I think he will not pursue it," said her grace. "Once Mr. Johns explained who we are and that my husband has property in Mr. Gully's district, I rather thought the light of battle faded, didn't you? Besides, my dear, Mr. Johns was speaking quite correctly. I have taken the liberty of engaging a chamber for you next to mine." She held up a restraining hand. "There will be no protestations of gratitude, if you please. I shall win any dispute in the long run. I am accustomed to that and have no inclination to change.

When you have had a good night's sleep amidst congenial surroundings, we shall talk about your future. I think you will not be displeased at what I have in mind."

Tyger Dobyn snapped his fingers with a roguish chuckle. "And that," he said, "is that."

The eager waiter hurried to the table. "Something, sir?"

Tyger grinned as he shook his head and put his offending fingers in his pocket.

=4=

WHEN ELINOR AWOKE late the next morning it was with a sense of guilt for not already being out in search of employment; but, when she opened her eyes and looked about the room, she hardly knew where she was. Certainly she was lying in a comfortable bed of the Hotel Peverly. However, instead of impersonal hotel accoutrements, she saw all the furnishings of her life which she had left behind at Mrs. Smeed's lodging house.

There on the table were her few books. In the corner was her familiar, battered old travelling trunk. Lying across the arm of a chair was her dressing gown and beneath it her slippers. How had they all come here? And there, just on the table beside the bed where her eyes would fall upon it as she awakened, was the cherished miniature of Papa, which she might have lost forever.

A light tapping at the door preceded its opening, and a chambermaid peered in. "Are you awake, miss? Do you want your tea?"

Elinor sat up in bed, pulling the covers around her. "Dora? Is that you?" Elinor remembered Dora from the days when she had merely served in the hotel scullery. "Come in. Why, you have quite grown up."

Dora, pleased at being remembered, smiled broadly. "If I may say so, miss, so have you." She stared at Elinor frankly. "You was allus a pretty little thing, but you've fulfilled your promise rarely, 'aven't you?"

She put the tray on the table, handed Elinor her robe

and moved her slippers where she could slide her feet into them as she swung from the bed. "What do you think of all this? Didn't we do a smashing job, miss? There was a dozen times I thought we would waken you, but you was sleeping the sleep of the innocent I expect. Even when Giles dropped the corner of your trunk, all you did was stir a bit and murmur something in your sleep."

Elinor looked about in unfeigned amazement. "It is all quite wonderful, but how in the world did they get here?"

The little chambermaid all but smirked at Elinor's surprise. "It were her grace, miss. She and the porters descended upon your old lodgings-keeper shortly after daybreak, I believe, and collected it all before breakfast."

Elinor could not but shudder at the memory of the state in which she had left her room, but she had to smile at the thought of Mrs. Smeed's expression as a duchess and two footmen appeared to collect Elinor's shabby belongings.

"I expect it was quite a shock to 'er, miss. Especially as they roused 'er out of sleep. But that ain't the 'alf of it, you know." Dora pointed to a stack of three corded packages on a chair near the door. "When you've finished your tea, p'raps you'd like to peep into 'em."

"Oh, another surprise? Do you know what it is?"

"No, miss, but I can guess They only arrived a little while ago while I was fetching the tea tray. Her grace slipped into the room and, when she saw you was still asleep, said as how she'd come back presently."

Elinor's face fell. "Then perhaps we should wait to open them until she returns?"

"Oh, do you think so, Miss Elinor?" Dora seemed inclined to protest, but then, as if realising it was, after all, not strictly her concern, said diffidently, "I expect you know best."

The girl could not help smiling at the maid's obvious disappointment which so echoed her own. "No, on reflexion, I think her grace might be displeased if she thought I had so little gratitude as to have no curiosity about her gift."

She put down her teacup and cleared a space on the table, while Dora scuttled quickly across the room to fetch the packages before Elinor could change her mind.

The cord was cut carefully, and Elinor unwrapped the first of the parcels. What she saw as she folded back the paper elicited a cry of admiration from both herself and Dora. Elinor lifted out a beautifully embroidered shawl of light cashmere with silk fringes and draped it about the shoulders of her dressing gown.

"How do I look, Dora? Does it flatter me?"

"Flatter you? Oh, no, miss. Nothing is needed to do that, but it does suit you marvellously, even over your robe. What do you suppose is in the other parcels?"

In the second, smaller package was the prettiest little Betsie collarette Elinor had ever seen, all made of the finest lace; but in the third was something which quite took her breath away. The sheer muslin gown had a squared neckline and softly puffed sleeves, but when she held it up against her, it was obviously too long by far.

"Oh, that is nothing, miss. The hem can be taken up in minutes, you know, so long as there is no ruching nor embroidery about it. Do just put it on to see how it suits you."

Elinor slipped quickly out of her dressing gown and pulled a chemise over her head, then donned the snowy frock. Except for the length, it fitted her almost as perfectly as if it had been created expressly for her. The chambermaid arranged the Betsie about Elinor's neck and draped the shawl about her shoulders, then turned her toward the tall looking glass. Both young women gazed speechlessly at the figure reflected there. It was Dora who finally breathed a tremulous approval.

"Oh, miss," she said simply. "Oh, miss!"

Then, at an imperious rapping on the door, she hurried to open it.

"Quite exquisite, my dear, as I knew it would be," said the duchess, coming into the chamber followed by two women. "I am so glad you did not hesitate to open the parcels."

She circled Elinor, eyeing her critically. "Yes, I knew the length of the frock would be excessive when I saw it on the dummy in Madame Larishe's establishment, but I anticipated the fit would be correct elsewhere." She turned to the older of the two women. "For whom did you say it was originally meant, madame?"

The dressmaker assumed a long-suffering expression and rolled her eyes heavenward. "For the Countess Walpole, your grace. I do not know what she will say when—"

The duchess held up a restraining hand. "Never mind. With what I paid you, I daresay you will come up with a suitable excuse." To Elinor she said, "That gown is, of course, just for the moment, my dear. Madame and her assistants are here not only to alter it, but to take measurements for the rest of your wardrobe as well."

"My wardrobe? Oh, but your grace, I do not see how I can afford—"

"Enough, enough. We shall discuss it later. It will be all for the best, Miss Hardy, I do assure you. I certainly do not think of this as an act of charity, but a shrewd investment on my part."

The dressmaker's assistant set about taking measurements while the duchess outlined what seemed to Elinor an extremely ambitious plan.

"We shall have little more than a fortnight in London, you see, so we must arrange very carefully to reap the ultimate advantage. There's Lady Monroe's garden party, of course. The muslin will do for that. One or two evenings at the theatre and the opera, but in a box only, never the pit. There is an exhibition of Landseer, and of course you must be seen in the new Burlington Arcade. That is the idea, you know, to be seen: always judiciously, but leaving an impression. You must become somewhat established in London before we go away.

"You are certain you cannot have the British net evening dress before Tuesday, madame?" she asked the couturier.

The dressmaker took the pins from her mouth and threw up her hands in despair. "I have promised you my best service, your grace. My entire staff shall be attentive to your demands, but I cannot make a miracle. As it is, I cannot think what my other patrons will say. Especially the dear countess."

Lady Augusta passed off the complaint with a wave of her hand as if it were no more than to be expected. "If one of the evening dresses is completed, we shall be able to attend Mrs. Patterson's rout. Everyone in town has been invited. I expect the crush will be intense. It is the *only* place to be that evening; and, since there will be no entertainment whatsoever, everyone will be looking at everyone else to see who is and who is not present. What a pity my dear husband is out of the country. It is always so distinguished to arrive on the arm of a peer, even if one does happen to be married to him. Don't you agree?"

"I am certain of it," Elinor replied faintly.

Her grace rapped her long fingers speculatively upon the table as she watched the dressmakers. "I have been turning it over in my mind, Larishe."

Madame looked about in what seemed almost to be fright. "What, your grace? You are not going to alter the design of the pelisse? The tailor has already begun the cutting."

"No, no, not the pelisse, but the blond lace. What would you say to a corsage of rose-coloured satin drawn tight and cut to display Miss Hardy's fine bust?"

"Very nice, duchess," Madame agreed with obvious relief. "And perhaps, sleeves of the same rose fabric?" She smiled up at Elinor. "With the young lady's colouring, the effect should be exquisite."

The duchess was gratified at the agreement. "Ah, yes,

my girl, I prophesy we shall turn you out very well," she said, half complimenting herself in the process.

In the meantime, Dora had been bustling about the chamber: tidying up the bed, removing the tea tray, beginning to unpack Elinor's trunk while the duchess watched her approvingly.

"I expect you would like to attend the theatre, would you not, Dora?"

Dora beamed. "Oh, yes, madam, I go as often as I can find the price."

The duchess seemed to consider. "It will be as well if Miss Elinor has a personal maid, one who can sometimes go out in attendance with her. Should you like me to arrange it with Mr. Johns?"

Dora made her bob excitedly. "Oh yes, your ladyship. Thank you. I should like it very much indeed." She shot a quick look at Elinor. "That is, if Miss Hardy don't mind."

"Not at all, if that is what your ladyship wishes. But I do feel this all requires an explanation, duchess."

"In time, my dear. In time."

When at last Larishe and company were gone, Dora sent upon an errand and the muslin frock removed and folded away, Elinor sat down with a sigh of relief. "I never knew merely standing still could be so onerous." Then she looked at her companion quizzically. "Now, Lady Augusta, do I not deserve an explanation of the way you have begun to regulate my life?"

"Poor child, have I made it so dreadful then?"

Looking about her, Elinor could not help but giggle at that. "Dreadful, madam? Not at all, but more than a trifle confusing, nonetheless. I sincerely appreciate your great generosity, but I should like to be reassured as to the cause of it."

Rising, Lady Augusta squeezed Elinor's shoulder. "Of course you would, my pet, and so you shall."

She moved restlessly about the chamber, poking at random among Elinor's belongings: picking up a comb, a ribband, a book, examining it and putting it down again.

"Ah, Miss Burney? I was not aware that she was still being read. I remember how, as girls, we all thrilled over *Cecelia*."

Still Elinor waited for her explanation.

The duchess lighted upon the small miniature by the bed and held it up to look. "And this is your dear papa?" Then she frowned at it. "To say the truth, my pet, I think it a wretched likeness. I don't remember that he looked like this at all. The same colouring, of course, and how could one not recognise the nose? But those are certainly not his eyes. Did he ever mention to you how it came to be done? He must have been very young to have still been wearing powdered hair."

"He never told me anything about it at all," the girl confessed. "I found it among his things after he passed away and I kept it to remember him, however imperfectly. I have always imagined he must have been too displeased with the rendering to put it on display."

"Then why keep it by?" asked Lady Augusta. She took it a bit closer to the window, peering at the frame. "But, I believe, these are small diamonds, girl. He could have sold or pawned it at any time for a pretty sum. Were the two of you not so much in Bleak Street as I supposed?"

Elinor had to laugh out loud at such an idea as that. "Diamonds, madam? I think it is hardly likely. Papa would have pledged it over and over again if the stones were genuine, of that I am quite certain."

"How very curious." The duchess replaced the little portrait where she had found it, then returned to where Elinor was sitting and drew up a chair opposite her.

"How much do you know of my life, Miss Hardy? Not much, I should imagine. Well, I was married very young, widowed soon after, and then took on the rewarding task of raising my beloved brother's two daughters. Like your father, my brother was a gamester who disposed of everything not entailed. When he died, we had only my own slim income upon which to live.

"I must confess that the task of finding my nieces husbands without a dowry between them was something of a challenge to my ingenuity. As perhaps you are aware, I found one for myself instead. Or, more happily, he found me. Lavinia, whom I had expected to have by me for some years to come despite the title she bears in her own right, married her cousin, Jack Mawson. For love, no less, which delighted all of us. My Lady Barbara, unfortunately, is another thing. How well do you know Barbara, my love?"

"Not very well at all," Elinor confessed. Then she added honestly, "If you mean me to be a companion to her ladyship, madam, I must say that I do not think it will do. Lady Barbara and I are quite unlike in our temperaments."

"Oh, good," said her grace surprisingly. "So much the better for my plan."

=5=

LADY BARBARA PENTREATH was something of a perfectionist where her own self-regard and comfort were concerned. She had, for some time after the marriage of her aunt and guardian to the prominent Duke of Towans, believed that her own life could not now fail to become a whirl of indescribable luxury. It came as rather a shock that, even with all the Towans riches at her command, the duchess was as careful as she had always been. Barbara's comeout in London had been as lavish and well attended as she could have wished, and the young bucks and swains had crowded around her and come to call in the days after. She was thus launched upon the sea of society. However, the liberty to live her life as she saw fit, the liberty to come and go as she saw fit, and, above all, the opportunity to *spend* as she saw fit, had, unfortunately, been denied her. Aunt Augusta had been most indulgent, but that was not quite the same thing. The remedy then, it appeared to Barbara, was merely to find a husband for *herself*: an indulgent husband who would ensure her nature was fulfilled, that part of her which longed for orgies of shopping and self-adornment.

It was not in her aunt's London house, however, that Barbara was this morning having breakfast, but in the establishment her guardian had taken for the season in Cheyne Spa. Lavinia had found herself a husband—not that Barbara would have even considered marriage to a cousin! Being a countess in her own right and a respectable married woman, Lavinia could afford to do as she liked and had joined them at Cheyne Spa. In effect Lady Barbara had *two* sponsors, her sister and her aunt. The drawback was that she had virtually two guardians as well, though it was a pretty sight to see how often she managed to play them off against each other. Only yesterday, after Aunt Augusta went up to town on business, Barbara had made an appeal to Lavinia for a wrap her aunt had decided was impractically expensive.

"But remember, dearest, it is your name-day gift in advance. I don't want to see any pouting when Jack and I present you with only some little token remembrance."

"My name day? But, Lavvy, that is not until autumn. It is a summer wrap. It will be quite old by then."

"See that you take care to preserve it, dear," the countess chided. "Money doesn't grow on trees beside the road, you know. . . . Unless you'd rather I took it back to Miss Roberta's shop?"

"Oh, no. I'll remember, Lavinia. I swear I will."

Money on trees? She knew that this was one of those falsely profound sayings with which her sister often armed herself. Barbara tossed her head impatiently. Why, if *everyone* had money, money would mean nothing at all. Thank heaven she was a Pentreath and had *family* to fall back on.

It was a constant source of puzzlement and annoyance to Lady Barbara that, despite the fact that she was the acknowledged beauty of the family, both her sister and aunt had married before her. And Aunt to a duke: a duke, moreover, who was considered to be one of the foremost peers of the nation and stood in such regard with the Prince Regent that he was, even now, on some sort of urgent diplomatic mission to Tsar Alexander. Something in Lady Barbara insisted that she must marry as well or be shamed forever: not a peer, necessarily, but certainly someone who could provide the frame in which she would be seen to best advantage.

She had admirers of course—too many, Lavvy seemed to believe—as if it were Barbara's fault that the young men, and many of the older ones as well, gravitated naturally to her side. It was true they were sometimes an annoyance and had to be shooed away like so many flies. But there were two who both admired and teased her fancy in a way she obscurely resented. They were the best of friends, always in each other's company; and she was attracted to both of them. Ben Weymouth, son of Lord Weymouth of Rye, was the favoured of Aunt Augusta who had actually gone so far as to urge Barbara to consider him seriously . . . and soon.

"I want you to be happy, my girl, but this shilly-shallying about while you bask in the admiration of men in whom you have no real interest is not healthy. Young Weymouth is well fixed and you can as easily find happiness with a rich man as a poor one. I have had both and I know."

"Do you really love the duke more than your first husband, Aunt?" Lavinia asked innocently in her namby-pamby way. Barbara snorted her disgust, but the countess had really meant the question to be taken seriously. Barbara could remember perfectly the look which passed over Aunt Augusta's face.

"No, my dear, certainly not *more*, but differently. I do not believe that love can be measured out like flour or spices, can it? Every time you love it must be different from the time before."

Why? Barbara had asked herself. It was all such a mystery to her. When she was by herself, alone with her thoughts, she had to admit that she had never really been in love. She had no idea what it meant when people talked of it to her. She had seen the look on the faces of the boys and men who declared their passion for her which, to her, meant only that now they were hers to do with as she liked. The trouble was, she supposed, that too often she wanted to do nothing with them at all.

Except for Trevor, of course.

Trevor Quenton was the other of the pair and Ben Weymouth's best friend since Trev was four and Ben was five and they had fought over a broken toy sailboat until Ben's nurse spanked them both. The high injustice of that incident had somehow forged a bond of camaraderie, and they had been bosom companions from then on. This was sometimes a great trial to Lady Barbara because it made for competition where, in other instances, her only rivals had been girls and women plainer than she.

It was irksome to have Ben always there when Trevor was trying to say diverting things to her, just as it was a bore to find Trev skulking in the shadows when what she craved was the brightness of Ben's wit and sophistication. She had to admit that each provided the perfect foil for the other, but enough was enough. She was seriously considering putting a stop to such behaviour; though of course, it was dreadfully amusing to promenade along the river walk with two strings to her bow and see out of the corner of her eye the envious looks of girls with only a single escort, or worse, another female for companionship.

Cheyne Spa was a spot well fixed for promenades, as Lady Barbara had long known. It was prettily laid out in respect to such matters. There were walks and paths along which to stroll, even a substantial trek up into the surrounding hills for those whose health and inclination allowed such things. In gentler moments there were the beautiful St. Gerrans's Gardens upon which a succession of head gardeners imported from Cornwall or the Scilly isles, had lavished such care as only comes with dedication and substantial remuneration.

Barbara waited in the breakfast room as the housemaid brought fresh tea.

"Oh, 'tis a glorious day out, miss. T' sky is like a robin's egg and t'air is soft as down."

Barbara allowed herself the familiarity of a smile. "You are very poetic this morning, Elsie. You may lay out my riding clothes, if you will, and remind Cook about the hamper I requested last night. I shall sample your glorious day for myself."

The girl blushed piously. "Oh, 'tisn't mine, is it? God made it, your ladyship, and I wouldn't presume to take the credit, though I'll enjoy it to the full." She began to leave the room and turned back. "Oh, and there was a message for you, miss. Mr. Ben sent round to remind you that you are riding out with him and Mr. Trevor."

"Yes, Elsie," said Lady Barbara with barely restrained impatience. "That is why I wish you to lay out the riding costume, you see." She sipped the aromatic jasmine brew. "Have you ever been to the caverns, Elsie?"

"Yes, miss. My friend took me once. Terrible damp place it is, very gloomy. I expect it did me good though, for they do say it is very educational." She giggled boldly, sneaking a sly look at Lady Barbara's face as she ventured, "What with two gentlemen in attendance, it might prove a bit of a education for you as well?"

Barbara smiled indulgently at the sally. "I do assure you, my girl, that two gentlemen are as good as a duenna, for each watches the other like a hawk."

"Yes, miss, I have heard they is safety in numbers."

"What is this about two gentlemen, Barbara?" asked the Countess Lavinia as she came into the room. "Are you still playing those two nice young men off against each other?"

Elsie made a discreet exit, and Barbara answered her sister with the slightest disdain. "It is nothing, really. We are taking nuncheon to the Warlock's Cavern at Palaceford."

Lavinia looked surprised. "Surely, not alone? My dear, is that wise?"

"I hope you are not thinking of forbidding it, Lavvy? I do assure you that everything is quite proper."

The countess sighed. "Yes, I suppose it is since rules are slighter here, but I do hope you will not mention it to Aunt when she comes back. I don't know what *she* would say."

By the time Lady Barbara descended the stairs to greet

her waiting suitors, she was handsomely arrayed indeed. The tailored riding costume was of a shade dubbed London Smoke and sported a full-sleeved cambric jacket, a full skirt over riding trousers and a pair of elegant boots complete with yellow gauntlets and silver spurs. Slowly she turned before her admirers.

"Do you think I will do?"

"Right as a ribstone pippin," Ben laughed. "I expect your mount will be honoured to bear off such a vision."

Trev merely glowered at the two of them, already sensing he would be the third party which turns the company into crowd. He sometimes thought he hated Barbara as much as he loved her, especially when, as now, she answered Ben with a cooing laugh that was at once silly, caressing and cruel.

"Have you no pretty compliment for me, Trevor?" he heard her ask.

It made him think what a fool he would be to let her play him so easily. It seemed to Trevor that he had loved Barbara Pentreath since the first time he laid eyes on her at the Cotillion Ball his first Thursday evening in Cheyne. Ben, unfortunately, had seen her at exactly the same time, and the pattern was quickly established. Although Trev very much doubted that his friend admired her ladyship with the same depth of passion which kept himself tossing restlessly upon his bed at night, he knew that the other had the advantage of shining prospects. Trevor had no prospects at all, shining or dull. Nonetheless, he resolved to remain amiable, although his heart was stabbed by every smile the beloved gave his friend.

"The day is quite glorious," he said cheerfully, "and the hamper is strapped and waiting."

Meanwhile, there was the sound of carriage wheels along the street; and Barbara moved to see who it might be. Lavinia, calling from another room, wondered the same thing.

"It is only Aunt Augusta returning from London."

Lavinia appeared in the doorway. "I was afraid of that," she worried. "If you are going to ride out, you had best do it now before she comes into the house." She paused at the window.

"But who on earth are those women who have come with her?"

"Oh, I say," Ben Weymouth murmured. "What a smashing-looking girl!"

=== 6 ===

HAVING NEVER BEFORE visited Cheyne Spa, what first impressed Dora was the church bells which pealed loudly for every arriving coach or carriage as it crossed the bridge.

"My stars, miss," she said to Elinor, covering her ears with her hands. "Do they do this every day?"

"Every day," Elinor assured her.

"And then have the face to ask you for a tip for the honour." The duchess laughed. "Everything costs money in Cheyne Spa, where they have discovered every possible approach to the pocket and purse."

"But can you imagine what harm it must be doing to the poor invalids?" Dora wondered. "I am sure I should not like to die with such a clangour in my head. Why, who knows where that din might send your soul? Straight off course, I shouldn't wonder, so that you would go down instead of upwards."

Elinor, for her part, was happy to see that the town had changed so little since she was last here with Papa. There were the famous Assembly Rooms with the Rotunda above them. Old Mr. Fortes could still be glimpsed standing behind the counter of the circulating library. The public breakfast tables remained immaculately set out in St. Gerrans's Gardens; and there, just along that little street was the lodging house of old Miss Hubbard and her companion, where Elinor and her father had always found such warm welcome. They had often been able to afford only the smallest and shabbiest of the rooms, but they were always treated as if they had engaged the main chamber and parlour. Papa seemed to have that effect on people. They went out of their way to do for him the very best they could. One day she would visit in that part of town.

"Be good enough to straighten your bonnet, Dora," said Lady Augusta. "And you, Elinor dear, pinch a bit of colour into your cheeks. I declare you have gone quite pale. I hope this task will not prove too much for you."

Elinor sat up straight and squared her shoulder. "After all you have done for me in the last fortnight, madam, I could hardly be so ungrateful. I do not pretend to be a femme fatale, but I shall certainly do my best to fulfill your expectations."

They turned a corner; and Dora, looking out of the window, sighed in a kind of swooning delight. "Will you just look, miss? I never seen anything so fine even in London."

Elinor observed that they were coming on toward the one landmark in Cheyne which had been absent in her childhood, and she was much impressed. She knew of Regent's Crescent, of course, for it had been in all of the illustrated magazines when it was completed a year or two ago. Now she could see firsthand that it laid just claim to being the crowning achievement of modern architecture. Its broad and majestic sweep was composed of thirty-five houses joined together in one magnificent, curved facade of Ionic columns. In full agreement with the maid, she found it awe-inspiring in its symmetry.

"How splendid," she said to the duchess. "I hope they are as wonderful on the inside as is the exterior."

The coachman turned the carriage through the handsomely wrought south gates and drew up a little more than a quarter of the way along. "Indeed," said Lady Augusta as the carriage stopped, "I am confident that you will think so." As they approached the door, she added quietly, "Please remember, my child, that you are to be called *Lady* Elinor."

"I still protest it, madam. I shall feel very uncomfortable, I am sure. As merely the daughter of a viscount I am not entitled to that designation."

The Duchess of Towans laughed understandingly. "But it has a much nicer ring, don't you think? It will put you on a better footing with Barbara. And, in any case, who will know the difference or dare to call us on it if they do? If we are to lure this young rascal away from my niece, we must use every weapon at our command."

The footman, who had run to the carriage to help them descend, now flung open the door. They stepped into the stately entrance hall just in time to see the last of Lady Barbara's London Smoke ensemble flick around the corner toward the rear entrance where the horses were being held.

"Barbara?" her grace called out. "Is that you?"

A moment passed before Barbara reluctantly reappeared with a patently false smile of delight. "Aunt, you have come back from London so soon?"

"Yes," Lady Augusta answered dryly. "So I have, and brought a guest as well." To the footman she said, "Lady Elinor will be in the green bedchamber if you please, Wilton."

Barbara gave a hard stare at the newcomer. "*Lady* Elinor?" Her pretty lips curled into an acid smile. "Why, I believe it is little Elinor Hardy!"

Lavinia poked her head about the door casing from the drawing room. "Why, of course it is, you goose. Lady Elinor, how have you kept since schooldays?" She came into the hall with hands outstretched in welcome. "How you have grown since we were all in pinneys, and what a beauty you have become. Has she not become a beauty, Barbara?"

It was Elinor's first look at the sisters in several years, though she had once seen Barbara from a distance in London. It seemed to her that the countess, who had not been particularly pretty as a child, had grown into decided handsomeness and that Lady Barbara's early promise of loveliness had been spectacularly fulfilled. Still, to Elinor's taste, there was a certain static quality in her looks.

"Yes, quite pretty," Lady Barbara answered her sister's question in a deliberately offhand manner, perfectly delivered. "But she was always tolerable as I recall."

To an outsider there would not have seemed the least unkindness in the way she said it. Yet, she managed very well to imply that she thought the whole discussion negligible in the extreme.

However, the two young men who had joined them made it evident that they did not share Barbara's indifference as they sprang forward animatedly. The brooding look had quite vanished from Trev's face, and Ben displayed unashamed interest.

"Lady Augusta, good morning. I trust you did not journey straight through?" he asked.

"No," she answered. "We broke at The Pelican."

"Ah, The Pelican." He chuckled and quoted:

> The famous inn at Speenhamland
> That stands below the hill,
> May well be called The Pelican
> From its enormous bill.

"I trust you were not overcharged, your grace?"

Lady Augusta gave him one of those looks which had begun in her family but made her famous far beyond it. "Believe me, sir, I always extract full value for my money."

His smile was as brash as it was open. "I am sure you do, madam," he acknowledged with admiration. "I hope you will one day teach me the trick of it."

Then he turned to Elinor. "I am Ben Weymouth, your ladyship. May I welcome you to Cheyne Spa?"

Behind him, Trevor cleared his throat ostentatiously once or twice, so that his friend was finally obliged to take notice.

"This lout is my friend, Trev Quenton, but you need

pay him no mind, I am sure. You have never met such a dull dog in your life."

Elinor smiled at the pair of them, recognising Ben's disparagement as the highest compliment of friendship. "Good morning, gentlemen," she began; but before she could continue, they were distracted by the tapping of Lady Barbara's yellow-topped boot against the wood-tiled floor.

"We had best be on our way, Trevor," she said. "Perhaps Ben should stay if he likes."

Trev sprang to heel at once; but Mr. Weymouth, if he was expected to follow suit, surprised the pair of them. "If she is not too tired of riding, perhaps Lady Elinor would care to join us?

"We are off on a jaunt to the caverns, you see," he said to Lady Augusta who made no protest at all.

Elinor pretended innocence of the caverns even though she had visited them many times in the past years. It had been a pet delight of her papa to explore their murky depths.

"I am sure our guest must be quite done in with the journey from London," Barbara said solicitously. "You should be more patient, Ben. I am sure Miss—forgive me, *Lady* Elinor—will oblige us another time.

"Especially as she is putting up right here in the house."

"How pleasant it will be to have you with us, Elinor," the countess said in what she believed was agreement with her sister.

Elinor sensed that Lavinia at least meant what she said, though Barbara viewed the idea with hostility.

"You are quite correct, Barbara," said the duchess. "I am sure that both Lady Elinor and I are tired to the bone. You will excuse us from the expedition, I am sure," her tone making clear that, for one, she had not allowed Barbara to pull the wool over her eyes, and, secondly, she understood she had been expected to remain docilely at home while the youngsters careered about the countryside. "Make sure you are home by mid-afternoon, my dear child. You will need all your energy for the Cotillion Ball tonight."

The duchess smiled engagingly and added, "Especially as you will now have a such a rival as Lady Elinor."

The barb struck home. The duchess strongly suspected that the trip to the caverns was destined to be brief.

When the others were gone, Elinor followed her mentor to the chamber where the footman had placed her boxes and found Dora was already unpacking. It was a pleasant room overlooking the park, with a dressing room where there was a cot for the maid.

"I am sure you will be quite comfortable here," said the duchess. "The bed has been freshly strung and tied. You must lie down at once, of course. Country dancing at our Cotillion is quite strenuous since we have a new master of ceremonies. Remember that you must make a good first impression upon Spa society. What are you going to wear? The pale yellow muslin I think will do it nicely, don't you? Rest well." But before the duchess had reached the door she paused and turned back. "You did very well downstairs, though there is one thing I should mention to you."

"Yes, your grace?" Elinor sensed a reprimand. She could not guess how she might have put her foot wrong already.

"Mr. Weymouth seemed mightily taken with you, I perceived."

Elinor could not help but smile. "That was rather my impression as well, madam. I hope I brought it off successfully?"

Lady Augusta allowed herself a wry grimace. "Wrong chap, my girl. Save your charm for Mr. Quenton. He is the reason I brought you here."

When the duchess had closed the door behind her, maid and mistress all but fell into each other's arms with helpless laughter.

"Oh, miss," Dora half sobbed, wiping the tears from her eyes, "this is going to be rum employment and never you doubt it. With her grace about you'll 'ave to be on your toes every second of the day, I can see. Nobbut what she ain't the grandest of ladies, you know. Still, with all the glory of it, I ain't too sure I'd care ter be in your dancing shoes this evening if you don't smash them all into a cocked hat, as they say."

Elinor, too, found the prospect a little daunting. Still, she had been a gambler all her life, and she guessed she knew when the game had turned in her favour. She had no reason to believe that luck would quickly change or that the odds of success would not be with her tonight.

= 7 =

THERE IS A well-recognised rule of fortune which dictates that whenever plans have been too well laid, too carefully prepared and too much trouble has gone into the pursuance of them, Providence will strike them down. So it was to be with the arrangements of the good duchess.

Her notion was that Trevor Quenton would be so stricken with Elinor Hardy he would at once abandon his hopeless, but potentially dangerous passion for Lady Barbara in favour of the newcomer. Perhaps, indeed, the failure of her plans lay in failing to provide for alternate contingencies.

When the Duchess of Towans and party arrived at the Assembly Rooms, the orchestra was already tuning up for that stately minuet which always opened the evening. The patrons were standing about in little groups of two or three, waiting impatiently, so that there was good and sufficient audience for the entrance of such a group of attractive women.

To be sure, when they came into the room, there was a gratifying sigh of appreciation; and all four of the women rather preened themselves. Their escort, Jack Mawson, husband of the countess, though he did not share her title, was much amused at this. He leaned close to his wife and remarked behind his hand, "Well, old thing, now I expect the festivities can begin? I swear, I am glad I am already so well connected. I never would stand a chance against all these titles and pocketbooks."

She squeezed his arm affectionately in reply. The attention being given them was certainly heady, even though she knew it was mostly addressed to Barbara and Elinor, rather than the two staid married ladies, as Lavinia smilingly called her aunt and herself.

Lady Barbara, in fact, was looking particularly lovely in cool, seafoam green with a mass of white ruffles about the bodice. It admirably suited her colouring, making her look like a veritable Aphrodite emerging from the froth of the sea. On the other hand, Elinor's chestnut hair was cast into particular prominence by the jonquil muslin the duchess had dictated she wear. Meanwhile, the duchess and the countess, being matrons, could afford to be arrayed in a somewhat more sumptuous style, though appropriate still to a summer holiday and the warmth of the evening. Her grace wore white gros de Naples with a narrow line, and her ladyship was in pale blue satin with an over-robe of lace. They made a striking quartet.

Elinor's first hurdle was, of course, to be presented to the sponsors. Grave Mrs. Wilcoxen raised her eyebrows a little when reminded of the girl's parentage; but tiny Lady Ekdall, who had been the beauty of her day and appreciated the newcomer's stature, spoke to her kindly.

"We little butterfly creatures must fly together, Lady Elinor, or we are like to be caught up in a storm," she said with a sweet smile. "Let me take you around a bit before you are rushed by all the young beaux."

Under such impeccable sponsorship, who could gainsay the young woman's position among the guests? Old Lady Penhale, who had been at Cheyne every year for a decade, condescended most amiably. The Duchess of Doddington allowed a deferential curtsey to be paid her; and that dessicated old rake, the Marquess of Lorn, eyed Elinor speculatively and allowed his feathery, old lips to linger on her fingers a bit longer than normal courtesy required as he bowed low over her hand.

Lady Barbara was at once surrounded by admirers. However, while the Duchess of Doddington as the oldest lady of rank was led out by Mr. Marshall, the master of ceremonies, it was Elinor's fortune to be taken to the dancing floor by Mayor Tobias himself: an event which incurred Lady Barbara's complete disdain.

"One would think that, as a guest, Lady Elinor would contain herself a little and not be forward so early in her visit," Barbara observed acidly behind her fan to her sister. "How long is she to be with us? Has Aunt mentioned?"

"Why, no," said the countess as, against protocol, she let go of the arm of her handsome and beloved husband, "but, I am sure, she may remain all season if she likes. I find her a most refreshing person to have about."

Lady Barbara's temper was not much improved by the men who had crowded about to fill her card. She thought them a clumsy lot. She smiled a little when Ben approached to remind her that the first valse was his, and Trevor attempted talking her out of the second reel as well as the first quadrille.

Barbara conceived that they were a little tardy and was not about to let her suitors off so easily. "I assume that Miss—no, I do mean *Lady*, don't I?—Elinor's card is already full or you would not be bothering me with your attention for further dances," she told Trev. "I think you had better allow a few of my other admirers a chance. Do you not agree?" she smilingly asked the waiting cluster of young men who had not been so fortunate.

Of course, they all acclaimed her decision and clamoured for the one or two spaces still vacant.

"Oh, Barbara, pray do not act the virago simply because you nose is a trifle out of joint." Ben Weymouth laughed. "You know that Trev excels as much in the quadrille as I do in the valse. Don't stint him because you have a rival for his affection, what do you say? I warn you, you must now begin to treat him with consideration or he will defect. Won't you, old fellow?"

Trev ducked his head and blushed. "You know, Lady Barbara, that I am your devoted servant at all times."

Ben punched him lightly on the arm. "Maybe this is why she treats you so capriciously, my lad. You are gammoning yourself if you think our Barbara, here, has a heart. Beautiful as the moon, she is, and cold as midnight."

"I take your jesting in very bad part, Mr. Weymouth," said Lady Barbara. "I am certain no other lady would accept such abuse from you as I do. Pray, do not presume upon extended friendships. I think that, after all, I shall award the first valse to . . ." She pursed her lips and considered the anxious faces. " . . . to you," she said, bestowing a warm glance upon a young cornet. "You have the look of accomplishment."

The cornet blushed and stammered, writing his name on her card with a tremulous hand.

Ben merely smiled in that maddening fashion which Barbara found both obnoxious and devastatingly attractive. He could be such a winning rogue when he chose, getting around her as easily as anything. He seemed sometimes so devoted, but she had never quite been able to pin him down to an actual declaration. Trevor, on the other hand, would fall to one knee at the drop of a handkerchief which, even if superfluous, was mightily flattering.

Pretending a nonchalance she did not feel, Barbara glanced once more at her card. "Why, I never! Somehow or other, I have left the next dance unengaged, Trev, dear. Would you care to escort me to the supper room for a bit of refreshment? I find that my throat is quite parched.

"Mr. Weymouth, I am certain," she said over her shoulder, "will excuse us."

Ben bowed ironically. "Enjoy the sunshine while you can, Trev," he warned laughing. "It has a habit of cooling quickly."

"And are you still continuing your childish teasing of Lady Barbara, old man?" asked a voice from behind him. "I should think she would be in the habit of cutting you by now."

Ben turned with a cry of pleasure. "Tyger! What the

devil are you doing in a quiet place like Cheyne Spa? Is there a mill scheduled hereabouts? Don't tell me that your liver is in need of the cure?"

He looked at the gentleman sportsman sharply. "Or are you in pursuit?"

The Tyger gave him a rather tight-lipped smile. "I am always in pursuit, as you put it, my boy. Somewhere, I know, there is an heiress or a rich, plump widow who can afford to keep me in my recognised style. Perhaps I have come to try my luck with lovely Barbara again. She is no heiress, but with the Duke of Towans for an uncle, that is all one." He gave Ben a quizzical look. "I know you are fond of her, you rascal. Why do you continue to rile her so?"

Ben looked almost serious for a moment. "Only because it sometimes amuses me . . . and, I daresay, because she annoys me as well. It may even be because she pursues her goals with such patent intent." He said this laughing, but there was a ring of chagrin in his voice. "I daresay the lady would do very well if she sheathed her claws a little and those pretty teeth were not so eager to snap. God knows she is one of His handsomest creations, but the notion of spending a lifetime catering to her whims is more than I myself care to contemplate. I surmise that at the end of all I shall leave her to some calm-natured fellow who is more besotted than I. Though tonight, for just a moment, I fancied I caught her in a moment of self-revelation." Then he almost sighed. "But the moment passed, I fear."

"Well, if you are so careless as to send her off with a handsome, young chap like Quenton, you may find your chance of reform has passed you by."

Ben's face grew quite sober. "I will tell you truthfully, old man, if I thought she would not lead poor Trev the very devil of a life, I would gladly step aside, for he is deuced in love with the wench. Her family would never allow it, of course, since the Quentons are poor as church mice, no matter how charming they may be. It is a great pity, for

Trev is prime husband material if ever I saw it. Far more so than myself, if the truth be known. But he needs must marry money. Nothing else will do for it."

Meanwhile, the early and obligatory country dances being out of the way, the little band of musicians took up the sensuous rhythm of the valse. Time had been only a year or two ago, when the dancing rage of society was entirely banished from the Cheyne Spa Cotillions and allowed only at the Monday Dress Ball, but the Prince Regent had put a period to all that by once requesting it when paying a visit. Now, though there was an initial nod to propriety, the valse madness was allowed sway. Even old-guard diehards entered into the spirit of it like tipsy widows. When Lady Lieven introduced the dance in London no one suspected that all of England would soon go so far with the fad that even those who were too old and frail to venture upon the floor would faithfully attend every ball as if it were a concert.

Elinor Hardy swept by Ben and the Tyger in the arms of some lucky wretch, and the eyes of each followed her with envy. Ben's response was tempered with some measure of security in the hope of following the wretch's lead. Tyger, however, possessed a sensibly pragmatic mind and a self-amused acceptance of lost cause. He could undoubtedly have danced with her, of course, but why tempt fate when neither had more than a pound or two to live on? Romance with a pretty girl was all very well, but there was little use in being foolish as well.

The two men, therefore, each reacted in his natural way. Ben moved to find himself another partner and the Tyger to scout out the land for whatever advantageous opportunity might present itself. For men like Tyger Dobyn opportunity was the very currency of life. As it fell out, the partner Ben Weymouth lit on was Lady Augusta Trenarry herself. Thus, the duchess was able to congratulate herself that if he was not with Barbara he was not, at any rate, falling into the hands of some rival claimant. She was, however, piqued by his choice of conversational topic.

"I daresay, your grace," he offered somewhat tentatively. "Since you are more or less sponsoring Lady Elinor in Cheyne, you must be the fount of knowledge concerning her?"

She was caught between amusement at his clumsy gambit and annoyance that it should concern Elinor rather than her niece. "Lady Elinor," she said as abruptly as she dared in hope of discouraging his interest, "is the daughter of an old friend of many years. She is a lovely girl of no prospects whatsoever."

Immediately, she cursed herself for her careless tongue. Young Weymouth would likely as not communicate that piece of information to his crony, Quenton. So much for her intentions in that direction. Trevor Quenton could scarcely afford a dowry-less bride any more than most second sons, especially those whose elder brothers had little enough of their own to begin with. Without in the least intending it she had just written finis to her own conniving. Perhaps Weymouth realised it as well, for he raised his brows just slightly and, though his expression was not in the least mocking, there was an annoying curl at the corner of his lip.

"Luckily," he said smoothly, "that is not something over which some must bother."

The duchess knew he was alluding to herself, but she remained undaunted. From what she had seen of Ben Weymouth, he might prove of benefit to her niece in more than one way. But only if Trevor Quenton were kept out of the picture.

Although one could scarcely expect Miss Hardy to have ridden into town and carried the field in one day, she must now certainly be reminded of the reason for her presence here. Or was it too early to be judging such a thing as her success? Perhaps the girl must first be allowed to find her feet? In which case, time might very well mend the result of the duchess's own slip of the tongue.

As Elinor and partner swept past, it appeared that the girl had perhaps found her feet rather well already. She was a splendid dancer, and Lady Augusta was obviously not the only one who believed so. There were many eyes on her, including those of Barbara Pentreath who stood at the edge of the dance floor looking as if her heart had turned to stone and her eyes to fire. From the intense way she was staring at Elinor Hardy, it was evident that Barbara was not pleased to have such formidable competition. The duchess stole a look at Ben Weymouth and saw that he too was gazing from one young woman to the other with an amused smile. He was not, after all, the sort to be so easily led as Augusta had believed.

When the waltz ended, the young men, and a few of the older ones, divided as surely as ever did the Sea of Reeds at the wave of Moses' rod. One half faithfully surrounded Barbara, the other moving irresistibly to her rival. For Elinor, who was quite conversant with her task, it posed something of a difficulty when Ben Weymouth came toward her, while Trevor, the one man she was obligated to entice, had gone into Barbara's camp. If Elinor were to fulfill her bargain with Lady Augusta, she must make an effort to rectify this state of affairs, even though it ran contrary to her personal inclination. Consequently, when the musicians struck up "The King's Brigade" ten minutes or so later, she gratefully accepted Trevor's arm and put herself to the task of charming him totally.

"I sincerely hope you will explain to me who all these people are, Mr. Quenton," she begged. "I have met so many and smiled at so many and heard so many names that my smile is tired and my brain has gone quite awhirl."

Trev looked down at the tiny creature and thought her fully as enchanting as did every other man in the room, his loyalty to Barbara Pentreath notwithstanding. He at once began a quick run upon the people in question. He pointed out the doyennes and called them by name, then the mere people of celebrity, and even a few of the less creditable who should be avoided.

As for the members of the corporation who actually have Cheyne Spa in their care: "There is the mayor, whom you already know. Next to him is Mr. Gavin Marshall, the new master of ceremonies, as you can see by his staff; and there, just behind him is the Earl of Glastonia, the man who supplied the money to begin in the beginning."

He was scarcely prepared for the reaction this drew from Elinor. She peered about and craned her neck as curiously as any unschooled girl just up from the country. "Where is he?" she asked urgently. "Which is the old earl?"

Trevor obligingly pointed out his lordship a second time, then began a detailed history of the earl's connection with the Spa, but presently discovered that all the flattering attention the girl had previously paid him had dissipated as surely as morning mist. For the remainder of the evening, whether together or apart, he was aware that the pocket beauty's attention focussed upon one person only, that proud old gentleman who stood head and shoulders above his companions.

Surprisingly, it made the young woman far more interesting to Trevor than if she had gone on in that pose of artlessness by which young women attempt to engage the exclusive attention of young men. Such wiles and gambits had been practised upon him as long as he could remember, despite his lack of fortune; and it was monstrously enjoyable not to be obliged to think up answers to empty questions about which no one in their right mind cared in the least. If Lady Barbara could be conceived to have any fault at all, it was that she was, too often, transparently given to such tactics. For the time being, however, this young original appeared to have forgotten him completely so far as he could tell, in favour of staring unabashedly at a man old enough to be her ancestor.

In fact, the old gentleman, though she had never before

laid eyes on him, was a delight to Elinor's eye. He had her father's head, her father's proud, erect carriage and even a few pleasant lines about his eyes which suggested that he had in some degree her father's sense of the absurd—or rather, the other way around—that her father had inherited these features from this gentleman. For there was no doubt in her mind that this handsome old patriarch was her own grandfather.

Deeply etched lines about his mouth told her something else as well. This was the same proud and relentless old man who had turned her father off for squandering his inheritance and had shown his back when the son brought his bride to his father's house. Elinor had never known her mother except from report, but she knew well enough that the young woman had never harmed this old man, save by making his son love her.

As if he had begun to feel the weight of her continuing gaze, the leonine head swung slowly in Elinor's direction. For a brief moment before his gaze passed on, their eyes met. His, she could see, widened in surprise. After a moment, he leaned down to the mayor and asked a question which made Tobias dart a quick glance in her direction. She answered with a smile, and the effect was immediate. It was as if a curtain had been drawn over the old gentleman's countenance, so cold and withdrawn did it become.

Above her knowledge of their relationship, there was something else about him that seemed uncannily familiar, though she could not, at first, put her finger upon it. Then it came to her and provided an explanation for a long-held mystery. It came to Elinor that *here* was the original of that miniature she had long assumed was merely an imperfect rendering of her father's likeness. It was instead a youthful representation of her father's father. It spoke a great deal of filial love that never in all their adversity had Papa put the brilliant-studded miniature out to pawn.

"I say, the old fellah seems to be in a fine taking about

something, don't he?" Trevor Quenton observed. "I wonder who it is about to feel the whip of his tongue this time?"

He was completely astonished by the sudden look of fury which marred the face of his partner. It crossed his mind that this gel had a certain interest of her own, over and beyond her beauty, and that she was becoming more interestin' by the moment.

=8=

THE LOWER ROOMS, as the gaming parlour of Cheyne Spa was known, were densely packed after the Assembly Cotillion, but this was not unusual. However popular and well attended the balls, routs, lectures, concerts, cotillions, masquerades or even the soaking in the waters themselves, it was the gambling which paid Cheyne Spa's way in the world, for the ruling corporation took a substantial bite from all proceeds.

In the days of old Beau Carlisle, the master whose social genius more or less established Cheyne, a certain laxity had been allowed until it was discovered that the Beau himself was acting as a shill. Despite an alarming tendency to fare quite badly at the tables, the gentleman had put away enough of a nest egg to retire comfortably from his position with a good grace. That advantage had not been allowed his successor nor the present social master, Gavin Marshall, which was all to the good of the patrons. Mr. Marshall was paid handsomely in an effort to keep him honest, and, insofar as anyone could tell "by eye or spy," this tactic had worked very well indeed. Mr. Marshall, in fact, having a lovely wife, was rarely even seen in the gaming rooms.

Nearly everyone else who was eligible, however, found it a lodestar. Some gambled because it was the smart thing to do and so made up a part of the throng at peak. Others, often out of desire to preserve a fictitious reputation, chose the hours when their friends were at the Assembly. Still others, habitually inflicted with a kind of insomnia which kept their eyes from shutting after midnight, made their way to the rooms only in the wee hours and played with an intensity which the smart set would not necessarily understand. Meanwhile, the house and corporation members profited nicely from all.

It is hardly to be supposed that Elinor Hardy, with her background, would shun the most popular diversion in Cheyne Spa; but she found she was, in truth, most diverted by the differences apparent here. To one who had observed in London the caste lines drawn between Almack's Club in Pall Mall or White's or Arthur's and the lower hells, it was amazing to see how persons of the best quality here sat side-by-side with any and all. Persons in ordinary or even servant's garb came hither to wager a hundred guineas or even two without any hindrance.

Wandering through the rooms, she saw that all the usual features were present: écarté, faro, an E.O. wheel, *rouge et noir*, even macao and vingt-et-un, which the vulgar called pontoon. There were, as well, certain variations such as silver Pharaoh and a Russian game of whist which went by the peculiar name of *biritsch*. All these were familiar to her; but, rather than put her skill to the test on an evening which had already been fraught with strain, Elinor drifted instead to the one table which offered a game of sheerest chance. In hazard both skill and knowledge were at discount which meant, of course, that the rankest beginner might successfully vie with the most case-hardened gambler on terms of perfect equality.

It was a disarmingly simple game to be shared by as many players as could squeeze around the circular table. Each took the box in turn and wagered against any or all of the company when the cast was made. The caster named his stake, which he placed upon the table. Those who wished to join the game then matched it with a sum of equal amount. The groom-porter then called forth the caster's main in a patois unique to the round table.

"Four and four. Eight it is. Let's see yer siller. Let's see yer siller. Let's see yer siller!"

Elinor played with a calm deliberation which much impressed the porter and he nearly gave himself up to watching over her.

"Six and six," he called. "Twelve it is, the number twelve. Ye've nicked it, miss," he said admiringly. "Take all the bets."

Unfortunately, only a little later he was forced to call, "One and two, unlucky three. I fear ye've crebbed it, miss, 'aven't yer? Ye've thrown out, miss."

"Your luck seems variable in the extreme, Miss Hardy," whispered Tyger Dobyn close to her ear.

She looked as if she were about to remind him that she was, at least for the moment, *Lady* Elinor; but she surmised from the twinkle in his eye that he remembered perfectly well and, believing he would not be overheard, was having a bit of fun with her. She gathered up the balance of her winnings and moved away from the table.

"What a surprise to see *you* here, Mr. Dobyn. I would have thought that your particular way of life would more or less confine you to London."

He grinned impudently at her, and the indentations in his cheeks grew deeper. "My busy life? Yes, I admit it is sometimes a hard scrabble to keep alive, but one may as well subject oneself to being rackety in Cheyne Spa as anywhere."

He offered his arm. "At least the company is superlative. How is your business here progressing?"

"My business, sir? What business is that?"

He only repeated with a wink the same impudent grin as before, as if he knew a secret which was not his to share. Then he spied Lady Augusta descending upon them with a troubled mien. The Tyger at once became more circumspect, bowing as her grace approached.

To Elinor he said, "So pleasant to have seen your ladyship again," and was off, moving through the crowd with the grace of a panther.

"I don't really trust that man," said the duchess. "I like him enormously, but I do not trust him the smallest part of an inch. You must be very careful now that he is here."

Elinor was sanguine. "I expect you have little to worry about, madam. I believe that Mr. Dobyn lives by some code of his own which does not encompass peaching on the plans of others. In any case, what could he do? I cannot imagine him warning grown men to be wary of a 'tiny butterfly' like myself."

"Oh, I can," said the duchess darkly. "Men are all in the same club, you know. They do that sort of tittle-tattle just as women do, though perhaps with less malice." She paused for a moment, staring about the room. "But where are your gallants? I expected to find you surrounded by at least three or four besotted fellows."

"That behaviour is for the ballroom." Elinor laughed. "It is when you come to the gaming rooms that society's mask is torn away, and it is everyone for himself. You must have noticed that the ladies painted on the cards are more alluring to many men than those in real life."

Elinor saw that her words were falling on the air, for the duchess was looking with alarm and displeasure at someone who had just come in the door of the establishment. Elinor recognised him as well and could not repress a shudder of distaste. It was Jasper Gully, M.P., got up to the nines in smart clothes that suited him not at all.

The collar of his coat was the merest shade too broad, his neck-cloth the smallest morsel too elaborate. The coat itself stretched too tightly across his shoulders and was pinched far too severely at the waist. Jersey pantaloons were certainly ill advised on a man with legs as spindly as those of Mr. Gully. In his hand he carried a gold-knobbed walking stick which he waved about in a fashion which suggested it had not been in his possession for very long. Above all, his lank hair had been teased about his face in a variety of elf-locks which were more appropriate to a miss of sixteen than a man in his middle years.

"Here, that's a 'rum duke,' ain't it?" asked Trevor Quenton as he joined the two women, then seemed discomfited. "Begging your pardon, your grace. I meant no offence by the term."

"None taken, I am sure," she answered with a laugh. "I have not been a duchess for such a very long time that I am jealous of the title." But she did not take her eyes off Gully.

"Are you acquainted with the gentleman, madam?" Quenton asked curiously.

The duchess exchanged a glance with Elinor. "Only slightly," she answered him, "and that too well. I believe he is of that new breed which rises too easily in times like ours." She shrugged and turned away. "I suppose it cannot be helped."

Gully had not looked in their direction, but toward the smoke-choked room at the far end where the deepest play was always to be found. There was a particularly greedy look about the Parliamentarian tonight, as though he were avidly contemplating great advantages which might accrue to him. He headed purposefully in that direction, rubbing his hands together and pulling at the joints of his fingers as if he were seeking to make them more supple by dislocation.

Suddenly he stopped, almost in mid-stride, and stood staring toward the faro table. He leapt purposefully forward and put his hand roughly on the arm of a curly-haired young man who was quietly watching the play.

"There you are, you young devil!"

The youth spun around. "I do not know who it is you may be, sir," he said in a lyrical Irish voice, "but I do resent bein' mishandled by complete strangers. So, if you don't mind, I'll be thankin' you to keep your hands to yourself."

Gully was not at all abashed. "You don't know me, eh? No, me lad, you don't pull the wool over *my* eyes. I remember you all too well, *all* too well. Where were you a fortnight ago? Answer me that, if you will. Well, well? Are you afraid?"

The attention of the entire establishment was focussed on them by now, but the Irishman answered him calmly. "Where do *you* say I was, sir, if you please?"

"I know demmed well where you were, you young blackguard. You were lifting my pocket in an establishment in Seven Dials."

By this time a small crowd had collected about the pair, and an unexplained ripple of laughter passed through it at Gully's words. He scowled angrily.

"You wouldn't think it so demmed funny, by heaven, if it were your guineas he'd got!"

The groom-porter had edged through the crowd and now stood before the furious and red-faced man. "I think you owe the young man an apology, sir. There are many people here who can swear to his whereabouts any night for some time past. It is impossible, sir, that he could be guilty of the crime you accuse him of."

"I say he lifted my purse," shouted Gully. "How dare you dispute me? Do you know who I am?"

"No, yer worship," the groom-porter answered smoothly, "but I do know who this young man is. His name is Patrick Tyrone, sir, and he has been appearing nightly at the Theatre Royal without letup, excepting the Sabbath. I think that even you, sir, will admit that it would be difficult to reach London and come back in anything less than three days, without flying as old Jane Wenham was said to do."

Gully blinked. "What? He is an actor?"

"Aye, he is that, and a very popular one, if I may say so. I myself have had the pleasure of seeing him a number of times."

Gully seemed unperturbed. He poked his gold-knobbed cane at the groom-porter's belly. "I believe you may be Irish, too, eh?"

The other man drew himself up. "I am that, sir, and proud of it."

"I might have known. All you Paddies stick together, I don't doubt. I should have expected as much."

The actor had thus far behaved quite equitably. Now, however, he paled. "I did not so much mind your taking me for a cutpurse, your honour," he said, "but I think I may not be persuaded to be so lenient if you continue in such a vein. I hope you understand me?"

Gully would not back down. "Are you threatening me? Do you imagine I would allow myself to be called out by a mere actor?" He said the word contemptuously and with an exaggerated roll of the tongue. "If you continue, I shall most certainly have you thrashed for your impudence to a member of Parliament."

"If you are a sample of what's in Parliament," scoffed an anonymous voice in the crowd, "then Gawd help us all."

That provoked a wide burst of laughter.

"Well, Mr. Gully, continuing your little war against the world, are you? Not a good way of being returned to your seat, I should think."

The duchess's voice, perfectly modulated, struck the man like the flick of a whip and it was his turn to pale. "Good evening, your grace," he said nervously. "I trust you understand the justice of my threat?"

The crowd parted, and she stood before him impassively.

"Well, madam, this young blackguard, you see . . ."

Her grace said nothing to suggest she would either accept or refuse his explanation. Her silence obviously intimidated him.

"What I meant to say, you see . . ." he began again, but trailed off impotently once more.

At last, she took some pity on him. "Since no harm has been done, I am certain I shall not be obliged to mention this unfortunate incident to the dear duke, Mr. Gully, shall I?"

"No, of course not! I mean to say, I would be much obleeged, so much obleeged, your ladyship—that is, your grace—if you would see fit not to—that is, your grace—madam . . ." He was turkey-cock red, much to the enjoyment of the crowd, and completely unmanned by the calm assurance of Lady Augusta.

"I am certain it can all be forgotten, sir, if Mr. Tyrone can find it in his heart to forgive such a monstrous accusation. Is that at all possible, sir?" she asked the actor.

He swept into a low bow of appreciation. "I am sure, your grace, that I would do far more to please you than this mere trifle," he said.

"Spoken like a true Irishman." She smiled. "Poetic and gallant." She looked down her nose at the politician. "There you are, Mr. Gully, you have been let off, but I think, if I were you, I would not press it. Good night to you."

"Good night to your grace."

He slunk off, but not without a pause at the door for a final resentful and pawky look which the duchess, of course, did not miss. She merely shrugged her shoulders. The crowd dispersed. Lady Barbara, drifting about with one of her admirers at either hand, paused for a moment beside her aunt.

"What in the world was that about?" she asked languidly. She paused, looking sharply at the handsome Tyrone. "But I know you, do I not? Ah yes, I saw you as Bob Acres, I believe."

He did not deny it. "I expect you may have done, Lady Barbara."

Barbara bridled. "You know *me* then?"

"Ah, who is not acquainted with the lovely Lady Barbara? You are a Cheyne Spa legend, your ladyship. Almost a nonpareil."

"Almost?" Barbara pouted. "How ungallant, sir."

Elinor and Trevor had joined them, and Tyrone looked about him, perplexed.

"Three handsome ladies, and I must choose? You place me at the Judgement of Paris, my lady." Irish charm overflowed from his eyes and smile as well as his words.

"So you are an actor, Mr. Tyrone?" the duchess asked. "What a curious occupation for someone who is so obviously of gentle birth. Is it possible to make a living in such a profession? To support a wife and children, say?"

His eyes had hardly left Barbara's face, but he glanced away long enough to reply to her aunt. "It all depends, madam. The public is notoriously fickle."

"Not only the public," said Trev with an unkind look at Barbara. Her other admirers watched hopefully and were gratified when he inclined toward Elinor. "May I offer your ladyship some refreshment or some air? It is becoming quite close in here, it seems to me."

Elinor held her tongue after accepting, waiting to see what he would say. Presently, he began to speak aloud as if he had been explaining the situation to her all along.

"It isn't easy, you know. I know what sort of girl she is, but it seems I cannot help myself. Demmed foolish of me, I expect." He shrugged. "But there it is."

=9=

"To be sure, I know about her," said the old earl testily, "but she has not asked *me* for anything. She may call herself Mary Queen of Scots for all I care."

Cecil Partridge stirred uncomfortably. His discomfort was twofold. For one thing, the heat emanating from the fireplace in his great-uncle's library was nearly overpowering on a summer's day even though the season had been uncharacteristically chill and rainy and this room was on the north side of the large and drafty old house.

The second thing was that, as heir to the title and the estate, he viewed with great alarm this sudden surfacing of Elinor Hardy, be she Lady Elinor or plain Miss Hardy. He felt it was necessary to take as strong a line in the matter as he dared, which was why he was braving the old man's famously uncertain temper in order to secure his own future.

Cecil moved away from the immediate proximity of the fire and paced about the room as though deep in spontaneous thought. "Still," he said, "it doesn't look at all well, does it, sir? I mean to say that people will soon enough know who she is, I am sure. I daresay she will even use it herself to gain some spurious advantage."

The old man snorted derisively. "I suppose you mean that she will parade the fact that she is my granddaughter? Well, so far as I know she hasn't done it yet. And what if she did? She has a perfect right to do so."

Cecil's sharp, little face took on an expression of horror.

"Well, my lord, think of the scandal. All that old business raked up again."

The earl regarded him frostily. "I fail to see, sir, that it can be your concern. What do you know of 'that old business,' if you please? You were scarcely born when my son and I fell out, and you know nothing of the circumstances."

Cecil understood that he was skating close to the line. It would be unpolitic to anger the old man; but, dash it, there were things that had to be said. He contrived to look pained and pushed on.

"It is a family matter, Uncle, which reflects upon me as well as upon you. I am next in line, after all."

The old earl gave him a disgusted look which spoke volumes. "You are heir to the title, sir, and that part of the estate which is entailed. Luckily, however, I have made most of my money myself and increased my holdings considerably."

Now Cecil quite beamed. "Yes, sir. You have certainly done wonderfully in expanding the scope of the estate."

"No, not the estate, my boy. Aside from the strict entailment, the rest remains to dispose of as I see fit. Keep that in mind whenever you are tempted to explain to me what it is that I should or should not do in the matter of my private life. It will be of great benefit in the long run."

His nephew's laugh was nervous. "Oh, but Uncle, you know the land and the money must go hand in hand if the estate is to be maintained. After all . . ."

"Yes?" asked the earl. "After all what?"

"Well, what I mean, sir, is that you cannot mean to make the mistake of separating the two?"

"Why should I not? Your mother has a goodly portion of her own, I believe, which comes to you?"

Cecil's lips did not exactly begin to tremble, but there was a certain quivering about the corners of his mouth which suggested they might do so at any moment."

"But . . . dash it all, sir, that ain't the thing, is it?"

Cecil received for this merely a dryly amused glance from beneath bushy eyebrows. "When I inherited the title, my boy, there were scarcely two shillings to rub together. The house was a veritable ruin, the stables were empty and, the property being entailed, no part could be sold to save the rest. Even without my money you will be inheriting a great deal more than I did." He waved his hand about the room. "The house is in proper order. The stables boast the best hunters in the county, and the land is more productive than it has been for generations. I think you will have nothing to quarrel with."

"You take me wrong, Uncle. I don't mean to appear greedy, but it seems to me that it is all one, the estate and the money. You couldn't have had the one without the other is how I look at it."

"So that is how it appears to you, is it? Interesting, quite an interesting point of view." The earl drew meditatively upon his long-stemmed pipe. "Tell me, my boy, what do you know of land management?"

Cecil in his innocence found the question hilarious. "Of land management, sir? I? Why, nothing whatsoever."

The earl nodded as if this confirmed some opinion of his own. "And those two farms of your mother's, how do you deal with them?"

The younger man laughed now. He understood that his relative was merely testing him, and Cecil was confident of the answer. "I leave that to a better head than mine, sir. Wilson is well known as a fine steward. I would trust him with my life, if need be."

The earl nodded. "Oh yes, I agree that he is a fine steward. It would be strange if I did not, for I trained him myself and recommended him to your mother when you were a boy, but that is beside the point, you see. A good master does not leave things completely in the hands of even the most trusted servant."

"I don't expect that you mean that I should toil in the fields with the labourers, sir?" Cecil arched his eyebrows and pursed his lips into an amusing moue. His laughter was hollow. For all he knew, that was exactly what the old eccentric had in mind.

"It certainly would do you no harm to strengthen up those lily-white hands. But no, that is not what I had in mind." The earl took another long pull on his pipe and stared meditatively into the fire. "The title and the estate do go hand in hand, my boy," he said almost kindly. "But they are not a mere advantage which sets you above the common run. They are a responsibility. I could have left the old place to rot away, but I did not. I saw the decay and the ruin as a challenge and a trust. When I go, I shall leave not merely the manor and the estate, but the ideals of them as well. Do you understand me?"

Now on sure ground, Cecil languidly waved a paper fan before his face and ran a finger about the inside of his neckpiece. "Oh, quite, sir. Family tradition and all that. A noble sentiment, ain't it? A noble thought. Never fear, I shall carry on."

The old gentleman had become notably quiet, and Cecil felt a moment or two of sympathy for him. It couldn't be easy for the poor old fellah, lingering there at the end of his life, unwilling to let go. Cecil hid a little smile and mentally rubbed his hands together. Well, as they say, you cannot take your worldly goods with you when you go, and what you leave behind belongs to someone else. Begad, *he* would know how to deal with it, when the time came.

Unfortunately, there still remained the imminent threat of that brash young woman who allowed herself to be improperly referred to as Lady Elinor Hardy. Something would have to be done about that.

Lady Barbara snapped at her sister, "I do not see why Aunt has decreed that jade to be quartered right here in the house."

"She says it is because Elinor's father was an old friend

and she wants to give her an advantage," answered Lavinia. "I see nothing amiss in that."

The acrimonious squabble had been echoing about the drawing room for a good ten minutes now and was no nearer a solution than it had been when they began, but Barbara's voice had not previously reached such a sharp pitch. The countess was quite taken aback.

"That is all very well, but I fail to see why she must be inflicted on us. Aunt may be the chit's patroness, if she so chooses, without carrying it to such an extreme."

Lavinia had at first been somewhat amused at her sister's evident discomfiture since the lovely Elinor had come to share their lives. Now she felt Barbara to be passing beyond the bounds of good taste.

"Why, child," she said reproachfully, "how can you speak in such a way of a guest? It is the most flagrant breach of hospitality I have ever heard. I sincerely hope you will confine such opinions to me and not repeat them to our aunt. She would be most disappointed in you."

Barbara tossed her lovely, dark head. "I don't much care, if you want to know the truth. I cannot see why we have to have such a sly minx in the house in the first place. She has done nothing but cause trouble since she arrived."

The usually calm Lavinia was a little ruffled as sometimes happened when her sense of fair play had been outraged. "What trouble is that, may I ask? Lady Elinor has been quite considerate and charming to everyone, so far as I can tell. Aunt is fond of her. I like her as I always have, and the servants cannot do enough for her. I expect she is as popular in society as any young lady in Cheyne Spa." She eyed her sister narrowly. "Or is that the root of this outburst? Could it be that your own nose is slightly out of joint, dearest, because you do not hold sway in quite your usual fashion?"

Barbara had the grace to look faintly chagrined. "Well, I certainly do not mind the general run of men who flock to her. They are scarcely of the better sort, a poor collection of fops and nedashes. What I do protest is that Trev Quenton and Ben Weymouth have been my particular beaux for years, and one would think that even such a creature as *Lady* Elinor would respect such rights."

The countess could not suppress a smile. "Rights, sister? I was not aware that you had entered into any sort of firm contract with either of the gentlemen."

"It has always been understood that I would marry one of them if no better fortune presented itself. I am sure I could have whichever I chose at a moment's notice."

"Why do you not choose then, if they are your particular property?"

Lady Barbara bridled at her sister's chiding tone. "I see that you do not believe me, but I assure you it is true. It is only that I do not wish to injure either of them by taking the other."

"How very considerate of you." Lavinia's dry humour was reminiscent of her aunt, the duchess. "What a pity you do not live in the East where, I believe, one may have as many husbands as one likes. Or is is the other way about? I am never quite certain because my own dear husband is quite enough for me to manage."

The fact that Lady Barbara was often out of sorts with her sister did not mean that she lacked affection for her, and now she said kindly, "If I found a man with whom I could be as happy as you are with Cousin Jack, I am sure I should marry him in a moment."

"If you mean that sincerely, then it seems to me you do not truly want either of your beaux and that is why you are so jealous of them."

"Jealous? I am certainly not jealous at all!" Sometimes when Barbara's temper flared she allowed herself the luxury of giving it reign, and now her voice began to rise. "It is just that Ben and Trev are my own particular friends and I do not care to see such a little opportunist as Elinor Hardy worming her way into their good graces by taking advantage of her presence in this house and often thrown into their company."

"I am positive that it is not the situation at all." Lavinia retorted. She would have continued but for a strangled sound from the doorway of the drawing room. Both sisters turned their heads to find Elinor white-faced and stricken. She stood there for a moment, then ran back up the stairway from which she had come.

"Oh, Barbara, how could you?" cried Lavinia and sprang up immediately to follow their guest.

Lady Barbara had turned beet-red, but she held her ground. "I am sure I had no notion she was creeping about listening at doorways," she said defensively. "In any case, eavesdroppers are bound never to hear good of themselves."

Lavinia was already on her way out of the room but she paused in the doorway long enough for a parting shot. "You are my sister and I do love you, but sometimes, Barbara, you can be a perfect beast!"

Barbara was immediately contrite but, being Barbara, had no idea how to mend the harm she had done. She was not much given to self-reflection beyond the image she perceived in her looking glass. Her beauty had always been a solace, and she crossed the room now to seek justification from the large mirror on the far wall. It was always a thrill to recognise once again what made such a broad variety of men cluster about her.

Smiling, she thought of the coming masquerade ball at the Assembly Rooms. She must take care not to disguise herself too well. It would be a pity to cover up this flawless face. The vision of Ben and Trevor, perhaps as knights to her Queen Guinevere, passed through her mind, followed by yet another face, far handsomer than either of her two beaux. It was that actor from the playhouse. She wondered if he would have the audacity upon such a night to mix company with his betters?

= 10 =

PATRICK TYRONE WAS well aware of his effect on women both young and old, and he was canny enough to employ it to great effect in the furtherance of his career. Actually, he was far from being a womanizer by temperament, but he *was* fully aware that the life of a professional actor can be lamentably short if he does not make full use of every advantage given him. There is, however, a great difference between the cultivation of a loyal following and that practice of some unscrupulous male actors who actively prey upon their feminine admirers. Patrick was not of that breed, and yet . . .

His thoughts flashed back to the moment when he had first encountered Lady Barbara Pentreath and her frankly admiring gaze. It set up a man to have a woman as lovely as that look at him so. It gave him ideas, perhaps even ideas a bit above his station. She was a real lady, no doubt about it. Wasn't her aunt a duchess an' all? But there was also no doubt in his mind that there had been in her eyes something more than mere appreciation of his art as a thespian. He was no womanizer, but he was also no fool. He knew when a woman found him attractive. Even when the woman in question was a highborn lady.

Mrs. Mudge, the character actress of the company, passed on the backstage stairs and gave him a surprisingly healthy swat across the backside. "Here, then, what are you standing about for, my young bucko?" she asked in silvery Shakespearean tones. "We've got a mort of fresh work to be done on scene four. Did you hear them last night?"

She meant, of course, the audience which was always her prime concern. This theatrical grand dame, much beloved by public and players alike, had grown up in Houndsditch, where her father was the purveyor of second-hand garments; she had long ago eliminated every vestige of the district from her speech. Her voice rang out like a trumpet. The words of the playwright were never blurred or mangled in the mouth of Mrs. Mudge, though ordinary conversation sometimes took on an incongruous importance which its intrinsic subject matter lacked, merely because every sentence she uttered was enhanced by the way it was spoken.

"In scene four?" Patrick struggled to remember. So far as he could recall, it was only a few brief moments on the forestage to carry the plot while the setting was changed behind the curtain. "No, I cannot say that I did hear them," he confessed.

She shook an admonitory finger at him. "My point exactly. There are at least three good laughs in that scene, and you caught not a one of them. Shame upon you, my boy. A scene is not merely a waiting period, you know. You call yourself an actor? I warrant you shall be one before Mrs. Mudge is done with you. Come along and I will show you what you must do."

Such was the old woman's prestige that he accepted her dictum without demure. If Mrs. Mudge said something must be improved, who was he to say her no? The whole theatrical establishment held the truth of that. Had she not seen every actor from the Great Garrick to little Master Betty?

They reached the narrow playing area before the curtain and she thrust him into place with surprising strength. "Now then, you stand there. Now say your line."

"Which line?" he asked stupidly. "Do you mean my first line or my main speech?"

"Which line begins the scene, you great lout?" she railed

kindly. "Say your first line, and I will be Lord Grafton discovered here."

He filled his lungs and took a half step toward her. "Good afternoon, my lord, though it be nearly evening by the clock."

"Stop. Did I tell you to move or stand?"

Patrick shrugged. "Well, madam, you originally said stand, but I have always—"

"Never, never move on a line, my dear. You kill it automatically. Do you take me?"

"Yes, madam."

She mimicked him exactly. "*Yes, madam.*" Then she gave a humourous little snort. "See here, my lad, if you move one inch before I give the word I shall cross the stage and stamp on your feet to make you remember, and you will not be able to do a thing about it," she added, "because I am such a frail old lady. Now stand and deliver!"

He repeated the line, feeling like a fool. He could not say why, but it *did* have a faint ring of comedy which he had never noticed before.

"Like that?"

"Better. Good enough for the moment, but you'll improve upon it when you find the feeling. Now, then, pay attention. Turn your foot out. No, no, your *right* foot, dearie. Always the right foot out when you are standing stage right. Try it again."

Patrick did as he was told.

"You see what difference it makes? You see what it does to your body? Makes it twist a bit, doesn't it? That stance is a great secret of Restoration acting. It will get your laugh I guarantee, and once they've taken the habit of it they'll laugh again even though they may not know why. And *that* will build to your main speech which is very funny if you come at it in the right way, you see."

"I hope you do not mean that I must keep in this spot the whole while?"

Her look could have been withering from anyone else. "I

should think not. But you must have a *reason* to move, bumpkin, or you will lose what you have gained. Oh, I have every faith in you, but you must learn the art of discretion. I daresay it would be something of a novelty to show a wooden post as player, but it would be a passing fancy."

She surveyed him once more, rather more sharply this time. "What is it, my boy? I fancy something is troubling you. A woman, is it? When a man of your young years goes off his regular manner, there is usually a bit of skirt at the bottom of it."

Patrick flushed. "Yes, I suppose it is." He hesitated, then blurted out, "I don't suppose you would give me a bit of advice in it?"

She shook her magnificent old head. "You men are all alike. If the wench is giving trouble, let her go her own way and you stick to your own, is always my advice. Some tavern slut, I'll be bound, who makes you think she is good as any lady?"

The young actor bit his lip. "This one *is* a lady, I am afraid. There is nothing yet, you see, but there might be."

"What, a real lady? Don't be a fool, lad. Do you think you'll outmark old Malvolio? No, no, the Bard knew what he knew. The classes do not mix. We players must not mingle with our so-called betters. It never goes well. Look at poor Mrs. Jordan. Taken up by that wretched Duke of Clarence with his silly pineapple poll. Fancy being mistress to a man with no money. The cork-brained trull supported him for years, gave him ten children and then found herself cast off when she became an inconvenience to him so he could marry someone of his own station. She died in France a few years ago, poor thing. Mad as a hatter, they say, and I shouldn't wonder."

Patrick smiled. "I scarcely think this particular lady would foster ten children upon me."

She winked rather rudely. "No, but if you are not properly wedded, fostering just one on *her* would bring your arse about your ears as they say. Especially if she *is* a real lady. Are you prepared for such a thing as that? Oh, no, my dicky-duck. Stick to your own kind, is what I say. Stick to your own kind, and if it goes awry no harm is done. Theatrical folk know what loneliness is and what it can lead to among them as is thrown together."

She patted him consolingly upon the shoulder. "Now, you just put your energies into exploring this little scene and see what you can do with it. Old John who plays Lord Brandon will pick up on your intentions quickly enough, though he is no innovator himself. You have the true stuff in you, you know. I can see it. I have been around long enough to recognise the gift when it is there, but you must work for it."

She allowed him one of those dazzling smiles which had contributed to her long popularity. "Whatever you set your eyes on, you can achieve; but it must be worked for. That is a part of the secret. It is no good otherwise, you see. It turns to fairy gold in your hand."

Hardly believing it could make all that much difference, Patrick followed her suggestions at the next performance and was not a little surprised at how accurately she had predicted the reaction. The first mild chuckles built into a laugh, and then, with his main speech of the scene, a collective guffaw.

John Gordon, with whom Patrick played the scene, was stupefied. "What the devil had got into them tonight? Was my wig askew or my smallclothes unbuttoned? I have been playing that scene for forty years, and all they ever did was to sit on their hands and wait until it was over." He looked quizzically at Patrick. "I kept me eye on you, young fellah, to be sure you wasn't mugging it up to entertain them. Well, you wasn't, so far as I could see. I cannot account for it, and that's a fact."

Nor could Gordon account for it the next evening when the laughter came in exactly the same places and in the same degree. In following performances he continued to be baffled each time the scene came around, although he also began to look forward to the gratifying warmth of the audience. What was more, he seemed to regard Patrick with a wary new respect.

"It must be you, my boy, for I know I am playing it in exactly the way I have done for all these years," he said.

Of course, that was not true. No advance is made alone; and, even if he did not realize it, he was, as much as the audience, reacting to Patrick's new understanding. In the theatre, as in life, the ground must be prepared before the blossoming can take place.

Word soon flew around Cheyne Spa that something rather interesting was happening at the Theatre Royal. There were many amusements to occupy the hours, but everyone likes to be abreast of the latest trend. Consequently, Mr. Tyrone was soon taken up by Cheyne society. In fact, one could speak of him in the same breath as the Duchess of Doddington or the old Marquess of Lorn without the slightest blush.

"I should like to go to the theatre again sometime very soon, would you not, Aunt?" asked Barbara artlessly, and Lady Augusta agreed.

"Why do we not send Wilton around for tickets for this evening?" she suggested. "We might make up a little party and take a box. Perhaps the five of us plus your two admirers?"

"What five?" asked the girl a little crossly, although she must have known the answer. "Whom do you have in mind?"

"You and I, Lavinia and Jack, and Lady Elinor, unless she has made some alternate engagement," said the duchess mildly.

"Oh, Aunt, I wish you would not call her Lady Elinor when everyone knows she is merely plain Miss Hardy. Don't you think it a little common to promote someone to a rank she does not rightly hold? I am certain Miss Hardy herself would agree if you asked her. I remember her as being a mousey and compliant little thing at school, always willing to defer to her betters."

Lady Augusta said nothing in reply, but raised her eyebrows in that way she had which made her niece wish the subject had not been broached. There was silence between them for a moment, while the duchess attended to a particularly difficult stitch in her needlepoint.

Presently she remarked, "They say that Mr. Tyrone is coming along more quickly than anyone had expected and that he is soon to be seen in some of the larger roles. I expect he has a natural talent for the stage to have progressed so rapidly."

It occurred to Lady Barbara she might not be alone in her admiration of the actor; but, of course, that mattered little. Attractive though she found him, such a misalliance was, to say the least, absurd. Sometimes she wondered just a little about the pleasures of ordinary people.

She sighed. It was an amusing game, but she knew that question would never have an answer.

=== 11 ===

THE THEATRE ROYAL, even when considered merely as a
building and not in terms of what was housed within it,
was generally acknowledged to be one of the glories of
Cheyne Spa. It had been designed by George Dance who
had built the facade of London's guildhall. By the time the
theatre had been completed public taste had grown to
deplore the early gimcrackery of the town, and the Royal
was deservedly praised.

Elinor loved it. It had just been completed when she first
came to the Spa as a child; and, whether their seats had
been fine or high in the gods, there had always been an air
of warmth and ease about the place which endeared it to
her.

The entrance to the boxes was by way of a private house,
adjacent to the theatre, with a convenient suite of retiring
rooms. As their party mounted the stairs, Elinor looked
about her with curiosity and pleasure. This was a special
night, and it seemed as if all the summer residents of the
Spa had turned out to see the favourite in a new role. From
where she stood midway up the stairway, Elinor could gaze
in both directions and look upon the cream of Cheyne
society at its most dazzling. There were the old Duchess of
Doddington with her majordomo. Their relationship was
so consistently outré that it had long since been accepted.
Also present were the ancient Marquess of Lorn, Lady
Sinclair, Lord Wilton, the inseparable Misses Thompson
and Coppinger and the popular Princess of Thoningen.

Lady Augusta said something to Elinor which was unintelligible above the noise of the crowd. Just as she was about to turn back to the duchess the girl's eyes were caught for a moment and held by those of a remarkably priggish-looking gentleman about her own age. He was approaching the bottom of the stair and regarding her with such intense animosity that she was quite taken aback, the more so since she had no idea who he might be. He said something to a faded-looking woman beside him, and she too turned a frown upon Elinor. It was most curious to be reviled by people unknown. She would have enquired of the duchess who they might be, but that lady was already engaged in conversation. Thus, the moment passed.

When they arrived at their box, Elinor was quite enchanted. She had never before been privileged to see the theatre from this particular vantage, and she found it delightful. Their box was almost in the centre of the second of three tiers and afforded a depth of rows to accommodate their party. Custom decreed that the ladies in their beautiful gowns should occupy the fore. Cast-iron pillars were placed at a distance of two feet from the front. Consequently, the first row of each circle appeared as a balcony independent of the main structure. The boxes themselves were individually enclosed by gilt lattice which provided a feeling of privacy while not in the least obstructing the view of one's neighbours.

In the moments before the play began, of course, there were a great many people staring about them through opera glasses, those clever, little binoculars which are so designed that no one can perceive who it is you are looking at. Even Elinor gazed about her when one of the gentlemen was not engaging her attention and spied a familiar face looking up at her with a smile from the stalls. She acknowledged Tyger Dobyn with a small movement of her head, hardly more than a brief nod. Nonetheless, Lady Augusta took note of it at once and leaned closer to whisper in her ear.

"Not that one, if you please, my dear. Smile a bit more

at Mr. Quenton. Perhaps you could manage to drop your fan or handkerchief?"

That made Elinor laugh, and her prettily painted fan was at once put into use with such effect that Mr. Quenton was quite enchanted. Her success might well have been measured by Lady Barbara's annoyance or, conversely, by the tolerant smile with which Ben Weymouth regarded Elinor's action. However, once the curtain had been raised and the prologue spoken, attention was completely centred upon the stage.

Old Mrs. Mudge was *The Marriage Broker* of the title and she made the most of the role. She had never been pretty enough to reach the heights as a young woman, but now the field was hers alone. Indeed, this role had usually been played by less venerable dames, but she convinced the Cheyne Spa audience that such casting had been mere shortsightedness on the part of the managers. Her comic timing, her very presence carried the play. However popular the rising, young juvenile, however much sage advice and tuition she had given him, it was to herself that the acting plaudits of the evening were gathered. The clever denouement of the fifth act, in which all the matchmaker's machinations are vindicated, delighted the spectators so fully they were all but brought to their feet.

The portrayal of Charles Kingston was the ideal role for Patrick Tyrone at this time. It allowed him to wear gentlemanly costume, behave with buckish dash and exercise that considerable Hibernian charm which was his greatest asset. He was the perfect foil for the old woman; and hardly a person in the theatre, male or female, did not succumb to the spell he cast. If he did not yet wield that mastery which was later to place him in the forefront of the actor-managers, he had well begun toward it.

Lady Barbara was entranced and made no secret of it. At the intervals she burbled on in such animated fashion that her aunt and sister stared at her in astonishment. Here was a new and unexpected Barbara. In place of the usual cool and disdainful exterior, her eyes sparkled and her lips curved into a succession of smiles so enchanting that nearly every gentleman within her purview was drawn to exercise his own greatest amiability in return.

"Is not dear Mrs. Mudge a marvel?" she asked of all. "Is not Mr. Gordon a paragon?" She reached the ultimate object of her enthusiasm by degrees and such oblique means that no one who did not know her intimately would have realised how ardent her admiration. "And Mr. Tyrone, is he not fine? Does he not move elegantly? Did you see with what finesse he used the handkerchief after dipping snuff?"

Her own admirers agreed. They had liked the young actor exceedingly well, but it was Barbara who now inspired them. They all but fought to get nearer to her—Trevor, for all of Elinor's efforts, succumbing with the rest. Ben Weymouth alone seemed impervious to her animation. At a pause in the conversation he approached Elinor.

"Are you as swept away by the performance as everyone else seems to be, your ladyship?"

Certainly, she was enjoying herself and was full of admiration for the actors, but she was not as blissfully uncritical as Lady Barbara. "Mrs. Mudge is very fine, is she not? I particularly liked the scene when she was bargaining for the dowry."

"I am sure that is a situation in which you need never fear for yourself," Ben said gallantly. "Any man would consider himself fortunate to win you, dowry or no."

Elinor smiled at his extravagance. "That is most fortunate, sir," she answered, "since I have no prospects whatsoever."

He gave her a quick, speculative look. Like most of Cheyne, he was aware who her grandfather was and had heard something of their history. Since her arrival at the Spa, her family situation had been much discussed.

"Nevertheless, I hold to my thought."

Elinor was so taken aback at the admiration in his voice

that she cast her eyes downward and blushed in a way which Weymouth found quite enchanting.

"And the performance of Mr. Tyrone who seems to have entirely taken everyone's fancy?" Weymouth went on.

"What of it, sir?"

"Are you as charmed by him as the others are?"

She felt that he was leading up to something but could not quite perceive what it might be. She looked up into his handsome, young face. He was scarcely more than a boy after all, older than herself by only a year or two, but much more youthful in terms of life experience. His schooling would have been academically impeccable, she was certain, while hers had been the hard education of a gamester's daughter. Their differences were more than those of mere situation. Meanwhile, over her shoulder, she heard Barbara's continuing paean.

"Mr. Tyrone is quite remarkable, is he not? I am sure I have never seen a player of his young years do such justice to a role. It quite makes one long to see him in the classics. Think what an Orlando he would make with those fine, wide shoulders."

"Or even a Romeo?" suggested another feminine voice, and there was a general sighing amongst the ladies.

Elinor saw that Ben had heard it, too. Dropping all pretence, she asked forthrightly, "You care for her very much, do you?"

She had caught him off his guard; and for a moment pride, caution and natural masculine embarrassment struggled in his face. Then he shrugged.

"It is difficult to tell," he said simply. "I suppose I have loved her in some degree ever since we met."

She laid an understanding hand on his arm. "I do not know that I can do much for your cause, but I will further it if at all possible."

Ben smiled and placed his own hand over hers. "I repeat once more, any man will be fortunate to win you for a wife."

"Thank you," she said and slipped her hand away with a guilty look in the direction of the duchess. Elinor's assigned purpose was to occupy Trevor's attention, not Ben's; but, to her great surprise, she found Lady Augusta beaming at her fondly.

Elinor excused herself from Barbara's suitor and returned to the box, where she borrowed the duchess's opera glasses to amuse herself by looking about. In the glow of candlelight, the theatre had a golden quality which she remembered from her childhood. Peering down into the stalls, she saw that Tyger Dobyn had left his seat and, though she watched casually for him when the audience returned, she did not see him again that evening.

The remainder of the performance passed somewhat uneasily for Elinor due to words spoken almost tenderly by Lady Augusta when she returned to her place. "We shall have a little talk at home before retiring, shall we?"

Elinor could not tell whether that boded for good or ill.

Her grace had organised a small supper party after the theatre for the seven of them, plus three or four old friends of impeccable reputation. It was quite informal, and the men were allowed to drift off to one end of the drawing room where they could huddle together, talking of horses, milling and politics. Meanwhile, the ladies, at the other extremity, chattered with similar mindlessness about fashion and society, subjects which were closely identified in their minds. It was all frocks and fans except for Lady Barbara who was not to be deterred from her infatuation with young Tyrone, and who went on and on about him until eyebrows began to be raised and Countess Lavinia was obliged to draw her away for a moment on the pretext of asking her advice on the purchase of some painted chicken skin.

When they were out of the hearing of the others, Lavinia maintained her pleasantly enquiring expression but spoke to her sister quite sharply. "For heaven's sake, my darling," she drawled in that exaggerated, country way she had adopted since her marriage. "You are becoming dreadfully tedious about Mr. Tyrone. I expect that all the ladies share your admiration, but they are less conspicuous about it."

Ordinarily, this would have been enough of a hint to dampen the fires of Barbara's enthusiasm to a manageable level because she was always concerned with the image she presented to the world. Tonight, however, she merely tossed her head and trilled a little laugh.

"I suppose you are all thinking I am nothing but a gillygaupus, carried away like any silly schoolgirl?" She made a pouting little moue. "Well, perhaps I am. Or it may only be a reaction to seeing Miss Hardy fairly throw herself a Ben Weymouth's head. I suppose you saw how she made a great show of going off by herself, expecting him to trail after her I am sure, though he did not, of course. I see that someone will have to take her in hand so that she will not entirely disgrace us when we go out in the evenings." Her colour had become uncharacteristically high. "Perhaps you could do that, Lavvy, since you profess such great friendship for her."

The countess watched her sister warily. This flightiness was not in the least like her usual self-containment. "I am sure that Lady Elinor is free to do as she sees fit," she retorted, keeping a weather eye on the other women across the room. "It is yourself and your own reputation with which I am at the moment concerned. Remember who you are, my dear. Lady Elinor may be allowed to 'throw herself' at Ben, as you put it, though I do not for a moment believe that to be true. But a lady and certainly a Pentreath lady, may *not* launch herself at the head of a mere player, no matter how talented and popular he may be."

"Richard Sheridan married Miss Linley," Barbara protested.

"Yes, and made her unhappy ever after. Is that what you want for yourself?"

Barbara blinked at Lavinia's tone. It was one which she

herself often employed with inferiors, but never before had it been used on her.

"Good heavens, Lavvy, issue me a little credit. I merely admire the artist and his talent. May not a lady become a patron without scandal? What a pother over nothing."

The two sisters stood for a moment, staring at each other. Finally, their old girlish understanding came to the fore. They returned to the other ladies in a more light-hearted mood, half-dissolved in a fit of giggles while their guests exchanged knowing glances. How pretty a thing it was to see sisters dwelling together in such amity.

In fact, the countess would have been dismayed to learn that her timely warning had inspired an opposite effect from that which she intended. Instead of allowing her sister's infatuation to run its course, Lavinia's words exacerbated it. They had initiated in her sister a process usually alien to her way of conduct. Lady Barbara had actually begun to *think* about her situation. It was a line which could easily lead her either to wisdom . . . or to folly.

$=$ 12 $=$

THE WIDOW PARTRIDGE, Evangeline to her friends, had in her youth been a pertly attractive young woman. Though she was now plump and matronly, she had never in her inmost heart relinquished the idea that she might, by some miracle, become that girl again. At the age of forty-three with a grown son it was, each morning looking in the glass, more difficult to maintain the memory of youth. Nonetheless, though long-since passed into the state of comfortable reliction, she continued to hope that, in the world's eyes, she might still be taken for her son's sister. It was in order to foster just such an illusion, and forgetting the languor of most young women, that she had begun to cultivate an animated demeanour which her son found vastly annoying.

"Really, Mama, could you not spare me a few moments of your undivided attention? I fear the situation verges on the serious."

Mrs. Partridge smiled brightly, opening her eyes very wide. "But I *am* listening, Cecil, dear. I have heard every word you uttered and I agree with you wholeheartedly. Your uncle is undoubtedly being very obstinate, but he is an old man and cannot have very many more years left in his allotment. Your place as his heir is assured, you know; the girl cannot possibly inherit."

Cecil's sharp nose quivered in indignation. "That is true. There is no doubt about the title, but my uncle has dropped some very worrisome hints about the money."

"The money? What do you mean? The title and the

96

money go hand in hand, do they not?" Evangeline was all attention now.

"When I spoke to him yesterday, he was at great pains to point out that, although the estate and the profits from it are entailed, the fortune he has accumulated in other enterprises is not. He may leave most of his money where he chooses, Mama, and there is no use in having the title if there is no money to maintain it."

"I had always understood that the estate was self-supporting. Heaven knows, I seem to have heard him boasting of it often enough," said Evangeline, sounding suddenly troubled. "Is that not true, after all?"

"I am no agriculturist, Mother dear. As you know, my talents have always lent themselves to more intellectual pursuits."

His mother refrained from mentioning that he had twice been sent down from school and made little use of the great library amassed by his late father. While it is true that law books and collections of sermons are not often stimulating to the minds of the young, it was a great pity to see the handsome volumes merely sitting there on the shelf, providing little more than opportunities to busy the downstairs maid with dusting.

"Well," said Evangeline, considering, "you know that Wilson has always done well with *my* little property, and he was trained by the earl himself. I daresay he could manage a larger demesne. It is not so bad as you think, I am sure. I believe your uncle is very fond of you, my dear. He has often intimated as much to me, I believe. Yes, very fond, I am certain. You have merely let it get into your head that he means to treat you as he did his poor son, but I think that is unlikely. If I know Edward Hardy at all, he is not likely to turn his back on a property which he takes great pride in having saved from ruination. The only danger I can foresee is if that young woman we saw at the theatre should marry and bear a male child before the old man dies. What happens in such an event, I wonder? Would the title pass to the child or to you? I cannot see, though, why you think he might change his mind at this late date."

"Sometimes, Mama, I feel as if I must speak to you in thoughts of one syllable. It is because Cousin Elinor *is* in Cheyne Spa, don't you see? If we saw her last evening, he probably did so as well."

His mother took up the new digression eagerly. "Oh, was that not amusing last evening? I quite adored that new, young actor, didn't you? It is easy to see why they are all gabbling about him."

"I am sure he is very fine, Mama, but that is not the point."

His mother giggled maddeningly. "Then what is, dearest boy? We were talking about the theatre, and I merely mentioned how much I enjoyed the players. Dear Mrs. Mudge, did she not do well? We were almost related to Mrs. Mudge at one time, you know. It was quite a near thing, I believe. Fancy, being related to an actress!"

Cecil was not to be drawn off along still another tangent. He was willing, in the interests of harmony, to pause a moment to discuss the play, but he was in no mood for one of his mother's endless digressions into the past. He launched upon a detailed exegesis of the play, of young Tyrone and his great reception in the hope that, by the time he had done, his mother's mind might have had the leisure to do its work and come to some conclusion about the problem of Elinor Hardy. He knew well that maternal concern would express itself one way or another eventually.

Brushing the matter of the play aside at last, Evangeline said, rather shockingly, "The answer is clear, of course. You must resign yourself to marrying your cousin."

This took her son quite aback. "But Mama, I scarcely know the wench. I only guessed who she was because the gossips all said she was acting as companion to the duchess and I quite disliked her at first sight. Marry? Impossible!"

"The way things stand now," said his mother with unaccustomed practicality, "there is little alternative. If you marry Miss Hardy, the title *and* the income will surely be secure, no matter what the law says or what the old man decides to do. As for the girl, the lapse of acquaintance is easily remedied. Aside from her grandfather and his sister, we are her only relatives. What could be more natural than that I should ask her to tea? She can hardly refuse to visit her dear old auntie, can she? Thank heaven she is at least not ugly. I should hate to have an unpleasant-looking grandchild."

"No," said Cecil, considering, "she is not that, though I have no great attraction to these kittenish faces which are so popular just now. At least she dresses well."

"Oh, I daresay she takes very great pains in that direction, since she is so well turned out. If only it is not mere extravagance, I quite like her already. Anything else for a pretty woman seems almost like flying in the face of Providence."

With this curious, though pious observation, the widow poured herself a little sherry and returned to the burden of her previous topic.

"Dear Mrs. Mudge is always so fine, is she not? Though it is extraordinary that such an old thing should suddenly be taken up by the public after all these years. Quite inspiring, really, when you think of it. Some small compensation for her great sacrifice, I expect."

Cecil wondered if his mama's mind was beginning to go at such an early age. "Are we still speaking of Mrs. Mudge, Mama? To what sacrifice of hers do you refer?"

"Oh, her marriage, my dear. Once years ago she was affianced to your Uncle Edward. You didn't know that? How extraordinary. Oh, yes, she was to have married him, but it was all spoilt when she ran away to seek her fortune upon the stage. He couldn't marry her then, you see."

"Why ever not?" asked Cecil with a show of sophistication. "Noble gentlemen marry actresses all the time. I mean to say, Mama, that it is awfully common."

His mother nodded. "I daresay it is. A gentleman may,

I suppose marry beneath him and raise the lady to his own level. However, what is the poor man to do when his beloved not only falls from grace, but also fairly *flings* herself over the precipice?

She sipped the Amontillado meditatively. Her eyes were unfocussed as if they gazed upon some distant horizon. "I always fancied that I could have been an actress, you know, if I had not had the misfortune to be born a lady."

All that morning Lady Augusta had been much occupied; there had been urgent correspondence to deal with, preparations for a charity bazaar to be held in a fortnight's time, a late breakfast for the deaconesses of St. Gerrans's; and, later in the day, the church deacons were coming to tea. It was not until early afternoon that she found a few moments to spare for Elinor.

"I am so sorry we did not have opportunity to speak last evening, my dear, but it was so late by the time our guests took their leave that I thought all of us deserving of a good night's rest." The duchess said this rather severely, as if she disapproved of people who had no idea when it was time to take their leave. "I simply wanted to congratulate you upon your change in tactics. I see now that you were quite right in your assessment of the situation and that my own judgement was flawed."

Elinor looked at her blankly. "Tactics, duchess? Whatever do you mean?"

"Ah, you slyboots. I mean your presence of mind in seeing that Barbara has shifted her attention from poor Trevor Quenton to that handsome actor. It is only a passing fancy, I am sure, but making her jealous of Ben Weymouth's attention to you will surely hasten things along to their logical conclusion."

"I must protest that you give me too much credit," Elinor began to say, but the duchess seemed not to hear her, her attention being occupied instead by the scribbled list in her hand.

"There are not enough hours in the day," she moaned in despair. "As well as the deacons, I must decide on the favours for the masquerade ball."

"Is there no way that I can help?"

"Oh, no, dearest. You must continue to fascinate Ben. Are you not seeing him today?" She peered closely at Elinor. "I would have thought that after the great attention he paid you at the theatre and again here at the house we would have him on our doorstep every moment."

Elinor smiled. "For most of that time we talked about Lady Barbara. I have a sympathetic ear, you see. He feels that I am the only one who can understand him."

Her patroness chuckled. "I pray you, do not allow my niece to know that she is your subject. We can only succeed if she believes you are a serious threat to her future happiness."

There was a pleasant smugness in her attitude that Elinor found quite enchanting. All the more so when the duchess added, "Not that *she* will ever bless you for your understanding heart."

"Ben has gone to Budolph with Trevor to look at horses, I believe," said Elinor. "I am quite free for any commissions you might care to entrust to me. I will find them welcome in fact because they will allow me to go out of the house. I may take Dora, I hope?"

"Dora? But of course you may, if you like. Although in Cheyne it is not considered a necessity as in other places, you know. I expect that has something to do with the high percentage of invalids to be found here. Actually, what I really need are the masquerade favours from the Assembly Rooms. Mrs. Parsons knows where they may be found. In fact, I would be most grateful if *you* would make the preliminary decision and then refer your choices to me. Do you mind doing that?"

"Not at all, duchess. Shall I change your books at the circulating library while I am out?"

"What a good idea," said her grace. "That new novel by

Mr. Kneitel would be most pleasant, if it is available, though I daresay it may not be. He is very popular, you know. Perhaps the new Alice Brannigan is in."

As Elinor turned away, intent on changing into a walking dress, the duchess called after her humourously, "Do not think I have mistaken your eagerness, my dear. Since you were so kind as to help with the deaconesses, I shall let you off the deacons; but there is still the committee for the masquerade. I don't know that rich, old women are much to be preferred over pious, old men."

In response, there was such a clatter of the door-knocker that they could hear it in the library. Presently the footman brought a tray carrying a *carte de visite* with one corner turned carefully down.

"There is a gentleman, your grace, asking to see Lady Elinor. I have explained that neither your grace nor her ladyship usually accepts calls on Wednesdays, but he informs me he is a near connexion of her ladyship."

The duchess took the card from the tray and examined it with amusement. "Cecil Partridge? My poor love, you have made a sorry conquest. How in the world do you come to know Cecil?"

Elinor was mystified. "Does he say that we are connected?"

Then a light seemed to break over the face of the duchess. "Oh, of course. He is your cousin. How very silly of me. I had quite forgotten."

"My cousin, madam? You astonish me. I did not know I possessed one."

=== 13 ===

DESPITE HIS NAME, Cecil Partridge, in grey coat and white smallclothes, looked more like a small, grey mouse than a feathered fowl. So marked was the resemblance that Elinor almost felt she should be able to see a long tail extruding from beneath his tailcoat.

He made his leg with a great flourish as he came into the room and said in a high-pitched voice, "Ladies, you do me honour in receiving me upon such informal application."

Elinor eyed him attentively. She knew she had seen him somewhere before. Then it came to her. At the theatre, this had been the gentleman who eyed her with such displeasure as they were ascending to the boxes. Yet, his malice seemed to have quite evaporated since then. Indeed, he was wreathed in smiles which he bestowed indiscriminately upon the duchess, upon herself and even upon Dora who came quietly into the room at that moment.

"You rang, madam?" she asked.

Lady Augusta assented. "Please fetch Lady Elinor's parasol and gloves, and bring a reticule. You will be accompanying her upon a commission or two for me."

"I apprehend that I have come at an inconvenient time," said the caller, purposefully removing the yellow gloves which were so fashionable that year.

Lady Augusta made no pretence of it. "It is a busy life here in Cheyne, Mr. Partridge," she said. "We must somehow draw your mother more fully into it. We must all shoulder our responsibilities, you know."

"My mother is a most retiring lady, your grace," he answered. "It is a miracle to persuade her to leave her own parlour."

"Do you know Mr. Partridge, Elinor dear?" asked the duchess. "He is heir to the Earl of Glastonia, you know. Though, of course, we all hope that sweet old man will be with us for long years yet," she added. It was difficult to say whether the delicate barb had penetrated Partridge's coat.

"Mr. Partridge?" asked Elinor uncertainly.

"Cousin," he corrected. "Your dear Cousin Cecil, Lady Elinor."

Bewildered, Elinor could only stammer. "I—ah—in what way are we related, sir? I mean to say, by what means have we become cousins?"

"Why, in the usual way I would expect," he answered with a faint smirk. He stared at her for a moment, seeming to gauge her reply, then drew back with an expression of complete surprise. "Do you really mean to say . . . Why, bless me, I believe you really do not know who I am." He paused, wrinkling his brow in concentration. "You *do* know that your father had a cousin born on exactly the same day?"

It was obvious that the young woman was struggling to recapture long-forgotten memories. "I think I have heard my father mention it, but it was so very long ago . . . Is he in good health, my father's twin cousin?"

"No, my father died some years ago. I was such a mere boy that I scarcely remember him myself. My mother is very well, though, and that brings me 'round to the purpose of my visit. Mama, that is Mama and I, would like you to come to tea one afternoon very soon. Perhaps on Friday, if you are free?"

Elinor exchanged looks with Lady Augusta who rolled her eyes heavenward. "I do not know if that is possible," Elinor answered. "We are arranging the final details of the

Masquerade Ball, you see. And since it takes place on Saturday, I fear there is hardly a moment to spare."

"You have no idea, sir, of the great number of things still to be done," the duchess interposed hastily to back up Elinor's story. "Lady Elinor was just departing on some commissions concerning it when you arrived."

He allowed his delicate hands an extravagant gesture. "Perhaps you will allow me the honour of accompanying you, cousin? What a good means of furthering our acquaintance, eh?"

His attitude in the theatre was not forgotten. Elinor was certain she had not imagined it, but she tried to mask her feeling toward him. "Oh, I fear it would put you to far too great a trouble, sir. My maid will be accompanying me, and I fear we will be too occupied for much conversation. As for Friday, I am afraid it is out of the question, but I shall be happy to make the acquaintance of my aunt one day next week, if that is convenient. On what days does she receive?"

He pulled a long face. "She will be disappointed at having to wait, but I am certain she will understand. Shall we say on Tuesday?"

Elinor allowed him one of her most charming smiles. "I am looking forward to it. It is quite exciting to find one has relatives one never knew existed." She took a deep breath, then added with as much casualness as she could muster, "I hope I may one day have the pleasure of meeting my grandfather as well. Will that be possible, do you suppose?"

His expression altered suddenly into one of disbelief and a certain apprehensiveness. "Do you mean to say you have never met the old fellah? Why, I would have thought that . . . Well, I daresay it could be arranged sometime. He is quite famous as a misanthrope, you know. Doesn't see much of anyone."

Perhaps suspecting that his words might merely whet her appetite for such a meeting, Cecil hastened to turn aside from the subject. "Well, then, cousin, I shall not detain you further. I shall tell Mama to expect you on Tuesday."

Wilton appeared in the doorway once more. "Mr. Dobyn, your grace."

In contrast to her coolness to Cecil Partridge, Lady Augusta at once became all expansive charm, moving forward with her hands outstretched. "Ah, my dear Tyger, what a pleasure to see you!"

The gentleman boxer seemed faintly surprised at such effusiveness but accepted it easily. "Good afternoon, duchess. Lady Elinor, I hope you are well. I trust I do not intrude?"

The duchess smiled in a tolerant way. "Good grief, is such a thing possible? Come in, come in." Then added, almost as if it were an afterthought, "Oh, do you know Mr. Partridge? Mr. Partridge, this is, of course, the famous Tyger Dobyn of whom you have perhaps heard."

Cecil stiffened as if his decency were outraged in being presented so casually to such an individual. He reddened; and his traitorous nose, disclosing his agitation, quivered. "I know the name, certainly," he said. "Good afternoon, sir." Then to Elinor, "I know Mama will look forward to your visit, cousin. We of the old families must stick together, do you not think? Duchess, it has been so very kind of you to allow me to break in upon your little circle. I hope you will allow me to visit again?"

"Thursdays, Mr. Partridge. I am sure we shall be most gratified. Perhaps my nieces will be present as well. They usually are, you know, on our regular at home day." She rang for the footman. "So kind of you to call, sir."

Cecil allowed himself to be shown out, but with a certain fury building in his breast. The woman might be a duchess and a Pentreath, but that was no excuse for such hauteur. She had acted as if he himself were no one at all. And to add to the insult, that ruffian had been welcomed so warmly. A pugilist was scarcely the sort of person one expected to meet on Regent's Crescent—and to find him an intimate of the household of such a personage as the Duchess of Towans was quite incredible!

So *that* was Cousin Elinor. When he had seen her at the theatre, he had not supposed she would be such a colourless thing. He could not for the life of him see why she was being spoken of all over the Spa as the latest rage who was setting all the young bloods' hearts atumble. She gave the impression of being quite biddable, in fact. Perhaps the task of securing Grandpapa's fortune would not prove to be so difficult after all.

Cecil tapped his hat to a more comfortable angle and swung his cane with a dashingly jaunty air as he made his way toward St. Gerrans's Gardens. He found himself vastly in need of a sudden cup of bohea to clear his mind. Besides, the Gardens might, as they had sometimes done before, provide a bit of adventure as well.

Meanwhile, back inside the house Cecil had just departed, Tyger Dobyn found the temperature descending to a more natural level. He accepted the alteration as easily as he had the previous, more effusive mood.

"I came by to enquire of Countess Lavinia about Black Davey," he explained. "I understand she is considering putting him on the block."

Lady Augusta pulled an expression of disbelief. "Put her stallion up for sale? Why, she treats the beast as one of the family. Where did you hear such a thing?"

"I had it from a not unimpeachable source," he admitted, "which is why I called to confirm it for myself. I would naturally be vastly interested if such were the case. I have admired Black Davey since he was a foal."

The duchess shrugged. "Perhaps you are right. I will send Wilton to fetch Lavvy." She reached for the bell rope, but Dobyn detained her.

"That will not be necessary. He has already told me that both your nieces are absent from home. I would not have forced myself upon you, but that he was off and running to announce me before I could make my escape."

The duchess raised her eyebrows, and even Elinor made a point of looking away across the room to keep from laughing. "Make your escape?" asked her grace. "What a honeyed tongue you have to be sure." But despite this, she looked at him quite kindly. "I hope you will believe that I am always happy to see you as a friend, Tyger, as my husband is. It is only that you . . ."

"It is only that you see me as no suitable match for Lady Barbara, I ween. Edad, madam, you set me high to believe that I need only crook my finger to have all the wenches coming at a run."

"It is not true?"

He snorted. "An aging cavalier who has retired from active, physical sport and grows more complacent about it every day? Would it surprise you, duchess, to know that I have never felt the slightest inclination in that direction?"

"You are aware of the dowry, of course." He made a face, but she pressed on. "All the same, between the three of us, you are much, much too fascinating with your air of wicked ways to be left unattended among impressionable young women. Elinor here is the only one I know with bite enough to outface you."

The Tyger turned to the young woman in question and shrugged. It was the gesture of an indisputable innocent man. "I have no idea what she means. Do you? When has a blameless gentleman been so maligned, I should like to know?"

Elinor knew when a gauntlet had been tossed down, and she took it up as effortlessly as he had thrown it. "I think even you must admit, sir, that a slightly tarnished reputation is a potent lure for any young woman."

"A much overrated attraction," he protested. "Young women—even perfectly ordinary ones—are quite a bit more sophisticated in matters of that sort than you allow.

In any case, I have it on good authority Lady Barbara has never been particularly impressionable in that direction."

Even Lady Augusta had to laugh. Though Barbara was her own close kin, she had to admit that young woman had been managing every member of the opposite sex who came into her view, from parson to plowboy, since she was seven.

"I do not seek to malign you, sir, but I suspect that even such a one as my ward is not immune to your sort of scapegrace charm."

His eyebrow arched. "Good heavens, madam, I had not an inkling that you entertained such views about me. No wonder you have always kept me at arm's length."

The duchess bit her lip to keep laughing yet again. "What a rogue you are. I have met your duplicates on too many occasions in the past not to have an instinct for self-preservation. I admit that you and your sort provide a certain spice in society, but I would never trust the judgement of any young woman where her safety is concerned."

"I hardly know whether to feel set-down or flattered," the Tyger said with a wry chuckle. "From the expression on the face of your pupil here, I have the impression that she too has absorbed a good deal of your prejudice toward impoverished, but high-minded gentlemen. I can see it from the look in her eye."

"That is possibly because I have been acquainted with too many gamesters, sir," answered Elinor. "You forget my background. I am aware that the truly dedicated gambler will play with anything: spades, clubs, diamonds—even hearts."

Dobyn all but whooped at this sally and threw his hands up protectively. "Help, help! I concede. No man could ever hope to win a match against the two of you together, I fear."

There was a soft clearing of the throat, and they saw that Dora had appeared in the doorway. Over one arm hung a wicker basket, and she was carrying Elinor's cashmere shawl along with a high-crowned straw bonnet with wide, blue ribbons.

"I beg yer pardon, miss. Was this the wrap you was wanting?" Dora asked diplomatically.

Elinor sprang up from her chair with alacrity. "How thoughtful you are, Dora. They are exactly the items I was thinking of.

"You will excuse me from further sparring, I hope, Mr. Dobyn. I have a dozen commissions about town, and the day wears on." To the duchess she said, "It was Mrs. Parsons I should see at the Assembly Rooms, I think, madam?"

"Yes, my dear. Phyliss Parsons will know what to put at your disposal. You need only make the selection, I think. Do not bother to bring them back for my approval since there is so little time left."

"Ah, if you are going to the Upper Rooms, Lady Elinor, perhaps you will allow me to accompany you? I am headed in that direction myself."

"I suppose it will be proper, sir, so long as Dora is with me."

The Tyger made a gesture of congratulations with the merest flicker of one hand. "Touché, dear mademoiselle. You have taken your lessons from her grace very much to heart, I see." He laughed as freely as a boy.

Elinor and Augusta exchanged a look of complete understanding.

"I have every confidence in your judgement, dear girl," said her grace, and both knew that she did not refer to the selection of party favours alone.

═14═

ON THEIR WAY along Wickham Street and around the Circle, Tyger began to question Elinor about Cecil Partridge.

"I had no notion that he moved in Lady Augusta's world."

Elinor thought of the duchess's reaction to Cecil. It had been distinctly cool, especially considering that she knew him to be Elinor's kinsman. It was almost as if, beneath her obligatory politeness toward a guest in her house, there lurked a deep and settled antipathy.

"I do not believe he moves in her circle at all," Elinor answered. "I think it is something quite the opposite, but I have nothing to give as a reason. It might even be something quite trivial. Have you not at sometime met a person who had done you no harm but whom you instinctively, nonetheless, disliked on sight?"

"Yes," he answered as he offered his arm at a corner. "That is part of a gambler's stock in trade. You must size up your opponent accurately in order to defeat him. However, in the real world, it is slightly irrational to dislike someone before being acquainted with their faults."

They had crossed the street, but he did not relinquish his touch beneath her elbow.

"Yes," she said with a smile, "and how very disconcerting if they turned out to have no faults at all."

"Everyone has faults, Miss Har—that is, Lady Elinor."

And she was amused by that as well. "I can see that one

of yours is a faulty memory. I daresay, though, even that can be trained."

She noted that Dora wore a faintly disapproving look, recognisable as that expression assumed by servants when they feel their masters are failing to live up to the responsibilities of their station. Elinor flushed and moved her arm away from the intimacy of Tyger Dobyn's solicitous assistance for the remainder of their stroll.

The Upper Rooms in the daytime presented quite a different face from that of the hurried hours of evening. At this hour they were the province of sedate, old gentlemen playing interminable games of silver-loo and pontoon, or respectably situated ladies who settled into the reading room amidst clouds of patchouli and social impregnability. Elinor enquired of the attendant where she might find Mrs. Parsons and Tyger declared he would beat a retreat to the smoking room where he could peruse the latest gazette in comfort while he waited.

"Oh, but there is no need to detain yourself on my behalf, Mr. Dobyn. I have only one or two small errands, and Dora will be with me. It is not as if Cheyne Spa ladies were in great danger, you know."

He looked straight into her eyes. "Are you sending me away?"

Elinor felt the wave of colour rush to her cheecks. "I . . . Dora . . ." She swallowed. "No, Mr. Dobyn, I am not *sending* you away. I merely do not wish to waste your time."

His voice became as quiet as velvet. "Perhaps you will do me the courtesy of allowing me to judge that."

The statement was said with such perfect equanimity, such composure, that she could only accept it for the reasonable request it seemed to be and nod in agreement. Dora cleared her throat rather loudly, and Elinor found herself drawing away almost guiltily.

"Will you send an attendant for me when you are done making your selection?" he asked, and Elinor nodded once more without speaking.

As each turned from the other, a particularly observant spectator might have suspected something more than a passing social acquaintance between them. Indeed, one such watcher read far more into what he saw than was strictly warranted, but that was in some degree a product of his own imagination. Cecil Partridge, on his way from the card room and seeing them there, was quick to draw his own conclusions. His small, sharp countenance took on a certain cunning and his small, sharp, ebony eyes appeared almost to snap with malice.

So she is no better than she should be, my little cousin? Very well; how much, much easier that makes things, eh?

Cecil returned to the gaming table where he had left his grandfather. At this moment, the old gentleman was crying, "Pontoons only!" and scooping in the cash of the disgruntled losers. The victor's face, so expansive in triumph, tightened as he saw his heir returning, but he kept his tone light. "I thought you had urgent business at home, my boy?"

Cecil's response was one of fatuous acquiescence. "Oh, quite right, sir. I must be getting back to Mama soon, but there is a certain person here. It came to me that you might be amused to see the sort of company she keeps. Rather ripe and quite amusing."

The old man scowled and glanced hastily around as if he feared the unseemly interest of his fellow players. "What is that to me, you young coxcomb?" he all but snarled. "Do you have nothing better to do than spend your time spying on your relatives?"

His voice carried, and now it was his great-nephew's turn to redden. "I say, Uncle, please. I was only trying to be of service to you, after all. I am sorry if I have been in error." He managed a beautifully aggrieved tone, but it fell upon deaf ears.

"Go home, sir, and be of use to your mother and her estate. You may tell Wilson for me that he is to take you in hand and teach you everything he knows—so far as you are able to absorb it."

Cecil turned pale. "Teach *me*, sir? The steward?"

"Yes, dammee. The steward," the earl fairly roared. "Who better than one I have trained meself? You want to inherit, do you? Well, I will be demmed if I cater to the idea of putting my holdings into the hands of an idiot. Do you think, sir, that I have worked like a navvy all me life only to have a gawk dissipate it within five years?"

The old men seated with the earl were endeavouring to look unconcerned and deaf to the conversation, but his lordship only scowled as Cecil tried his best to dissimulate his inner fury. The strain of the effort was monumental and showed, as it always did, in his telltale nose which paled and pinched and at last began to quiver with indignation as did his lower lip.

Cecil collected himself to the best of his ability and said stiffly, "Your servant, sir."

He edged away from the gaming table as from the gravest sort of danger. And who is to say he was not right in that assessment? If a recklessly proud man will stoop to disinheriting a beloved son, how much less will he stick at the undoing of a nephew?

As the young man blindly rushed through the lobby of the Upper Rooms, it was his inevitable destiny to run full tilt into the very chap he had been prepared to malign. Instead of even a perfunctory apology, there passed from Cecil's hard-bitten lips something that sounded to the gamester mightily like a curse.

"Be devil to you then," Tyger called laughingly after the hastily departing figure. Meanwhile, to himself he wondered, *What has put him in the wind, d'you suppose?* Then, resuming his usual lack of inquisitiveness concerning other people's affairs, he collected his gazette and settled into the smoking room to peruse its pages.

* * *

By the time Elinor decided between the silk-flower posies and the curled-ribbon rosettes as favours for the masquerade, the best part of an hour had passed. In fact, she observed with a guilty sense of relief, it had been so long that Tyger Dobyn would scarcely have waited. It was not that she did not enjoy his company. She could think of no one since the death of her father with whom she felt so much at ease. Perhaps, indeed, that was the problem—she *too much* liked being in his company and that fit uncomfortably with the task she had undertaken for Lady Augusta.

The attraction had little to do with the coincidence of their mutual choice of calling. Although it was likely that a similarity of character was what had drawn them each to gaming. Nor was it a surface resemblance to her father that drew her, for she saw in Dobyn a strength that went beyond her papa's nature. The Tyger was a sporting man, it was true; but she deduced a level of responsibility in him that the old earl's son had rarely exhibited.

When Papa was in the grip of a gambling fever, he would forget all else, even his daughter. This was a fact of life she was forced to recognise, but to which she had never become reconciled. When she first understood it, she had been crushed. Later she learned to benefit from the knowledge and, unknown to her father, put away small sums of money against the lean times. The only time he ever raised his hand against her was once when he suspected she had money but refused to disclose its hiding place. He had taken his pistol with him when he went off to wager the only half crown she would admit to possessing. Within an hour he had parlayed it into a small fortune and hurried back to their rooms to pour guineas over her feet. Laughing and crying, he had chided her for her lack of faith; but she continued to squirrel away gold whenever she could manage it.

She suspected that the Tyger could never be driven to either extreme of behaviour. However much she loved her father—and that had approached worship—she had, from childhood, recognised his frailty in respect to gaming. Somehow that recognition gave her insight into the lengths to which her grandfather might have been driven before casting off his elder son. She felt that, in his place, she would not have done the same; but she had a certain sympathy for him all the same.

Meanwhile, aware how time had slipped away and still wishing to reach the circulating library before Mr. Fortes closed up shop for the day, she hurried along the corridor with Dora only a step or two behind. As they passed the open door of the tearoom, Elinor hesitated for a moment. She had heard a peal of laughter which sounded oddly familiar, although she could not for the moment identify it. She and the maid had gone a few steps beyond the entrance when Elinor stopped in her tracks, listened once more, then returned to the doorway to look in.

The establishment was only sparsely occupied. A scattering of customers sat near the windows, one or two couples near the door; and three single ladies of indeterminate age were there alone each at her table. In the far corner, only partially hidden by the waiters' service table, Elinor spotted the all too familiar dark head of Lady Barbara Pentreath. With her was a most surprising companion.

Barbara's laughter trilled once more, and one or two heads turned toward her. Suddenly, Elinor realised why that laugh had seemed unfamiliar to her. Quite simply, she had not often heard it. Lady Barbara prided herself on her perfect social composure, and excessive mirth seemed to have little place within those strictures. Delighted peals rang out yet again, not so loudly this time, but with more freedom of spirit than Elinor had ever associated with her ladyship. The difference was, undoubtedly, because of her companion. Elinor had recognised him at once, of course, as did Dora.

"Good Lord, miss, that's that actor, ennet?" she asked, all the patina acquired so carefully at the Peverly Hotel gone in the flash of recognition. "D'you see him, miss, with Lady Barbara? That's that actor . . . ah . . . what is his name?"

"His name is Patrick Tyrone," Elinor answered sadly.

"That's right, miss, Patrick Tyrone. Whatever is our Lady Barbara doing with the likes of him?"

What, indeed, Elinor wondered; and did the Duchess of Towans have any inkling of such an association; and did she, Elinor Hardy, have any business whatsoever in informing her grace of it? Overcome by a wave of shame, as if she had set out to spy upon the couple, she hurried Dora along the passage.

"This is none of our affair, Dora dear. I believe that the less we meddle in it, the sooner it will all come right, don't you?"

The maid seemed doubtful. "It isn't proper, you know, Miss Elinor. They shouldn't be there together where everyone can see them, and well you know it."

"I know this much," Elinor answered sharply, "it is a great deal better that they be taking tea in a public place, under the watchful eyes of Cheyne Spa, than in secret."

Dora had the grace to blush at her gaffe. "Why, Miss Elinor, the things you say! I never in the world meant to suggest that . . ." Seeing the steely glint in the young woman's eye, the maidservant let her words trail away and reminded herself that silence was at *least* as valuable as gold.

As they turned into the main corridor and approached the lobby, Elinor was not at all certain whether she hoped Mr. Dobyn had waited for her or if she would be relieved he had not. She was even less certain how she would feel about being seen once more in his company in the streets of Cheyne. Would not such an association link her name with his to the possible detriment of her position with the duchess?

Elinor still had time to make her escape, if she so chose. There were alternate means of exit from the building, but she continued on her current path. Looking ahead, she saw that the Tyger was even now emerging from the smoking room, carefully refolding the gazette he had been reading. He had not seen them yet, for his back was turned as he greeted another gentleman emerging from the card room across the hall.

"Ah, Tyger, my boy, there you are," Elinor heard the other man call out. "Well met, sir. I need a bit of advice from you about this Prince's Folly of Weldon's. D'you know the nag at all?"

"Well, your lordship," Dobyn answered, "I've only seen the brute running once and that was at the Marymead Meet. You know what that track is, sir. I am not sure a horse can be fairly judged on it."

The older man was about to reply when he looked across Dobyn's shoulder and Elinor saw who it was. She caught her breath and swallowed nervously. Too late to think of escape now. His gaze had fallen upon her; and she could tell that he knew who she was, although beyond that his expression was unreadable.

The Tyger followed the direction of his companion's stare, then broke into a smile. "Here you are at last, my dear," he said to the approaching girl as if he had planned this meeting.

"My lord, may I present Miss Elinor Hardy? Miss Hardy, his lordship, the Earl of Glastonia."

The two relatives said nothing for a moment. They merely stood there peering at each other as if to dissect character. At last the old man unbent enough to make a slight inclination of his upper body: a stiff movement, but close enough to be reckoned as a bow.

"Miss Hardy," he acknowledged, his bright, blue eyes unblinking.

Elinor drew air into her lungs very slowly, then let it out again with the same care, trying to keep from trembling. It was not easy to face up to this proud, old aristocrat's examination; but it was good to be able to look straight into his countenance at last and meet him eye to eye without flinching.

"Good afternoon, Grandfather," she said.

"I say, Glastonia," called another masculine voice from inside the card room. "Have you deserted us? It is your bid, old chap."

The earl glanced toward the source of the summons, then back at his granddaughter. "A pleasure to have met you, Miss Hardy," he said. Still, he did not turn away. Instead he seemed to be searching her face for an answer to some unvoiced question.

"We will meet again," he said at last heavily, as if it cost him great effort. He turned away, his back straight and reentered the card room.

=== 15 ===

PATRICK KNEW Mrs. Mudge was in a pet from the reserve with which she replied to his greeting as he entered the stage door. He at first assumed it had to do with his performance; but, as the company made ready for the evening and she still had not spoken her mind, it came to him that it might be something more personal that was disturbing her. Since her first major scene in the play was with the character woman and he wanted nothing to stand in the way of the execution of it, he sought her out in the green room a brief moment before the lifting of the curtain.

"All right, old dear," he said with breezy affection as he came in. "I can see that you are in a miff with me and I mean to have it out. What have I done? Stepped on a line of yours? Upstaged your big speech?"

The elderly woman surveyed him with indifferent mien. She sat very straight in her chair, relaxed and yet austerely dignified. She could have been some regal majesty out of the old time, the old tales. Her voice, when she spoke, had resonance and authority a queen might have envied.

"I am sure I do not know what you mean, sir," she said. "I keep my own counsel so far as I may, and what I think about the behaviour of others is, I am sure, my own affair."

"Come on, then," he said persuasively. "Out with it. "What have I done?"

"No, no," she protested. "I am perfectly serious. I believe in giving all the help I may where it is needed, but purely in regard to the profession. Stop me if I ever meddle where I am not wanted."

He half knelt beside her chair. "But your advice *is* very much wanted," he said. "You have been as dear to me as my own mother, and you know I value what you have to say."

She was not to be so easily placated as all that, however. She gazed off into the distance. "I am sure your behaviour outside the theatre is your own concern."

Remembering how she had lectured him in the past about his attraction to Lady Barbara, he leaned forward and kissed her velvety cheek. "Perhaps you are right, old thing. If you are about to rate me for lapping congo with a certain lady today, I agree that some things are better not discussed."

She rose to the bait as eagerly as a trout to a fly. "Just listen to you. What sort of language is that for a coney-catcher like you to be using? 'Lapping congo,' indeed! That is the talk of the ton, I suppose? That is how they converse among themselves? Oh yes, I daresay that is the sort of thing said in all the most elevated circles." She sniffed again and made a face. "Not likely, I shouldn't think. You'll have to change your jabber, my lad, if you are going to mix with your betters. That sort of thing may be all very well for your common sort of player. But if you mean to ape Garrick or Sheridan or even, God help us, Colly Cibber, you must become more genteel than the mere top-diver you are now."

Her words stung even though he had been half-prepared for them. "I cannot quite divine your views, madam," he said a little stiffly. "One day it is that I should avoid the quality, and another it is that I should outdo them at their own game." He threw out his hands in a despairing gesture. "I do not know how or where I stand in the matter. You seem to blow cold then hot."

She laughed scornfully. "Pray, do not turn it to me, boy. You might learn by my own mistakes, but I suppose you will not. My advice to you is, if you insist on mixing with the likes of the lady with whom you drank tea then you might choose one who does not have a reputation for carrying a heart of stone within her breast. Lady Barbara will chew you up and spit you out before you know what is happening to you. Stick to your own kind is my advice and will ever be. The gentry do not accept those who seek to climb into their ranks."

The callboy thrust his head in through the door. "Time, if you please, Mrs. Mudge. Time, sir."

The two players began their last-minute rituals before going onstage. Patrick put himself through an elaborate series of body shakes, twists, head rolling and flopping of his wrists in an effort to become as relaxed and limber as possible while Mrs. Mudge surveyed herself in the glass one last time and touched up her hair and make-up.

She was still not resigned to letting this promising young fellow player make a fool of himself over an outsider as she herself had done so many years ago. How curious it was that even after all these years the memory of her liaison with Edward Hardy still had the power to bring on melancholic megrims. She had never decided whether, in fact, she made the right choice or the wrong one. Her life in the theatre had been fulfilling on many levels, but it had also been lived all alone, with no one to share her triumphs. On the other hand, if she had married handsome Edward and given up the stage to become the Countess of Glastonia, how much she would have missed. The rub would have come when they wed . . . *if* her loss of the crowd's adulation had not been balanced by the love she received from her husband. She had seen marriages founder on less formidable rocks than those. All in all, she had not been sorry for her choice; and she would not willingly see her young friend, Patrick, ruin himself over such a thing.

"Time, Mrs. Mudge, time."

The handsome old creature arched her neck and threw back her shoulders, drawing in a deep breath before she stepped upon the stage to greet her true lover: the audience of the Theatre Royal.

Lady Barbara Pentreath had no inkling that she and Patrick Tyrone had been observed in the tearoom by anyone other than the strangers sitting nearby. Certainly, she had no idea that she had been seen by two members of her household on Regent's Crescent. Having defied convention in inviting the handsome actor to join her for tea, the knowledge would undoubtedly have been met with a haughty lift of her chin. Barbara's ways were her ways; and she considered that, in most things, to be a law unto herself.

She knew, of course, what a daring thing it had been to take the initiative with a member of the opposite sex. She had never needed to do so in the past, but she was certain the man in question would have hesitated to approach her and she very much wanted to further their acquaintance. Besides, it was precisely the daring quality of the thing which added a touch of spice to the situation; for she knew very well how quickly the most innocent intrigue could be debased by the gossips of Cheyne Spa. She had often contributed to such gossip herself and found it vastly amusing. Well, it might be equally amusing now with the shoe upon the other foot.

What a juicy tidbit it would be for some she knew. What would they say to the spectacle of Barbara Pentreath pursuing a mere actor? Of course, she was doing no such thing, as any thoughtful person could see in a moment. Still, there were those who believed it reprehensible for a young woman to be seen alone with a man outside of her usual circle. No one thought anything of it if the man in question was a servant, of course—for one was not social with servants; or a gentleman considerably advanced in years who could be assumed to have no more than a fatherly interest; or any male member of one's family no matter how distant. However, chatter was bound to ensue if one of these conditions was not the case. Barbara understood perfectly that any who *chose* to gossip would do so even more avidly because of the position she held. She also knew that it was wiser by far to pursue the acquaintance in public than in dubious privacy.

And she firmly intended to pursue it. There was not a man of her acquaintance who offered such a challenge. Ben and Trevor, of course, were old and trusted friends. She might even consider marrying one of them one day, but they offered no excitement. There was nothing particularly stimulating about their company. More to the point, she had never felt with either of them the thrill that stirred within her at the slightest thought of Patrick Tyrone. Each time she saw him emerge upon the stage, she felt her heart swell in her breast with a peculiar flutter that left her breathless and confused. If, in the Assembly Rooms, his manner had not been as refined as his character in the play, well what was that? He would prove clever and adaptable, she was sure.

Abruptly aware where these considerations were leading, she brought them to a halt. Yet, as she was dressing for the Thursday Cotillion Ball, such thoughts so occupied her mind that she was scarcely aware when her little maid, Elsie, stopped her ministrations to answer a light knock at the dressing room door. It was the duchess, resplendent in a gown of peacock green and blue.

"May I come in, dear? I have scarcely seen you all day."

"Yes, Aunt, do come in," said the girl warily. "I have been out, I fear. I hope you did not need me for anything important."

The maidservant stood waiting for her next instruction, but the duchess waved her away with an airy hand. "I will help her ladyship finish, Elsie. You may go down to the servants' hall if you like. I am sure your tea is ready."

Elsie looked apprehensively toward Lady Barbara who seemed annoyed, but resigned. "Very well, Elsie, run along. I will ring when I need you again."

The duchess held the prettily ruffled gown above her niece's head and guided it down about her shoulders, straightening and smoothing as it settled.

"I had hoped we might find the time for a little chat."

"Hardly now, I think, Aunt Augusta," Barbara protested mildly. "We must leave for the Assembly Rooms within the hour." A discontented sigh escaped directly upon the heels of her words. The duchess noticed it at once.

"Whatever prompts such melancholy, dearest child? Do you not wish to attend the ball? Have you something you would prefer?"

Barbara tugged petulantly at her hem which did not seem to be hanging properly. "I am bored to distraction with the country dances at the Thursday balls, but I cannot think of an alternative unless it be to attend the theatre again. The company leaves tomorrow to play in Budolph for a week while the management brings the Budolph players here."

"You will hardly be missing anything, will you? We have just seen *The Marriage Broker* for the third time in a fortnight. I admit to a vast admiration of Mrs. Mudge, and that new young man—what is his name? The handsome one."

"His name is Patrick Tyrone," said Barbara with a touch of spirit. "After having seen his wonderful performance three whole times, I am surprised that you can forget him."

"It seems obvious that you have not," her aunt remarked shrewdly. "I hope it is not an unwarranted interest in an *actor* which is causing you to act so peculiarly?"

Lady Barbara could hear the underlying thread of steel within her aunt's unruffled tones, and she dissembled quickly. "An actor? How silly that would be. Not but that he is a pleasant enough gentleman and quite presentable." She then turned the subject adroitly. "It is only that the days here in Cheyne seem different this year somehow. They seem to be all of a piece and unendingly tedious. Every week brings the same round of engagements, the same amusements even, and the same faces or ones so much alike that it is no matter. On Sunday we go to service, then stroll about or listen to a concert of sacred music in the Assembly Rooms. On Monday it is the Dress Ball. On Wednesday another concert. Tonight the Cotillion Ball, and tomorrow the Card Assembly. I do not at all care for cards or for sitting in a stuffy room listening to the stuffy conversation of those who are not actively engaged in throwing down their pasteboards."

She flung herself about. "Oh, Aunt, I am so dreadfully bored. Cannot we go back to London?"

Her aunt laughed chidingly. "What, and leave behind all your crowd of beaux? You would find London a dull place as well without the attention you receive from Ben and Trevor, I am sure. Not to mention all the others. And I have only just come from London. It is quite impossible at this time of the year."

"Beaux, beaux." Barbara shrugged petulantly. "There are always beaux. One never has a moment to draw a breath to oneself."

The duchess's face took on an air of concern. "Why, my child, I think you are serious. The pleasure of allurement has faded. Surely some one of them must mean something to you—Ben, for instance?"

Barbara began clumsily putting the pins in her hair. "Really, I wish you had not sent Elsie away so quickly. I cannot make this into anything but a bird's nest."

Her aunt unpinned the hair, took up the brush and began to shape the tresses into a soft and becoming chignon. "You must be thankful we have abandoned the use of powder. Life is so much less distressful these days, do you not think?" Then she turned unerringly to her previous topic. "Do you mean to say that you do not care for Ben just a little?"

Barbara stared into the looking glass as if trying to read the mind of her hairdresser, but the duchess kept her eyes carefully upon the little ringlet she was shaping at the girl's temple. Her niece gave a pretty but mirthless laugh.

"I know you too well, Aunt Augusta. You are still trying to secure my future, even at the cost of saddling poor Ben with a wife who does not love him."

The duchess slid a hairpin deftly into place, securing the ringlet she had created. "Then you do not consider him your private preserve?"

Barbara's amusement was as genuine as she would allow it to be. "Private preserve? Ben? Good heavens, what a thought! He and Trev have been part of my life for far too long. I could not think seriously about either of them in the matrimonial way."

"Still, you must marry someone, you know."

"It will not be Ben Weymouth, of that I can assure you, madam."

"Ah, good," said the duchess as she lightly patted the last of her handiwork into place.

"Good?" Barbara echoed suspiciously as she turned her head from side to side, critically examining her reflexion. "You could have hired out as a lady's maid, Aunt, had you not married a duke."

"I shall come to you for a recommendation when I do, dear," said the duchess smoothly. "At least I am able to put up my own tresses without distress. You are lucky I was able to steal little Elsie from your Aunt Christabel. I might even take the girl for my own when you marry."

Barbara put down the hand-mirror in which she had been admiring her aunt's artistry. "What is all this talk of marriage? You have scarcely left it alone since you entered the room. Was this the subject of the little chat you sought? If so, I beg to disillusion you. At the present time I have no immediate plans for matrimony with anyone—not to Ben, to Trevor or even to Mr. Tyrone!"

"Mr. Tyrone?" asked her aunt. "I should think not. Whatever made you think of him? I hope you will marry a gentleman."

Barbara's face was hidden for a moment as she rose from the dressing table, but there was an unmistakable warmth in her voice. "Why, I am sure he has as many gentlemanly manners as many of the male sex one finds in Cheyne Spa." Then she quickly clapped a hand to her head to save a falling lock. "In any case, it was not so very long ago that the relationship between the stage and the aristocracy was cordial in the extreme. Perhaps that time is coming again."

"Yes," Augusta agreed, "there was many a lord married an actress, but I do not remember that many actors crossed the line. However, it is of no moment. As you say, Mr. Tyrone apes the gentleman to perfection on the boards. Perhaps I shall invite him one evening to observe how he does in private." She caught back Barbara's recalcitrant curl. "In any case, I am not in the least hurrying to dispose of *you;* I wished merely to be certain of your indifference to young Weymouth. Since you will not have him, I have in mind another bride. You know how it is with us old married women, my dear, we wish everyone an opportunity to share our bliss. It is high time Ben was wed, I think, before he makes a wrong choice."

"And you have made the choice, have you?" asked Barbara with a nervous flutter of her eyes. "Who may that be, pray? Some plain-faced tuft hunter, I daresay, who longs to be Ben's countess when the father has passed into his just reward? You are incorrigible, Aunt. It is the daughter of some old friend, I will be bound." She wrinkled her brow in mock concentration. "Who could it be?" Then she actually giggled aloud. "It is Aunt Christabel's Hermione, isn't it? That is why you mentioned my other aunt a few moments ago, because she was in your mind."

"Christabel is your cousin and only your aunt by courtesy," said Augusta with a shudder, "and I would not inflict Hermione on anyone for whom I did not have an active dislike. In any case, I believe she is to marry Lawyer Withering." She waited a moment, then tapped her cheek reflectively. "But what say you to matching Ben with dear Elinor? Would they not make a fetching pair?"

Barbara seemed stunned. "Elinor? You are not serious?"

"Why ever not? She is a charming girl and, of course, with Ben the dowry is of no importance."

"But surely they could not love each other?" asked the girl weakly. "They have scarcely met."

"Oh, fiddledeedee, what has love to do with it? Nothing, as you very well know. They enjoy each other's company, and love will come in time."

"But Ben loves. . ." Barbara began.

"Yes? Ben loves someone? Who?"

"Ah . . . I am sure he must love . . . ah, someone . . . I am sure he does."

"What a pity, but everyone knows that love and marriage have nothing to do with each other really. Do you not agree?" asked the aunt. "I am sure I have heard you say so."

═16═

DURING THE LAST few years, since Mayor Tobias had stood at the helm of the Corporation, Cheyne Spa had moved into the modern world with gratifying speed. It was now not merely a watering spot, but a place where the social genius of the late Beau Carlisle combined with the natural advantages in a provocative mixture of fashion, elegance and the best sort of scandal to rival, not only Cheltenham and Bath, but also, in certain respects, London itself.

As far as thespian pursuits were concerned, in addition to the Theatre Royal, Cheyne's mayor operated the little jewel of a theatre at Budolph, a mere ten-mile journey. The Cheyne company generally played there on Mondays and Thursdays when the Assembly Rooms' balls made operating the Theatre Royal generally unprofitable. The theatre company was not particularly enamoured of this circumstance, but they accepted it with the lack of inclination to rock the boat which comes of regular employment in a notoriously unstable profession. Still they groaned as much as they dared. Mrs. Mudge alone was cheerfully philosophical.

"Well, it makes for a change, after all, dunnit?" she would enquire in her elegantly enunciated Houndsditch dialect. "There is a great deal to be said for a fresh audience two nights a week, you know, me loves. I has no shame in admitting I sometimes miss the days when I was sleeping under a haystack while me company was on the road. It was a hard life, doncher know, but it was never a dull one."

"Oh, I am grateful enough to be settled here in Cheyne, I admit—at my age I'd be a fool not to be—but a change is nice, ennet, once or twice a week?"

Tyrone was something less than sanguineous in respect to the arrangements, however. Given his way, it is likely that the Irish actor would have elected to choose his best roles and play them over and over again until he had wrung every nuance from their lines. In this he anticipated the modern thespian, but his was not a time friendly to such considerations. As events fell out, he might have been happier in one of those less fortunate companies upon whose virtues Mrs. Mudge so happily enlarged, one of those companies whose fate was to be eternally peripatetic.

It was at the stage entrance of the Austen Street Theatre in Budolph that an almost forgotten face presented itself to Tyrone, floating up out of the gloom of the alleyway into the fading sunlight. The voice it employed, though, was far from doleful and had a lilting Hibernian charm.

"Ah, there you are at last, Paddy," the girl said as if they had an appointment to meet before he prepared to go on the stage. "Sure an' this part of the world is a difficult one for a girl to be finding her sweetheart."

The simple, ingenuous statement could scarcely have had a more marked effect upon the actor. He looked, in fact, as if he had been accosted by a spectre and staggered as if poleaxed.

"Why, what . . . ? Mary, is it you?" He reddened, then paled and shook himself into a semblance of welcome toward this far-traveller, but the girl was not deceived.

She chuckled softly. "Has it been so long then that you have quite forgotten the look of me? It appears that I have arrived in the very nick of time. Who knows what another month or two might have done?"

Tyrone looked about to be sure they were unobserved, then drew her into the shadow of the alley. He took hold of her shoulders and peered into the pretty, Irish countenance.

"But Mary, me darling, what in the very devil are you doing here of all places?"

"Where else should I be, Patrick?" she asked softly. "I came to find you."

"But why would you be doing that? Is something awry at home?"

"No," she said, "nuthin'. Me ma died and then the cow died and Squire Hennery found me more appealin' than I thought altogether necessary. Truly, Paddy, I was like to have died in that boggy ruin of a village, so I set out lookin' for you. I never had an inklin' that you wouldn't be glad to see me."

Now that the initial shock of the meeting had abated, young Tyrone was able to take a slightly firmer grasp of the situation. "Sure and did you not think I would be coming back for you? Did I not promise that as soon as ever I could manage it, we would be together? And have I ever broken a promise between us, Mary, me own?"

He asked it with a charming cock of the head which he had recently learned and used with great effect in the role he was playing that evening, but she was not taken in.

"Broken a promise? Aye, you have done it a time or two," she answered without rancour. "But I have never held that part of your nature against you. I know full well that it is a man's way to be slippin' the halter of responsibility if ever he can manage it. The fact is, I had it come into my mind that after all these months you might find me as refreshing to your eyes as you truly are to mine." She moved closer to him and stretched up her fingers to stroke him along the cheek. "Have I waited too long then? Have I come so far and am not offered even a kiss by my lover? Are you not glad to see me, Patrick Tyrone?"

"Glad? Of course I am glad, Mary, to be sure of it. I am as glad as you could hope to find me."

She looked doubtfully into his face. "I wish that I could believe what you say is true. If it were even just a little of the case you would have sent for me before now, instead of

leaving me there to grow old among the pigs and potatoes."
She pressed her body against him and lifted her mouth to
be kissed, raising upon her toes to do it. "Never mind, I
will make you happy that I am here."

The reluctant Patrick drew back involuntarily. "No, you
must not. You don't know how things have changed."

Mary understood it quite well. "Oh, do I not?" she
snorted derisively. "I can tell very easily they have that
indeed, Paddy, me-boyo. There is no more now of your
coaxing words. No more of 'Mary, me darlin', I must have
you or I will die.' No more of—what was that thing you
said? Ah yes, 'The very angels will watch over us, Mary,
and bless our union as surely as any priest can do.' No,
there is no more of that talk, is there, Patrick?"

The light, quick step that Patrick recognised in panic as
that of the character-woman clicked along the cobbles and
turned into the alleyway. Mrs. Mudge almost collided with
them before her eyes grew accustomed to the shadow.

"Patrick, is that you?"

"Yes, madam. I was just going in."

She peered toward him. "And who is that with you?"

"Me name is Mary Monaghan, if you please, mum. I
have come all the way from Donegal to—"

"Mary, not just now, if you please," Patrick pleaded.

The girl tossed her curls. "And why not, if this lady is
your friend? Should she not be knowing that we are to be
married?"

"Oh, God," he moaned. In his mind's eye he watched
the vision of Lady Barbara receding at a fast clip.

"Married, is it?" asked Mrs. Mudge with a sharp look at
the two of them. "That is as it may be, I am sure, but why
are you hanging about here in the damp? Come inside, and
we will have a cup and a chat. This news is very interesting,
and we must not waste it in a poor alleyway like this."

She tugged at Patrick. "Come along, boy, and you, too,
my dear." She took Mary's arm. "I am certain this can all
be sorted out to everyone's satisfaction."

"Ah, Mr. Tyrone," the stage manager called out as they entered the theatre, "just the person I wanted. May I have a word with you, sir, before the performance?"

Patrick held up a warding hand. "Not just now, Mr. Tweed, if you please."

"No, no, dear boy," Mrs. Mudge contradicted him. "You run along and settle up with Tweedy. Mary and I will just pop into my dressing room and acquaint ourselves with each other, shall we, m'dear?"

Mary aimed an amused smile toward Patrick. "Oh yes. Let us do that. Paddy, me darlin', I do not mean to stand in the way of your job, you know. I am sure that whatever it is the gentleman has to say is important."

Mr. Tweed, himself an Irishman, bowed lavishly. "A thousand thank yous, miss. May the wind be always at your back. I shall not be keeping him long." He turned back to Patrick and dropped an arm across his shoulder. "Now, then, it may not seem an important moment to you, my boy, but if . . ." His voice trailed off as he led the anxious actor a little ways off.

The two women went on into the dressing room and Mrs. Mudge at once began her unvarying routine. The kettle was put to boil, the window shut tight.

"It will be stuffy for you, I know, not being of the profession and being a country lass," she explained to Mary, "but I must think of my throat, you see." She stroked that still handsome column tenderly. "It has served me well, but it requires a bit of cosseting these days." She waved the girl toward the only free chair. "Settle yourself in, m'dear. Move that pile if you must and sit down." She herself took a seat before her looking glass and regarded the reflexion distastefully. "Can you believe that I was once the toast of London?" she asked, pulling a face.

"Yes, ma'am, if it please you, I *can* believe it," Mary answered. "There is a kind of beauty that keeps until the grave. Me mother had it and so do you. Age has nothing to do with it at all. It is bred in the bone."

Mrs. Mudge stared at her. "Why, bedad, you sound almost sincere. I would believe you implicitly if I did not recognise those lines from *The Marriage of True Minds*. Where the devil did *you* come by them, I wonder?"

The girl flushed. "Truly, madam, I . . ."

Mrs. Mudge batted a wrinkled old hand at her. "Truly me no trulies, girl. I am beginning to smell that something is a bit rotten in Denmark, as the Bard says. I cannot imagine that you sat of a long winter evening in that cob of yours studying over old plays. What are you up to? You've learned to say that line a bit too well to fool me. You're one of us, aincher? You have had a bit of time on the boards? Where was it, Manchester? Truro?"

Mary blushed again and dropped her eyes. "St. Albans, if you please, madam. I was two seasons there as a general dogsbody and one as ingenue."

The old woman let out a screech of laughter that would have served admirably for Mad Margaret or the Witch of Endor. When it had diminished to a cackling wheeze, she pointed a boney finger at the Irish girl and demanded, "What you are wanting from poor Patrick is not the fulfillment of some foolish promise at all, is it? What you were hoping for was a bit of influence with the management."

Mary nodded. "I hoped that if he put in a good word for me I might be taken on."

"Oh, never fear, my dove. *I* will do that. Anyone who could cozen Patrick in the way you have done deserves an opportunity on a broader stage." Mrs. Mudge began her laughter all over again, and the tears formed in her eyes. She breathed deeply to restore her equilibrium. "If I go on in this way, I shall have no voice tonight," she explained. "But it *is* such a joke, you know, to find the charmer caught in his own trap. I think poor Patrick half expected you to pull an infant out of your shawl and name him the father."

She stared at the girl shrewdly. "And you meant him to think all that, didn't you? I can see it in your eyes, you bad creature. What a jewel you will be. We should have been sisters. In my day I was just the same. We are alike in temperament as two peas from the same pod. In fact, if you are willing, I shall enlist you in a scheme of my own to save Patrick from himself. "Have you seen him play?"

Mary admittted that she had not, but that his growing reputation had drawn her to Cheyne Spa and Budolph.

"Well, he is very good and likely to become better if he don't spoil his future with unsuitable alliances. I take it that in the old days you were slightly more than mere friends?"

"He used to say that he loved me," Mary admitted. "I think he cannot completely have forgotten it."

Mrs. Mudge nodded in agreement. "It comes to him by nature," she allowed. "He certainly does not seem to have forgotten the principles of it, though now he reaches rather too high in my opinion and I fear he will bring about his own ruin if he ain't careful."

"I shall do what I can," Mary promised, "if I am allowed to remain."

"Oh, you shall stay," Mrs. Mudge promised. "Oh, poor Patrick. Poor lamb. You will lead him a merry jig before we are done, of that I am sure."

=== 17 ===

THE EARL OF Glastonia sat in his library all the next morning with his foot upon a gout stool, musing upon the vagaries of fortune. How unlikely a place to have been introduced to his granddaughter was a mere hallway in the Assembly Rooms, and how unlikely a chap to perform the introduction was Tyger Dobyn. Not that there was anything wrong with the fellah. Everything the earl knew about Dobyn was to the good. A bit wild in his youth, perhaps, but then, all the best fellahs were. The Dobyns were, at least, of good English stock: honest yeomen whose name went back a good way.

The origin of Edward Hardy's own title was, literally, lost in the mists of British antiquity, the name deriving from the Old Celtic *glasto*, meaning "woad" and "Glastonia" by extension implying "the place where woad grew." Couldn't go much farther back than that, back to those old fellahs who painted themselves against the cold. Weren't called earls, then, of course, just some sort of local dynasts who cannily kept the power in the family.

However that might be, Lord Edward was the seventh to hold the title; and he granted precedence only to Mar and Sutherland. It was a great pity, he found himself reflecting, that the chap entrusted to bear the weight of it was such a fool and a stubborn old fool at that. Too proud to bend, too shy to seek détente with his own kin in order to avoid leaving his hard-gained heritage in the hands of an even lesser representative than he considered himself. Each time the prospect of being succeeded by such a mealy slag as Cecil Partridge occurred to the earl, it made him shudder with revulsion.

It was not, of course, that the long line of his ancestors had not been speckled with a variety of villains. How could it be else, the law of averages holding as well as it demonstrably did? But, damee, earls or churls, they had all proved themselves to be men, not like the creepy-crawly petit-point worker that he knew his great-nevvy to be. God knows, he had tried to allow the chap ample breadth to shape into something capable of supporting the family honour; but that seemed doomed to prove a losing game. The fellow would rather tag along at his mam's skirts than sit astride a stallion for the chase. Petit point, be demmed, and proud of his skill, too, they say. Was it to this that the line of Glastonia had descended? Perhaps it was then to be hoped that with Cecil the strain would die out.

What a pity it was that the old rules could not be invoked which allowed the current nobleman to select his own successor from any among his family. In ancient times the title had not descended by primogeniture, but by gift. He laughed to himself. *Dash me*, he thought, *from what I have heard of the gel, she would be the choice of the two. And would that not cause a great hubble-bubble?* The notion so amused him that he laughed aloud. *What a glory it would be to be able to set that po-faced ninny aside. Impossible, of course, but tantalising.*

As if on cue, the door of the library opened, and a woman's face appeared in the shadows of the hall at a surprising height above the floor. "Well, Edward, into the port again? You know that the doctor has forbidden it."

The earl frowned at the prospect of still another lecture from his sister. Gad, but he knew to his cost the price of overindulgence. His afflicted foot had only recently survived a fit of that wretched inflammation. The gout stool had become a standard item of furniture in every room where he took his leisure. He waved his hand about with a grandiose sort of gesture. "Do you see any telltale evidence of indulgence, you demmed harpy? Come in and poke about, if you like. Search and seize, if you can, search and seize. You have my full permission."

The woman in the doorway sniffed self-righteously as if grossly insulted but came resolutely into the book room nonetheless. She took the chair opposite him, a straight-backed old Jacobean piece which had been in the family for two hundred years, and sat primly, shoulders back, hands folded in her lap the way she had been taught as a child.

"You were off with your gambling cronies all day, I expect. When you come home reeking of tobacco, I know you can have been up to no good."

"Quite right, m'dear. You should unbend a bit one evening and join us. It might possibly provide that indefinable touch of lightness which, if you will forgive me, your nature has always lacked."

As this was said not at all spitefully but with a certain dry humour, it immediately elicited the response he had anticipated. Lady Elspeth drew herself up even straighter and stared at him across the rim of her spectacles with a cold eye.

"The day I so forget myself as to enter the precincts of hell, brother, will be the day when there is ice upon the pools of brimstone."

Even when seated, the earl's sister was a towering figure of a woman. Her invariable costume of black corded silk relieved only by a bit of lace at throat and wrists, accentuated rather than diminished her stature. Seeing her for the first time, unmannerly strangers had been known to stand gawking in a most unseemly way, since her six feet of height, topped by such a long-jawed, Roman-nosed face and that mass of elaborately dressed, iron-grey hair, gave rather the impression of a retired army brigadier garbed *en travesti*. Her uncompromisingly severe expression was lightened only rarely by a wintery smile which did little more than play about the corners of her mouth.

"What devilment are you up to now, I wonder?" she speculated, almost to herself. "I have not heard such a yelp of delight from you since before your last attack. Since you were well into your cups at that time, as I recall, is it any wonder that I am suspicious of you now?"

The earl leaned back in his own chair, slouching comfortably. "Ah, my girl, I had such a day. I won three yellow Georges in a row from old Kinnaird, the banker, and had the inexpressible pleasure of an encounter with my heir when he thrust his way uninvited into the card room."

"I cannot think how that could have given you much pleasure," Lady Elspeth observed, "since you profess a distinct anti-doting for the boy. I expect you set him down in some way or you would not be so set *up* about it now."

He grunted comfortably. "Am I so much of a bear as all that?" he asked as if he knew full well it was true. "I am most sorry to hear it and must seem a very grim old monument to the rest of the world. I am surprised that you are able to put up with me, Elspeth. Truly I am."

"I daresay it is the innurement of the years," she replied coolly. "The rest of the world may not hold you in the same affection I do. We make allowances beyond the ordinary for those we love, I am sure. It is an unhealthy trait, but a sadly natural one."

He eyed her slyly. "I met someone else yesterday, as well. Tyger Dobyn presented her to me in the hall."

"If she was with *that* rantipole, I imagine she was no better a creature than she should be," her ladyship observed. Seeing that her brother's deep-set eyes still held a suspicious twinkle, she drew her own brows together in concentration. "There is more to this than you are allowing me, I wean."

"Yes," he admitted, "and I fear your aged sibling did not acquit himself so well as might be expected. The truth is, m'dear, that I was so taken off guard that I quite acted the country clod and backed away like an old curmudgeon. I daresay, if you had been present, you would have turned the situation into a pretty sort of thing, but I made quite a dog's dinner of it."

His sister's thin-lipped mouth fell open. "You do not mean to say . . ."

The earl nodded with a kind of embarrassed self-satisfaction. "Exactly. I was finally introduced to the gel. I *thought* it would stun you, and it did."

"You actually talked to her?" Lady Elspeth unbent enough to lean forward in her chair. "Well, man, what is she like? Is she a trollop, or is she presentable? Pretty, I hope? How was she dressed?"

Edward shifted and hunched his shoulders. "I really cannot say, you know, Ellie. It is just as I told you. I was so overset that I bolted like a fool."

He sniffed suspiciously and drew his hand across his face for a moment as if to shield his eyes from the glare of her attention. When he took it away, his sister could have sworn she perceived a telltale residue of moisture there. She so forgot herself as to reach across and pat his hand, something she had not done since they were in pinafores.

The old earl pulled out a handkerchief and trumpeted through his nose, nodding understandingly to his sister as he did so. "As to her looks—she is the exact image of Mama, Elspeth. The very sight of her took me back sixty years. Do you remember how beautiful Mama was when she would come in to kiss us good night before she went down to dinner? The lass is as beautiful as Mama was then."

Lady Elspeth stared at him disbelievingly. "Come, come, Edward. You know perfectly well that Mama was generally acknowledged to be the beauty of the county."

"It is true, what I say," he insisted. "The image of Mama."

Lady Elspeth rose from her chair and strode about the room, pacing the long book-lined chamber, coming to stop at last before the portrait of her lovely mother.

"You are my brother, Eddy, and I confess to an overwhelming fondness of you, but like many men you are sometimes a great fool. How could you have walked away? How *could* you have let her go? She is family, Edward, and as fantastical as all of us, I expect. Supposing she were to take it into her head to go back to London? Suppose we never again had the opportunity of seeing her?"

The earl sighed. "I know. I deserve all that you are heaping upon me, Ellie." He nodded contritely. "I have been telling it all to myself these past three hours."

Her ladyship crossed back and stood above him, seeming taller than ever as she stared down then patted him kindly upon the shoulder. She stood for a moment in that position before reaching out impulsively to tug the bell rope. In a moment the footman, Meese, was at the door of the library.

"Tell Hammond that I shall be wanting the carriage."

"Yes, your ladyship. For what time?"

She stared at him as if he were a fool. "Now."

Meese gaped at her. "What? Now, madam?"

"Now?" echoed her brother. "Where in the world are you off to at this time of day?"

"*Now*, Meese, if you please," she repeated, ignoring the earl. "Say to Hammond that I shall expect to be roiling up the dust within half an hour, is that clear?"

"Quite clear, your ladyship," the footman answered hastily. The entire staff knew what Lady Elspeth was like when crossed. "Within half an hour, madam!"

"Good gad, Elspeth. What are you up to?" the earl demanded. "I have a perfect right to know."

"After the silly way you behaved today, I am not at all certain you have any rights at all," she answered rather cruelly. "However, if you must know, I am off to pay a much overdue social call."

"A what? No woman of fashion would be caught dead paying a call at this hour," he protested feebly. "What are you up to?"

Lady Elspeth tossed her magnificently coiffed head. "If

you must know, sir, I am off to Cheyne Spa where I have an overwhelming desire to pay my respects to my old friend, the dear Duchess of Towans."

The earl frowned. "To my knowledge you have never unbent enough to call upon the Duchess of Towans since she has lived in Cheyne." He peered out at her from under bushy eyebrows. "What the devil are you up to, woman?"

"I may not spend my time carousing in town all night like you do, my dear, but even I know it is with the duchess that your granddaughter is at present residing. If I cannot find means of meeting her there, I shall find another way. You may be such an old fool as to let her slip through your fingers, but I certainly have no intention of doing the same."

= 18 =

ELINOR HARDY WAS not overly fond of the social ritual of the mineral baths. She found the smell nauseating and lolling indolently about in the tepid water while fully dressed even to hat or bonnet, ridiculous in the extreme. Lady Augusta, who equally disliked it, objected for other reasons.

"If I am to be thrust amongst any and all," she observed, "it is by preference in some proper place such as the gaming rooms, not a dank cavern where I am intimately conjoined with people about whose personal habits I know nothing whatsoever."

Certainly much of what she said was true—except that the gamblers, being night birds, kept to their beds until noon like the veriest invalids, while the sick were aroused at dawn to be wrapped in flannel against the chill and carried off to the baths in little, black sedan chairs the size of upended coffins. The earlier, the better, pronounced the physicians upon no basis whatsoever, in that tone of informed authority which doctors have used since time immemorial.

"Yes, Lady Blessington, if you will soak every morning and take your powders every night at bedtime, you will find yourself rejuvenated beyond belief. And your ladyship, no more of the white lead, if you please. If it does not fade from fashion very soon, we may have no society left. It is a veritable poison, madam, and has an ultimate effect even the baths and powders cannot alleviate."

If diurnal immersion was considered the most effica-
cious, it was the mid-morning hour that society chose.
Who, after all, would choose to listen to the tiresome
complaints of hypochondriacs when the fetching repartee
of the ton was available a little later in the day? No one, of
course, thought of conversation with the genuinely ill. If
such chose to speak at all, it would surely be of matters
inimical to the spice and gaiety for which Cheyne was
famed.

On the other hand, if one had sharp ears and a taste for
scandal, one was in sheer paradise as society soaked away
the excesses of the previous evening and ammunition was
also gathered for the exercise of back-chat and speculation.
Gossip flourished more freely in the cavern than anywhere
else. Even at the Assembly balls, there was at least dancing
to take one's mind off the activities of one's neighbours.
Here there was no occupation at all. One merely floated
gently with one's little tray in front to hold handkerchief,
comfit-box and cloved-stuffed citrus as fortification against
the stench. One could not read or do one's nails or one's
letters. There was nothing to occupy the time but conversation.

"Did you see that horror worn by Mrs. Spokes? And has
Mr. Abelard no recourse against his valet in the matter of
those shocking allegations?"

The men were equally as trivial-minded. They would
flounder their way about and speak of exactly the same
matters from the masculine point of view. "Dastardly
accusations against poor Abelard, don't you think? Can't
imagine what has come over the lower classes these days.
Ten years ago that wretch of a valet would have been
flogged within an inch of his life instead of standing up in
a court with a lot of trumpery accusations that anyone
knows don't matter in the least, what? The truth? What
the devil does that matter? Are you some sort of a radical,
sir? What has the truth got to do with it? The fellow is a
mere minion. What's he want to be taking oaths in a

demmed witness box for? Dashed impertinence, is what it is, if you ask me."

None of this chatter interested Elinor in the slightest. If anything, the sheer banality of the conversation made her even more aware than she already had been of the essentially trivial natures of the highly born as she remembered all too well. In fact, it was unlikely she would ever forget her feelings at the prospect of having nowhere to lay her head at night.

Idly watching the people arrive and depart, she witnessed the entrance of an elderly woman of such astounding height and masculine visage that one or two unmannerly bathers actually snickered and passed remarks. The old woman did not indulge in the conventional pride of seeming to ignore her detractors. Instead she turned her magnificent head slowly from side to side, fixing each ridiculer with a fierce, falconlike glance. Titters of merriment died in their throats; and, as her gaze continued to rest upon them, each appeared to discover he had some business in another part of the pool which urgently required attention.

Now there, thought the girl, *is the sort of person one wants to know, not all these pampered ninnyhammers.*

As if Elinor's thought had carried into the mind of the other, she found herself, for a moment, the sole object of that falcon-gaze. The dark eyes fixed upon her, and she felt a thrill, an unusual and disconcerting sensation, yet somehow pleasurable. It felt to Elinor as if she had been put to some sort of test and, for reasons unknown, had passed with colours bravely flying. Though she had no idea who the elderly doyenne might be, she felt that there was a possibility they would become fast friends if ever introduced.

This moment of speculation passed quickly, however. In another part of the vast pool a masculine voice was raised to berate an unfortunate attendant for the heinous crime of not being at elbow when required.

"This is certainly not the way things were done here in

the old days," Jasper Gully complained in a loud and haughty tone, looking about for the approbation of all others within earshot. "I could have you sacked, my friend. Inconsiderate chaps like you should not be allowed the privilege of ministering to ladies and gentlemen."

Unfortunately for the prestige of the complainant, Mrs. Mudge was floating nearby in an effort to alleviate aching muscles brought on by the previous evening's jolting coach ride to Budolph. The actress knew perfectly well who Mr. Gully was and had very little use for the Parliamentarian. This morning in particular, she also had little inclination to curb her irritation. Consequently, she did not so much say what she thought as let the world share her personal reactions to such flummery.

"Gentlemen? Oh, pshaw!"

The politician turned slowly in the redolent water. "And who, madam, are you?" he asked, looking down his nose in the affected fashion which he took to be aristocratic.

"It ain't so much who *I* may be as who you believe yourself to be," she answered. "Pollock there has been in attendance in Cheyne baths for twice as long as you have been 'gulling' your constituents and, to my thinking, has made a far better job of his employment than you have done with yours. So mind your manners, if you please. The ways of Cheyne Spa are not dictated by the likes of you."

Whatever Gully might have been—opportunist, rogue, social climber—he was not fool enough to believe that a middle-aged M. P. in direct confrontation with a feisty old lady could come out any fashion but bloodied. He, therefore, contented himself with giving her a hard look of some length, as if to impress her visage upon his memory for possible retribution in the future. He then drifted away with as much dignity as it was possible for him to muster under the circumstances.

Lady Elspeth Hardy was, of course, witness to the incident; though she could not quite place Gully. She knew the face but had for the moment no name to attach to it. Meanwhile, she guiltily recognised in Mrs. Mudge the sere remains of a young woman to whom she had once done a great wrong through a misplaced sense of family pride. The remorse Lady Elspeth felt had to do with the fact that she had long ago raised strong objections to a plan of her brother's which involved marriage to this very woman. Elspeth had seen Mrs. Mudge many times upon the stage since then and never without a twinge of guilt. She had been, as she privately admitted to herself now, a stuffy prude. Unfortunately, it had taken the spectacle of her brother's lonely life to bring her, years after the fact, to her senses. Though she had never acted upon it, the regret she felt was genuine. Only she had never been able to humble herself enough to admit that aloud.

Well, the time had come. Lady Elspeth began to bob and float across the pool toward the elderly actress. To do so, she had to make her way through a cluster of silly young girls twittering amongst themselves. Her ladyship had never felt at home among young women such as these. When she was their age, she had been disastrously plain and out of place in more comely company. She was no less uneasy with them now that she was old. All the insecurities of her distant youth came thrusting forward as she was forced to listen to their prattle. The voices might have been echoes from her girlhood. One, she recognised, was that of the duchess's lovely niece, Barbara. Lady Elspeth hardly knew whether she was annoyed or pleased to find even this acknowledged beauty as trivial-minded as her ring of toadies.

"Oh, I admit it," she heard the girl saying as if describing an accomplishment of which she had right to be proud, "I adore to be spoiled. I cannot imagine how dreary life must be without cosseting, and if a gentleman is not able to understand that part of my nature, well . . ." She rolled her eyes drolly as her audience squealed in shallow admiration. "Farewell, sir, and go quickly upon your way, if you please, is what *I* say."

It was evident from their admiring coos and cries that her coterie supported her every step of the way. Sharp words of censure sprang to Lady Elspeth's lips; but she bit them back, knowing she would only be sorry if they were said. She passed the young ladies with her eyes trained steadfastly ahead, aware that they had not even seen her. She had no existence for such creatures as these. To them she was no more significant than the servants or the paint upon the walls.

Meanwhile, Mrs. Mudge had engaged herself in conversation with a neighbour; and the moment seemed unpropitious for a reconciliation. Something else now captured Lady Elspeth's attention. Her eyes fell upon a girl who could be no other than her grand-niece. Brother Edward had been quite right in saying that the girl was a clear reproduction of their long-dead mother. Her ladyship thought of her brother's recollection of their beautiful mother coming into the nursery for a good-night kiss before she went down to dinner in her velvet gown and jewels. Mama had always spent more time with Edward. She had no time for a daughter who even then gave evidence of never outgrowing her plainness.

Now, it appeared, Mama had come again. It was impossible that this could be anyone but Edward's granddaughter. Elspeth began to propel herself in the girl's direction instead of toward Mrs. Mudge but then, to her chagrin, saw that she should have paid more attention to the other bathers. Headed straight at her with a determined gleam in his eye was the relative she disliked more than all others combined.

Cecil Partridge, upon first spying his great-aunt bobbing unsteadily about, had wondered how he might avoid a meeting with her. Then, when such an encounter seemed inevitable, he had decided to turn the situation to his own advantage. With that in mind, he purposefully assumed his most unctuous smile and pretended she was the person he had most wanted to see all along.

"Why, Aunt, I had no idea you were in town. I find you here in the baths, but it is evident that you have no need of them for you are looking better than I have seen you in some time. When are you coming to pay us a visit? My mother and I were speaking of you only yesterday. The rose-canes you gave her have acclimated splendidly, especially those that Uncle Edward brought from France."

Elspeth remembered very well when her brother had smuggled in the cuttings after Waterloo. They were said to have come from Josephine's famous garden at Malmaison and to be quite a horticultural prize. Lady Elspeth herself had never had the touch for roses, nor for any other flowers. She left such things to the gardeners and merely enjoyed the results. Some people, she knew, were said to have a green thumb and could make anything grow. Hers was more likely, she suspected, black. Still, she would enjoy seeing how the Malmaisons had turned out, even though she would have to put up with an afternoon of Evangeline's insipidity to do so.

She allowed Cecil a restrained smile, scarcely more than a polite acknowledgement of his presence. "What are you doing at the baths, nephew? I had thought you took great pride in the excellent state of your health?"

It was a subject he could warm to. "Indeed I do, madam, and I mean to keep healthy. There is nothing so good as prevention, in my estimation. The time for treatment is before you have become ill." He glanced about secretively and leaned closer to Lady Elspeth. "*She* is here, you know. The cousin. I hope you will not let it spoil your morning."

The earl's sister looked amused. " 'The cousin'? How baroque you are, Cecil. One would think you were intriguing at the court of the Medicis. Yes, I believe I must have seen her a little while since. If she is the gel I have in mind, she bears a distinct resemblance to your grandmother." As if to test him, she did not point to the correct candidate at all but toward the bevy of giggling girls. "That one in the cherried straw?"

Following her glance, Cecil smiled disdainfully. "So that is what grandmama looked like? No, alas, that is Lady Barbara, last year's great beauty, though she has fallen off a bit. The whisper is that she has a *tendre* for some mountebank or other, if you can imagine it. My cousin Elinor is the girl over there in the corner with the rather jaundiced look. I expect she is one of the few who have come for their health and not merely the gossip."

Her ladyship nodded contentedly. He had pointed out exactly the girl she had thought her grand-niece must be. Barbara Pentreath she had known from a child and was quite happy to be unrelated to her. It seemed to her, however, that Elinor's look indicated not so much jaundice as discontent and found that observation confirmed when the young woman's expression changed instantly to one of interest and animation as she saw an acquaintance at whom she smiled and waved discreetly.

Lady Elspeth recognised Tyger Dobyn immediately. So that was the way the land lay: a disinherited girl and a penniless adventurer, doleful combination to say the least. Elspeth determined to bide her time by listening a little longer to what Cecil Partridge had to say. Meanwhile, she would watch to see how the girl conducted herself.

"She seems drawn to the Tyger," said Elspeth to her despised relative.

Cecil put on a scornful expression and made a gesture of dismissal that almost upset the tray floating in front of him. "Small advantage in a liaison of *that* sort, I should think. I cannot agree with the lionization of people of that stamp, can you? How *do* they manage to work themselves into good society, I wonder? We shall be inviting pit bulls next and setting them at each other's throats in the Assembly Rooms."

"I suppose it must be tedious to be in a place like Cheyne

and have no fortune," answered Lady Elspeth with a sympathy she knew would be likely to distress Cecil.

Indeed, it had the effect of causing him to sniff disdainfully and toss his head in a spirited manner. "It has not seemed to impede my cousin in the least. She has half a dozen young Corinthians hanging about her most of the time. They say she would soon be set-down by Lady Barbara, but that her ladyship will not risk it while cousin is a guest of the Duchess of Towans, her ladyship's aunt." He giggled maliciously. "Cousin Elinor, you know, has committed the crime of flirting with both young Ben Weymouth and Trevor Quenton who have been Lady Barbara's private stock for, lo, these many years." He dandled himself smugly in the water. "Yes, I think we may expect to see dear little Elinor quite devastated one of these days when Lady Barbara puts her mind to it."

"I take it you have no love for your cousin?" asked his great-aunt a shade too pointedly for dissimulation.

Cecil, hearing the suggestion in her tone, was quick to tread water. "Oh, quite to the contrary. Mama has invited her to tea. I mention her behaviour merely as a commentary upon the social scene, don't you know? Means nothing at all to me, does it? Oh, no, not at all." A crafty expression lit his beady eyes. "I say, Aunt, why do we not arrange so you visit Mama and her roses upon the same day Elinor is coming? Then you may acquaint yourself with her and form your own opinion, eh? Isn't that a capital notion? I daresay Mama will think it a great jape to have you both there at once. Though, I know she will ask you not to be too hard on the girl, her being a blood relative and all that."

Lady Elspeth eyed him speculatively. He was precisely the priggish fool she had always thought him to be. "What a good idea, Cecil," she agreed. "Do ask your mother to arrange it, without mentioning my name, perhaps. Let it come as a surprise to the gel. And now you must excuse me, for I see the dear Duchess of Towans to whom I have not spoken in such a long time that she must almost have forgotten who I am."

"Oh, certainly, Aunt. Certainly."

He watched as she made her undulating way through the water. What a queer old thing she was to be sure. Still, she might be turned into an ally if he played his cards in just the right way, and it would be no bad advantage to have a friendly voice within his uncle's household.

19

As it happened Lady Elspeth was not the only one to notice that almost secretive exchange between Elinor and the Tyger. Lady Augusta had made her own assessment and was far from pleased. Despite her previously tacit sanction of their acquaintance, she now realised what a disaster the friendship could be for the girl. Tyger was a charming fellow, no doubt, but hardly an advantageous catch. It was the sort of thing which must be nipped in the bud.

Her grace propelled herself toward the far edge of the pool where the gamester lounged in conversation with the disreputable old Marquess of Lorn. The Tyger, seeing her bobbing in the shallows with one slim hand against the tiles to retain her balance, made his way to her at once.

"What a pleasant meeting, Duchess," he greeted her with a winning smile that almost turned her from her purpose. "Are you ready to come out? Shall I fetch an attendant?"

"No, I merely seek a word or two with you, sir."

Dobyn's eyes widened slightly at her tone, but he continued smiling. "Sounds ominous, ma'am. I hope I am not in bad straits?"

The duchess did not respond to his charm. "I had thought, sir, that we had an understanding considering my gels."

But he was not to be pulled down. "You say that in the

plural, your grace. Am I to understand that I am believed to have designs on the countess as well as her sister?"

Lady Augusta's eyes snapped. "I do not care for verbal fencing, sir. I think you know my thoughts. I mean Lady Elinor."

Tyger's handsome face began to take on that wary impassivity every professional gambler knows how to assume, useful in any sphere, of course, but particularly at the gaming tables or with outraged matrons.

"Perhaps you will be a bit more explicit, Duchess?" he suggested. "I have no knowledge of a prohibition save that against courting Lady Barbara which I would not have done in any case."

He spoke calmly and without a hint of insolence or even irony, but it did nothing to placate her ladyship. She turned her head to be sure that no one was nearby, then said firmly, "I will not allow you, sir, to set that poor child's life awry. You can have no serious interest, and I have grown too fond of her to let her form an unsuitable attachment."

The Tyger did not respond for a moment, merely regarded the still handsome woman with a level gaze. "I, too, have a fond regard for Miss Hardy, madam. I fear I do not agree that her interests will be best served by placing her on the block as if she were in some Carib market."

Lady Augusta had to admit, even in this stressful moment, that he was certainly an attractive man. She could feel her own defences waver. It was easy to see why a younger, less experienced girl might be fascinated. She listened to his next words with a degree of sympathy.

"As it happens, your grace, I agree that Miss Hardy—or Lady Elinor, if you please—would best be matched up with some amiable man of substance, but I cannot agree that fortune alone should be the deciding factor."

The duchess felt an actual twinge of sympathy as she scanned his face. "You care for her, do you not?" She saw a shield go up behind his eyes. "Oh, not love, necessarily, but you have a concern for her welfare."

"Elinor and I are friends," he admitted. "I daresay I remind her of her father, but as for anything else . . ."

Lady Augusta adopted a more urbane approach. "I expect, sir, that there are many such impressionable young women who are drawn to you. Can you not find it in your heart to deal kindly with this one by being cold?"

"I have a certain honour in matters of this sort, your grace, despite what you think of me. I am, as you have suspected, much drawn to Elinor Hardy but have already admitted to her that I have no money. It seems that she has no more than I, whatever her family connexions." A wry smile curled the corners of his mouth. "The honest truth is that, though I manage to support myself nicely in my chosen profession, it is a life of enormous variation. I doubt that it would extend to the comfortable maintenance of two. All of which hardly matters, in any case, as I expect I shall be quitting Cheyne Spa for London in a fortnight at the latest."

"I do not suppose," said the duchess as winningly as a swift transition would allow, "that you could be persuaded to hasten your leave-taking? If it is a question of finance, perhaps something could be arranged."

The Tyger was so taken aback by this blatant attempt at bribery that his customary gambler's control quite slipped, and he broke into loud and easy laughter which echoed and reechoed within the confines of the bath, turning every head in their direction.

"Indeed, madam," he said, "you go a step too far even considering our difference in station. I have not yet sunk to being bought off to secure my absence. With all due respect to your wishes, I fear that my business in Cheyne cannot be postponed and the date of my departure is dependent upon it rather than upon any whim of my own . . . or of yours."

This was said so good-naturedly that the duchess took

no offence and almost forgave his obstinacy. "Can I at least hope that you will not seek·to entangle the dear girl in the meanwhile?"

He bowed ironically. "One is always free to hope, your grace, but I think I am not prepared to make any promises. I daresay that Miss—that Lady Elinor's innate common sense will set your fears at rest."

He then turned away without farewell, and the duchess was left to be satisfied with only such a faint concession.

With a distinct sense of regret, she watched him walk away. She liked, even admired, the Tyger for his code of honour. She had heard whispers that such was not a universal view of the man; but, despite the cynics, she was of the belief that people change. If he had been a rogue in the past, she did not believe he was one now. Certainly he was devilishly attractive. Smiling to herself, she wondered how many of the gossips watching them had misinterpreted their meeting. How lucky that she was still contentedly in love with her own absent husband. How fortunate, as well, that he would soon be returning to England to enjoy the remainder of the summer. Life at Cheyne Spa, with all its irridescence, might be joyously diverting; but it could never hold a candle to the felicities of a marriage of like minds. She wondered, with a faint pang, if the duke longed for her as deeply as she did for him?

Meanwhile, Tyger Dobyn found himself looking into the smirking countenance of Jasper Gully. Tyger tried to brush past the man without acknowledgement, but the M.P. was having none of it.

"Well, well, did I detect a bit of trouble in Paradise? I had thought that you and her grace were as thick as thieves, Dobyn, but I see that even cronies can fall out."

Tyger clenched his fists, not in threat but to restrain himself from knocking the man aside. "What you thought is of no concern to me, Gully."

The politician pulled a sympathetic face. "Here now, my lad, there is no reason you and I must always be at odds, is there? Why, I daresay we could even prove mightily useful to each other at times. I will confess to you—and you may use it against me, if you will—that years ago I followed much the same profession by which you live. I did rather well by it, I must say, until greener pastures beckoned."

Dobyn smiled unbelievingly. "Are you telling me that you once followed the fancy? I cannot see you in a mill, Gully. You would be beaten to a pulp in the space of three minutes."

Gully sneered. "Boxing? Not likely. I think too well of my face, ugly as it is, to be such a fool as that. I meant to say that I was once of the gaming profession. I daresay we have used many of the same tricks, old son."

"We may each *know* certain tricks, but that don't mean we need to stoop to using them." He scrutinised the M.P. carefully. "What are you up to, anyway? It isn't your sort of amusement to be soaking up the minerals. There is no profit in it that I can see."

"That is where you are pitifully shortsighted, Mr. Tyger Dobyn. You do not recognise the chances that lie all about us. You would be surprised at the uses to which I can put the information I gather here. An amazing amount of which there is for a man with sharp ears, especially if one has nothing more to do than float from one place to another. I tell you, this mineral bathing has more to it than is readily suspected. Would you care to hear a few of the juicy tidbits that have come my way this morning? Nothing earthshaking, mind you, but tidy little pieces nonetheless."

"No, thank you," said Dobyn distastefully. "There are certain advantages which do not interest me."

Gully was not to be put off. It was his nature to be incapable of concealing a secret once he had gathered it to him. Whether this gave him reassurance or some other form of gratification is unclear, but it is certain that a good deal of pleasure was involved. He peered slyly into the Tyger's half-averted face, even went so far as to catch at his arm in order to hold the boxer's attention. It was not a very dignified posture for a member of His Majesty's government; but then, His Majesty, being old and mad, had probably never seen the likes of Mr. Gully.

"That granddaughter of old Glastonia, for instance, there is a mort to be said about *her*, as I am sure you know."

"I trust I will never hear *you* repeat it," said the Tyger in a tone sharp as the fine side of a sabre. "Lady Elinor does me the honour of calling me friend, and I would consider a slight upon her honour as one taken directly upon mine. I hope I make myself clear?"

Another of his fatuous smirks spread across Gully's face. He had acquired just the bit of corroboration he needed. "Oh, quite clear, old fellow. But you misinterpret me, as usual. I have been a friend of the young lady for years— friend of her papa, at any rate. Do you remember that a moment ago I was speaking of following your profession? Young Hardy, her papa, and I were partners. Worked hand in glove, the two of us, and fleeced many a farmer of his sheep money, I dare to say. Pity he came to such a bad end, is it not? Quite wasted away of disease, they say. He always was a delicate sort of chap, you know. Enormous amounts of energy sometimes, bright-cheeked as a boy and with the same sparkle in his eyes. Then he'd go into a collapse and be out of the way for a week at a time. Well, a partner cannot go along with that sort of behaviour, you know, so we parted. I would have helped him if I could, but I was rather in strait-street myself at the time. It was before I went into the service of my fellows, you know."

Dobyn frowned. "In the service of your fellows? What do you mean by that?"

"Why, politics, my friend. Who serves in the Commons is sworn to serve the dear old land as well as he can, ain't he? Of course, it works to my advantage now and then as well. I ain't so much of a saint as that."

I expect you take every advantage you can, thought the Tyger, but aloud he merely asked, "So you knew the old earl's son, did you? When would that have been, I wonder?"

The question might have seemed abrupt, but Gully took no notice, merely screwed up his face in thought. "Oh, seven, eight years ago, I should think. The girl was just growing up then, you see. That was another thing, not wanting to have the child about all the time. It restricts one's chances and opportunities. I am sure you see that. We worked together, though, until the luck turned, and we parted amicably enough."

You mean that you deserted him, thought Dobyn. *Left him and the girl to fend for themselves as best they could. Even you must have seen that he was dying.*

"I say, my friend," suggested Gully, tucking his arm through that of the taller man. "Why don't you and I go somewhere and have a quiet chat about the old days? Perhaps we might exchange a useful bit of memory or two."

Tyger Dobyn agreed warily. As they walked away, the M.P. felt that peculiar sensation as when someone is staring at your back, a faint tickling at the nape of the neck. He turned to see who it might be. No one was watching them. No head was even turned in their direction except that of a very tall old woman with disconcertingly masculine visage, and she was not anyone worth bothering about so far as he could see.

═ 20 ═

BEN FOUND HIS friend standing disconsolate beneath the three blue balls of the pawnbroker's shop in Marsden Street. "Good grief, old fellow, has it come to this?" he asked jocularly as he approached, then wished he had kept his mummer shut as he saw that Trevor's expression was not merely coincidental.

Quenton nodded toward an elegant, bullet-shaped silver teapot, the lid of which completed the round outline. It was obviously old and not very valuable. It was also obvious that it meant something rather special to Trevor.

"That once belonged to my grandmother," he said sadly. "I haven't set eyes on it for the ten years since she passed on, but I'd recognise it anywhere by that small dent near the handle."

"Come on, old fellow, by a dent in the handle?"

Trevor brightened. "Did I never tell you that story? My Uncle Richard flung it at my head one teatime because I said I favoured Maximus over his own horse in the Epsom Derby."

"Can't say I blame him, you know. Not a nice thing to hear over tea. So he flung the pot at your head, did he? Good for him. He didn't scald you, I hope?"

"No, it was empty by that time. Uncle Richard was never one to waste good bohea."

"But how do you suppose it sank to this estate, the poor thing? Rather a nice-looking old piece."

Trevor shrugged. "I expect it was when Uncle hit upon

hard times. The family generally ain't done too well in the last few years as you know. Wish I could redeem it and put in into my mam's hands. Wouldn't she half go off her crown?" He managed a strangulated little laugh at the thought of his mother's probable astonishment.

"Come away," Ben advised. "You'll only upset yourself with the longing. Perhaps you will come across some rich heiress at the Masquerade Ball tonight and be in a position to redeem the family's fortune entire."

Trevor shrugged. "You, of all people, know who it is I want to marry."

His friend had the grace to look uncomfortable. "If I believed that Barbara cared for you as more than a good companion, I would gladly step aside, you know that."

"You believe that she loves you?"

Ben shook his head. "Not in the least. I sometimes doubt that the lady of our affections is capable of loving anyone."

"Except herself," Trevor observed with uncharacteristic bitterness.

"I do not think even that is true. Perhaps there is something essentially absent in her. It is not so much a matter of self-love, but no acquaintance with love whatsoever."

"One day perhaps you will awaken her with a kiss like the prince in the fairy story."

Ben hardly knew what to answer. "Nothing in this world is certain, is it? Some other chap may come along who will know the magic charm."

Trevor turned away, and Ben followed toward the High Street. "Oh, she will marry you," Trevor prophesied. "She'd be a fool if she did not."

They made a shortcut through a lane so small as to be almost an alley and came upon a tiny, hidden square just large enough to support a plane tree with a wooden seat encircling it. Upon this bench a couple sat, locked in deep embrace, seemingly oblivious to the world about them, devoid of either caution or sense of convention.

Trevor touched his friend's arm. "My God, is that . . . ?"

"I fear it is," said Ben sadly.

He had recognised the frock the young woman was wearing. He had, in fact, been with Barbara when she had her final fitting for it at the dressmaker's shop. She had pirouetted before him, and he had thought that vastly becoming. He was not certain what he thought just now.

The young creature half glanced toward them, but Ben turned his head away without looking into her face.

"Should we not do something about this?" Trevor gasped. "It is quite public, after all. Why, the duchess would—"

"What would the duchess do?" asked Ben. "Are either of us privy to the mind of her grace or of the duke, for that matter? Is it our business?"

They had moved from the square to the passage leading out toward the High Street.

"By God, Ben, you do not mean to say they should be allowed to carry on in that fashion? Anyone might see them."

Young Weymouth stopped. That was a consideration. The friendship he and Trev had enjoyed with Lady Barbara over the years entitled them to certain rights and endowed them with certain responsibilities, no matter how distasteful. He hesitated, then turned back.

"I daresay you are right, old fellow. I hate the thought of interfering, but I suppose it is necessary in this instance."

Even if Barbara cared nothing for herself or her own reputation, a friend must look at it in a different light. She deserved that much at his hands, though he did not approve or even understand her behaviour.

Ben hurried back to the little square with Trevor at his heels, but the bench beneath the plane tree was quite deserted. All that remained as evidence of the romantic tryst was a small scrap of linen. Ben picked it up and held it to his face, inhaling the distinctive fragrance which was

Lady Barbara's personal identification, made exclusively for her by a famous perfumer in London.

"I say, old fellow," he heard Trevor ask, "what do you have in mind to do?"

"I hardly know," Ben Weymouth answered.

Elinor Hardy entered the house in Regent's Crescent in a state of deep confusion. She and the maidservant, Dora, had decided to take advantage of the fine day to walk about the town. They wandered in and out of shops eyeing the well-arranged displays in the windows, visited the library for a new novel, returned a bunch of silk violets which did not quite suit the bonnet for which it was intended, and generally whiled away the afternoon bearing in mind that one must not become too tired to enjoy this evening's Masquerade Ball.

They had been strolling along Stall Street when it was their fortune to encounter Tyger Dobyn emerging from the White Hart Inn. Elinor was delighted, of course, for she counted that gentleman among her affectionate friends and had high plans of inveigling him into inviting her to drink tea in the pleasant surroundings of St. Gerrans's Gardens. However, she was almost immediately aware of an unaccustomed formality in his address.

It was not in the least improper, of course, in fact quite the opposite, but there had over the weeks of their acquaintance grown up a kind of easy familiarity which she had found most pleasant. With the Tyger she felt she could be herself, free from the requirement of pretending to a background and rank which were not rightfully hers. Yet, this afternoon he bowed deeply and even tipped his hat to Dora but then evinced an almost unseemly haste to depart their company.

"If you will forgive me, Lady Elinor, I fear I have a previous appointment for which I am very much in arrears."

She was quite surprised. "La, sir, 'Lady Elinor' is it? I

had thought that between us such pretence was unnecessary."

He bowed again almost perfunctorily. "If you will excuse me? I am already quite late."

Elinor blinked at this brusqueness. It was behaviour quite unlike any she had grown to expect from him. "Certainly, sir," she said diffidently. "I would not for the life impede you in your social rounds. I daresay they are as necessary to you as breath."

She was aware her voice was trembling a little as she said this, but that seem to pass unnoticed by Mr. Dobyn. "I expect we shall meet at the Masquerade Ball?" she asked him, somewhat surprised at the note of hope she heard in her tone.

"Perhaps we shall," he conceded reluctantly. "Although I cannot be sure of it. I find I have urgent business in the city which may require my departure on the evening coach." He bowed again as if to bring their conversation to a close. "I hope, however, that you will find it diverting and enjoyable. Now, if you will excuse me?"

"Why, my stars," said Dora as they watched him stride hurriedly away. "Whatever has come over the gentleman, miss? There was a time only a day or two ago when he could have hardly have been pried from your side, and now look at him."

She peered up under the shadow of Elinor's bonnet and, oblivious to the implied impertinency, asked, "You an' him hasn't gone and had a dust-up has you?"

The girl returned her look blankly. "None that I am aware of, Dora. Unless such occurred, and no one bothered to inform me. It is really quite curious, isn't it?"

"Yes, miss," the servant agreed. "But, then, you knows men. Creatures of chance and change they is in my experience."

Elinor turned the incident over and over in her mind all the way back to the duchess's house and, even now, had no answer. She ascended the handsome stair to the first floor and passed along the hallway, intending to consult with her benefactress concerning the man's odd behaviour; but, as she neared the door of her ladyship's boudoir, she was stopped by the sound of Lady Augusta's voice berating a servant with quite uncustomary sharpness.

"I can imagine, my dear girl, that you may consider your private life on your free afternoon to be your own and that, once you are out of my sight, you may conduct yourself much as you please. I fear I must explain to you that such is not always the case. Whatever you do casts its reflection upon this household."

"Yes, your grace." Elinor could hear Elsie beginning to reply. "But I fear I do not understand your complaint."

It seemed that the duchess was now returning to her customary good humour. "It never crossed your mind, I know, but the spot you so unwisely selected for your romantic dallying lies just within the eye range of one of the most dedicated old gossips in Cheyne Spa."

"Does your grace mean the Duchess of Doddington?" Elinor could hear the dismay in the servant's voice. "Oh, Lord, madam, I never thought. It is not a private square, after all, and we were not doing anything but a bit of kissing, you see."

The duchess's reply was a mingling of understanding and irritation. "But *look* at you, girl. When I saw you coming home I quite mistook you myself, wearing Lady Barbara's frock and Lady Barbara's bonnet, even smelling of Lady Barbara's own scent."

"But, madam, her ladyship gave them to me herself only yesterday. She said she was going to create herself over into a new person and that these all belonged to the old. I only wore them to please my friend."

"I am sure you did, but since you and Lady Barbara are so much of a size and colouring . . ."

There was a brief and horrified silence as the import of this observation sank in. Then the maidservant's stricken voice spoke. "Oh, your grace, you don't mean to say that the old lady thought that I was Lady Barbara? Oh, but she couldn't have done, could she? Oh, your grace!" Was there a certain pride in her voice that she might have been, however erroneously, mistaken for one of the gentry?

The amused regret of the duchess was clearly conveyed through the half-open door. "I very much fear that such *was* the case. I daresay by this evening it will be all over Cheyne Spa that Lady Barbara Pentreath was seen snuggling in broad daylight. The worst of such rumours is that they cannot be denied without giving them credence. 'No smoke without fire,' folk will say, and say it very greedily, I am sure."

"Oh, madam, if I had for a moment thought . . ."

Now the duchess seemed merely resigned. "I suppose there is nothing to be done but to wait out the storm."

"And my position, your ladyship? Am I—?"

"Are you to be discharged? No, not for such foolishness. Though, in future, I trust you will behave more circumspectly?"

"Oh, I will, your grace. And I shall have just a word or two to say to my Alf for getting me into the situation, that I do allow."

"I do not think you should be too hard on the poor man," the duchess cautioned with a small laugh. "It requires a pair to exchange kisses, if I remember."

"Yes, madam."

The pretty maidservant fled the chamber so hastily that Elinor was almost forced to flatten herself against the wall in order to avoid being run down.

Considering the circumstances and her own culpability in eavesdropping, Elinor decided that perhaps another time might better serve to speak to the duchess about the strange behaviour of Tyger Dobyn. Not to say that it did not still trouble Elinor, but she wondered if consulting with her grace would provide any real enlightenment. Perhaps this was a situation in which Elinor would have to look to herself for wisdom.

=== 21 ===

By SIX-THIRTY IN the evening they had begun to ascend the hill toward the Assembly Rooms: kings, queens, jesters, historical figures from every clime and time, ranging from ancient Egypt to the Merrie England of Charles II. There were representations of natives from Goa. There were Cherokee chiefs and Mandarins, and there were more than a few figures of phantasy which had no factual home of provenance save only in some geography of the mind. All of the costumes were lavish and elaborate. Even the clothing of the peasants was of velvet and silk.

Every face bore a mask; although some were so abbreviated as to conceal little of their wearers' true identity. Perhaps this was intentional and meant to draw some parallel between the impersonator and the impersonated. The old Duchess of Doddington, for instance, was gotten up as Elizabeth of Russia; the Marquess of Lorn was an antiquated Casanova; and the Lord Mayor Tobias, in a grand effort to make some mark upon the company of notables, had enlisted the aid of his wife and her sisters to appear as Henry VIII with his consorts. All were garbed in the tradition of the Holbein portraits, but a delicious and imaginative touch was that about the necks of Anne Boleyn and silly Catherine Howard were slender scarlet ribbands to denote their not dissimilar fates. It was a well-conceived notion but utterly disregarded in the crush.

* * *

Naturally, no one was yet ready in the duchess's household, although they easily could have been. It was not sloth which held them back, but calculation. Lady Barbara, in particular, knew the value of making an entrance. Nothing could have induced her to arrive earlier than seven-thirty, and sometime past eight would be even better. Let them anticipate her.

Looking into the pier glass, she was more than satisfied with what she saw. She was, in fact, quite aware that by any standard she looked ravishing in the silver tissue she had chosen to wear as a representation of an Arabian houri. The design had undergone certain alterations from its original conception. Aunt Augusta had categorically forbidden harem trousers, which was rather unfair since she was allowing her pet Elinor to dress in a dashing adaptation of the uniform of the Queen's Light Dragoons. The wretched creature would probably attract a substantial following of undiscriminating admirers, Ben and Trevor among them. Yet, when she stopped to think about it, it was almost amusing how one could change so quickly. Only a month ago Barbara had been quite upset at the thought of Elinor Hardy taking up with her own discarded beaux. Now she fervently hoped that Ben in particular understood that he was discarded. It would make things so much simpler.

Lady Barbara was not learned. She had read very little, and that merely the light novels of the day. Certainly any sense of introspection was far out of her usual line of country; but it was beginning to become evident, even to her, that she was behaving in a most unusual way. It was not simply that she regarded her feeling for Patrick Tyrone as being outside the bounds of convention, for she had never much regarded rules as applying to herself. When she had observed them, it was merely because it seemed the easiest way to proceed. Perhaps it was that she had never *cared* very deeply about anything, but had allowed her attention to dwell on what was essentially ephemeral— gowns, parties, beaux, attention to her physical beauty.

Now all that was changed, and changed as well was her own viewpoint which had, in fact, multiplied.

Self-dedicated as she was, her infatuation made her see the actor from two directions. On the one hand, he stood before her enwrapped in all the glamour of his stage presence, endowed with the virtues of the heroes he played, gifted with all the wit they possessed. On the other, Patrick Tyrone, the real man, was nothing like those well-spoken gentlemen. He was in some respects rather like a figure of papier-mâché which by some chance had become animated. He was handsome in a way which made her sometimes feel quite giddy. His manners were serviceable if not fine. However, he had no conversation unless it was given him; and he seemed, at times, almost intimidated by her attention.

None of that mattered. She meant to have him; and, if she had to fill him out with her own spirit, she would do so. She was beginning to believe she had a good deal more of that commodity than she had ever suspected.

Elinor, meanwhile, was not at all certain she approved of the breeches costume Lady Augusta had ordained that she wear. Elinor was no romantic; but it would have been a pretty thing to attend the ball as a princess or some fairy tale creature, even some figure out of history. She made a leg and forced herself to salute smartly as she had seen young ensigns and subalterns do. The effect was not *too* terrible. Perhaps she would not look foolish trying to carry it off.

There was a light tapping on the door of her chamber, and she heard the voice of Countess Lavinia, Barbara's sister. "May I come in, my dear? We are all of us nearly ready to depart. Jack has dressed up like a highwayman and is determined to drive the coach up the hill as if he had just taken it as a prize. He is waiting in the Crescent now, impatient as any jack-a-dandy."

The countess herself might almost have passed as a

beauty on this occasion. She was got up in a court dress of the last century. With powdered hair and patches, her rather brownish outdoor complexion covered by paint and powder, she presented a sweetly nostalgic appearance.

Laughingly, she indicated her wide panniers. "I think I shall not come in for it might be too much trouble to edge through the door. I hope I shall not take up all the room in the coach." She giggled infectiously. "Would it not be a pity if Barbara were forced to walk up the hill in her curl-toed slippers? You haven't seen them? Quite adorable with a tiny bell on each toe. I daresay, 'she will make music wherever she goes.' "

Elinor made one or two last-minute adjustments to her uniform. When she joined Lavvy in the passage she could not help observing. "I think we make rather a handsome couple, don't you, Countess? Who can say? I may steal you away from your highwayman."

The Countess Lavinia smiled sweetly at this sally. "Even such a Cherubino as you could not do that, fetching as you are."

All the world knew how deeply in love were Lavinia and the cousin she had married. Theirs was a quiet alliance, but mutually satisfying.

It was quite a parade that made its way out of the Regent's Crescent house and along the walk to the waiting carriage: Barbara in her glistening silver tissue, Lavinia in her hoops and panniers, Elinor jaunty and insouciant, endowed by her costume with a greater sense of freedom than she had ever known in Cheyne Spa, and the duchess herself, splendid in a red, tightly curled wig, the Virgin Queen to the life.

Their highwayman leapt down from the box of the coach to assist them while the real footman held the door; then, just as they were about to roll off around the crescent, Barbara flung open the door of the carriage and flew back into the house.

"What on earth is the chit up to now?" demanded the duchess of no one in particular, and no one answered.

She had voiced the question for all. In a few moments her niece reappeared, without either apology or explanation; and the old-fashioned coach began its lumbering passage through the streets to the Assembly Rooms.

The press about the Upper Rooms was astonishing—a tangle of coaches, carriages and sedan chairs. It appeared that the Masquerade Ball was already a grand success. Not only were there fancifully dressed legitimate ticket holders jostling for position, but also the addition of a great number of interlopers who hoped to slip past the guards in the crush. Nothing like this particular spectacle had been seen in several seasons, and the staff of the Assembly Rooms were caught quite unprepared. However, upon the arrival of the duchess and her party, a passage opened up spontaneously, as if the crowd instinctively recognised the superior right of the gentry to skim the cream of the evening.

Jack Mawson had surrendered the reins to the real coachman, and the party entered the grand salon amidst oohs and ahhs of appreciation. The rooms were so transformed for the evening as to be scarcely recognisable. The usually barren walls had been draped with silken fabric gathered to the center of the ceiling, creating the illusion of a vast and luxurious tent. The Corporation was obviously making a determined bid to rival Cheltenham and Bath.

Hundreds of waxen tapers were at the ready to illumine the rooms once the fading summer light had gone, and the septet of musicians in the gallery had begun to saw away at their instruments in a fair approximation of one of the Boyce Symphonies. The dancing, of course, had not yet commenced.

Several spectators stood on chairs to observe the Towans party as they came into the room. Pretty comments were murmured at sight of the Countess Lavinia, her sweet face surrounded by a powdered wig. The onlookers also smiled amiably at the countess's not particularly menacing highwayman-husband and was vastly diverted by Lady Barbara's slightly shocking silver tissue and turned-up toes. Nonetheless, it was the duchess herself who most impressed the crowd. If Barbara resembled the moon in her silvery clothing, how much more did her grace represent the sun in cloth of gold? Below her huge Elizabethan ruff hung every necklace and her fingers bore every ring she had brought to Cheyne, so that she shot dazzling sparkles of light in every direction.

As patroness of the ball, the duchess made her way through the crowd to a sort of dais opposite the gallery and ensconced herself, with her family ranged about her, until the long line of homages had been paid. The gentry acknowledged her precedence over them by bowing and curtseying. Even the mayor and his 'wives' bent the knee, which was amusing since, historically, Henry VIII was Queen Elizabeth's father and would have as soon decapitated her as kneel. All of this delighted her grace no end.

"Do you remember," she whispered to her nieces from behind her fan, "how they all fought to gain entry to my gambling house, then looked down their petty noses? Just look at them now!"

While the great chandeliers were lowered and the tapers lit, the musicians took their only respite for some time to come. When they returned, the strains of the minuet heralded the official opening of the ball. Even in disguise, Lady Barbara was claimed at once. Lavvy stepped daintily out with handsome Jack Mawson; and her grace, with a flicker of amusement on her lips, allowed herself to be led onto the dance floor by a slim figure in the uniform of a cornet of the 4th Light Dragoons. This was scarcely noted at first, but then the covert whispers began.

"I say, who is that young chap with the duchess? I don't like to be naughty but . . ."

"Oh, I say, not too sturdy a fellah, is he? Don't know what the army is coming to, do you? Can't think how a young reed like that would have stood against old Boney."

"Looks more like a young gel than a chap, what?"

"It *is* a gel, you confounded toads! Can't think how you ever managed to . . ."

"Oh, I say, you don't mean it!"

There followed a chorus of guffaws, not entirely free of a certain salaciousness, and a general placing of monocles and a lifting of quizzing glasses.

"By Gad, I believe that is Glastonia's gel, the protegée of the duchess. By Jove, what a lark!"

The identification swept like wildfire about the crowded room, scattering a delicious impropriety in its wake. Some, of course, sniffed and pretended to disapprove. The ancient Duchess of Doddington, who lived, as everyone knew, in a state of marriage with her majordomo, coughed delicately and spoke of certain biblical injunctions against such travesty. However, most of those present indulged themselves in a good deal of farily innocent merriment.

The salacious old Marquis of Lorn cackled to his cronies and stared impatiently. "Goin' to be a treat to see who dances with her. Demmed if it won't seem as if we have two fellahs treading the steps, eh?"

To their credit, his cronies merely stared at him as blankly as if they did not take his meaning.

The evening wore on with a kind of languorous intensity. No dance cards were used at masquerades, the better to heighten the illusion of mystery. Therefore, any gentleman could ask any lady in the room to dance, irrespective of position. Social barriers did not exist for the length of the evening, and a countess might well be dancing with a candlemaker, without lèse-majesté, and thoroughly enjoying herself.

Ben, as Robin Hood, and Trevor, as a Turkish pasha in garb brought home from the East by some ancestor, searched the crowded room in an effort to locate Lady Barbara.

"I say, could that be her with the tulip headdress?"

"No, no, you fool, she is in silver tissue. Elinor told me so."

Trevor laid a finger aside of his nose. "Ah, Elinor again? Fine gel, that Elinor. Have you thought of taking *her* into the Weymouth family? You get along, don't you?"

"And leave a clear field with Barbara for you? Why don't *you* marry Elinor? She'd make any chap a capital wife."

Trevor looked at his friend as if he had taken leave of his senses. "You know perfectly well why not. It is a question of cash, my friend. Two can live cheaper than one, perhaps. Still, I daresay it is deuced difficult to live on no money at all."

Ben, rich, young ruler that he was, had the grace to appear abashed. "Sorry about that, Trev. I quite forgot the money. All the same, she would make a demmed fine addition to any family."

"Not to mine, unfortunately. Only another mouth to feed. But, Gad, look at her over there. She's stepping out with Mrs. Mudge. Don't they make a couple." His gaze continued to roam lazily over the crowd.

"Oh, I say, look over there. Lady Elspeth and the duchess. What the devil can be going on in that direction?"

Lady Augusta had danced nearly every dance with scarcely a free moment to enjoy her royal state upon the dais, where she might have avoided being jostled and trodden upon in the crush. In this situation well-wishers could come forward; but, fortunately, mere toadies were given no opportunity to slaver over one's hand in the disgusting way they fancy to be ingratiating. That dreadful Mr. Gully, for instance, had been a great source of revulsion to her, though he was a parliamentary member. God help England if it was to be governed by men like him.

Now, however, she saw approaching her, cutting through the crest of the crowd like some tall galleon of a previous century, an old woman with visage so masculine in tone that her grace was irresistibly reminded of the painting of

Horatio at the Bridge which had hung above the library fireplace in her childhood home. Severe eyes trained unswervingly upon Lady Augusta, and there could be no doubt that the woman intended to have a word with her.

"Lady Augusta, the Duchess of Towans, I believe?" asked the new arrival.

"I am," her grace acknowledged tentatively, suspecting that this might prove to be an unfortunate encounter.

The woman gave the definite impression of being very strong-minded, as if she had upon her mind matters far too serious for these surroundings. There was a faintly evangelical look about her, and the duchess had no stomach to be preached to other than on a Sunday.

"I believe you are acquainted with my brother, the Earl of Glastonia. He speaks very highly of your generosity and good sense. I fear I am greatly in need of both."

So this was Elinor's great-aunt? Had the old creature come to make more trouble than already plagued the girl?

To her credit, Lady Elspeth adroitly read the expressions which rapidly replaced each other in Lady Augusta's face. "I have come on a mission of peace, your grace. Elinor has been slighted far too long in my opinion. I am here in Cheyne Spa with the intention of rectifying that to some extent."

The sudden change in the duchess's demeanour was noted by every spectator, and there were many. Some, aware of the tale of the Earl of Glastonia and his once-beloved son, had watched the earl's sister approaching the duke's wife with a good deal of interest. Was this the beginning of a reconciliation? That interest heightened as the duchess reached out a hand and drew Lady Elspeth to the seat beside her.

"How very exciting, Lady Elspeth. Do tell me more."

Elinor's cousin Cecil and his mother noted this scene with great discomfort. Jasper Gully lingered, meanwhile, as near the pair as he could in hope of picking up a stray word or phrase, then slid through the crowd like a pickpocket or cutpurse to hover ingratiatingly at Tyger Dobyn's elbow.

"The gel might be yours, after all, eh, Dobyn? The old crow seems to be making the first moves. Little Elinor might have a bit of change in her fortunes, after all. I daresay you'll find that a good thing."

Even Gully knew enough to be intimidated by the ferocious look the Tyger gave him. "Keep your tongue off Elinor Hardy, if you know what is good for you. Her business is her own and not for the likes of you."

The M.P.'s eyes narrowed. "Why, I swan. I believe you have formed a *tendre* for the gel, haven't you, old fellow? Fancy that. Tyger Dobyn, the ruination of many a poor girl, fallen into his own trap. Stap me, if that don't beat all. I say, my friend, I hope you have better fortune with the Hardy family than I ever did."

Gloating visibly, Gully melted into the crowd as quickly as he had appeared. Meanwhile, he had implanted a shard of doubt in poor Tyger's breast. If what the cull implied was true—if the conversation between the duchess and the earl's sister *did* concern Elinor and her future—his chance with her was even slimmer than before.

Gully, despicable as he was, had been correct about one thing, nonetheless. Tyger Dobyn, gentleman pugilist, gamester and man about town had indeed fallen into his own trap. He let slip a short, humourless bark of a laugh. Should Elinor Hardy be reconciled with her family, she would be farther out of Tyger's reach than ever.

=== 22 ===

PATRICK TYRONE ENTERED the Assembly Rooms almost furtively, decked out in Highland kilts and spooran. His knees felt indiscreetly exposed, and he was occasionally disconcerted by the vagrant breeze sweeping up under his skirts. Only the semi-concealment of his plaid domino enabled him to retain a semblance of social equilibrium as he made an effort to chat with the young cornet standing beside him. This chap in the uniform of the 4th Light Dragoons looked a decent enough fellah and responded easily to the actor's proffered friendship, though, for the life of him, Tyrone could not get away from the notion that there was as much amusement as cordiality in his smile.

"Quite fancied up tonight, isn't it?"

The cornet nodded agreement. "They seem to have gone to tremendous expense. I expect it was worth it, though. I have never seen the place crowded."

"Oh, you've been here before? I wonder if I have seen you before and don't recall?"

"Yes, I would not be surprised." The young dragoon smiled openly, a friendly smile, without condescension. "I have had the pleasure of watching you on the stage a number of times. You are very effective, if you don't mind my saying so."

Tyrone blushed prettily, even his knees suffusing to a faint pink. "Ah, you know me despite my disguise, then? Strange that I cannot place you. Uniforms are not all that usual in Cheyne, I believe."

"I don't wear it all the time, you know. I daresay you might recognise me in my usual attire. This is merely fancy dress. I have always yearned for the adventure afforded an army man and, like many others have taken advantage of the occasion."

"Of course, of course. I should have guessed, since in my world we change our appearance all of the time. It is only that you wear the uniform so naturally that I assumed . . ."

"Only borrowed for the occasion."

"Visiting for the season are you? Stop backstage one evening after the play. There are one or two cast members you might like to meet."

The cornet responded eagerly. "I say, I should like that. I have long been an admirer of Mrs. Mudge."

Tyrone looked askance as if the young fellow had made a dashedly clever remark. "Oh, yes, I daresay. Mrs. Mudge, is it? And not at all interested in the younger jilts I had in mind, I expect?"

The young officer laughed in a suspiciously light voice. "Oh, I see what you mean. Young ladies. How interesting."

Tyrone chuckled. "Well, not exactly 'ladies,' you understand, but jolly types for all that." He nudged his companion as he said this and winked broadly.

"I shall certainly bear it in mind," said the cornet. "It should prove most instructive and amusing."

The musicians struck up one of the new waltzes. "I say, would you care to dance?" asked the cornet casually. "It seems a pity to waste the music."

Tyrone's mouth dropped. "What d'you take me for?"

"Oh, but it is just a masquerade, isn't it? Doesn't matter who dances with whom."

"I daresay, old man," Patrick Tyrone blustered. Good Lord, was this what the upper classes were like? "Surely there are limits, sir?"

"And what have we here?" asked a deliberately merry

voice from behind them. Turning, Tyrone saw a familiar dark head.

"Can you imagine, Lady Barbara," asked the cornet. "This gentleman has just refused me?"

Barbara Pentreath raised her eyebrows and contrived to look both arch and spiteful. "I expect the poor chap does not wish to be made a guy and a laughingstock."

Elinor Hardy was equal to such a poor riposte as that. "I should like to know why. Since he is in skirts, it seems admirably appropriate that he step out with someone in breeches like myself."

The conception was so comical that even Tyrone had to laugh in chagrin. Now he thought he recognised the young officer, though he had never actually met her, and appreciated the joke even though it was on himself.

For a brief instant there was something almost approaching camaraderie between the two young women until Barbara's innate territorialism reasserted itself. She linked her arm possessively through that of the pseudo-Scot and drew him away just in time to be accosted by Trevor Quenton, looking classical in a Greek chiton and fillet as he hurried up to claim her.

"I say, Barbara, this is *our* dance. You promised it to me a half an hour ago."

Barbara surveyed him scornfully. "Certainly I did, but you are such a laggard that I have engaged with Mr. Tyrone in the meantime." Her prettily spiteful face lit up with happy inspiration. "But you shall not be left out, sir. Here is your skirted partner, Lady Elinor. I am sure he has among the finest legs in the room, although, I must say, they seem a trifle hairy for my consideration."

Barbara swept off on the arm of the actor.

"How unkind of her ladyship to desert you in such a fickle way, Mr. Quenton," Elinor consoled the young man. "But I daresay you have other entries on her card or she would not have been so cavalier." Trevor merely sighed.

The Duchess of Doddington danced past, observing

them haughtily through her lifted quizzers which she fancied gave her a fashionably dashing appearance. She said something in an undertone to her partner as Trevor indicated her with an inclination of his head.

"Well, my lady, I hope you will not disappoint both me and the dear old duchess, who is so eager to manufacture a scandal of our costumes. Will you have me for the dance?"

Elinor curtseyed as well as she was able in the buckskins. "To be sure I will, sir. This is an evening for scandalous behaviour, I believe. Everyone expects it. Is that not the very reason we are all masked and tricked out so frivolously, so that we may act as if no one can identify us?"

"No one would dare try." Quenton laughed. "They would only leave themselves open to ridicule."

They stepped out in a sprightly fashion to more admiration than censure, for both were accomplished dancers. The room had begun to fill now and the press of spectators along the sides soon forced couples to escape to the floor. Some of them found that elaborate costumes, though eyecatching, were a decided hindrance. Elinor noted with pleasure how easily the Countess Lavinia manoeuvred her wide panniers while being partnered by her highwayman-husband. The two danced in a perfect harmony which attested to the quality of their mutual admiration in a world where marriage was as often a social contract as a sacrament. This observation inspired Elinor to look about her with a sharper eye and wonder for the first time about the significance of some of the costumes she beheld. What secret longings and ambitions did they represent? She blushed as she reflected upon what her own choice of uniform might say of her to others.

The still novel rhythms of the waltz had an almost hypnotic effect. The dancers whirled and dipped; and Elinor found that she and Trevor were admirably suited to each other as partners, seeming to anticipate each other's every move. It was a distinct pleasure to abandon herself to the music, letting it carry her along as though in the bosom of the sea, lifted and carried by eddies and tides.

"Oh, I say," Trevor murmured in her ear. "Who do you suppose can be that smashing looker with Ben Weymouth?"

She followed his eyes and perceived at once what had so attracted him. Neither had previously been exposed to the Celtic charms of Miss Mary Monaghan, decked out for this evening as a fetching milkmaid, complete with wide-brimmed straw and tucked-up skirts which showed her pretty limbs. Ben appeared to be vastly enjoying her company. His head was bent as if to capture every word from her lips, and there was upon his face that silly smirk which young men often assume when in the company of such a delightful creature as this.

Patrick Tyrone and Barbara were also watching the pair. The actor experienced distinct discomfort as he saw his erstwhile fiancée toss her head flirtatiously and turn coquettish glances upward at this scion of wealth. Though he no longer felt any romantic attachment to her, Patrick retained the responsive interest of an old acquaintance. It seemed to him that there could not be good for her reputation in risking condemnation by too forward a presentation of herself. It would never do for a lass as fresh and untouched as Mary to be burdened with the stigma of light behaviour. Not that he cared, of course, except as a friend; but he liked Mary, he really did. He *hoped* they were still friends. She had none of Barbara's ravishing beauty, but she was a dear little thing and a part of his memories of home.

He was jolted back to the present by a sharp pain in his instep.

"Oh, Mr. Tyrone, how clumsy of me."

He glimpsed a spark of something in Lady Barbara's eyes which suggested that her misstep had not been entirely accidental.

"The floor is becoming so crowded I fear I am quite

giddy. Could we slip out to the balcony for just a quick breath of air?"

Such an opportunity was not to be turned aside. He became immediately all solicitude. "But of course, my dear lady. What a lout you must think me not to have noticed your discomfiture."

He danced her toward the tall windows, and when they were in the open air hovered over her to enquire about her comfort. "Are you sure you will not be chilly without a wrap?"

She gazed up at him with fond patience.

"Really, Patrick, have you no imagination?" She moved closer and lifted her arms to place them about his neck. "Must I always be the one to take the initiative?"

Slow though he might be in some things, Patrick Tyrone was a quick study; and he knew at once what the moment required. Bending his head, he allowed his finely molded lips to rest lightly upon hers as he struggled to recall some appropriate line of dialogue. It was a pleasant discovery that Lady Barbara's education had not been lacking in certain social skills. She kissed far too well to be a mere tyro at the game, and he submitted gratefully.

"Do you care for me at all, Patrick?" she whispered. "Or am I making a terrible fool of myself?"

A rush of feeling almost swept him away, and he pressed more closely against her. "Oh, dear girl," he moaned, "if you only knew how much I adore you. I wish that you might be mine forever."

"Oh, Patrick, I knew we were destined for each other." She kissed him again in that exciting way of hers.

Tyrone leant into it, fully prepared for a long and pleasurable moment, but he bolted like a shying horse from the audacity of her next proposal.

"It must be tonight, then, darling," she breathed sensuously in his ear.

The young actor was wise enough to want the issue

clarified before committing himself. "What must?" he asked worriedly.

He had never known a girl so headstrong. She rode roughshod over suitors and conventions alike. It was quite exciting, actually. Yet, he knew they must not become carried away upon a storm of mere passion.

She kissed him again. "To elope, of course, my darling. They will never let us marry in the usual way. So we must run away to Budolph." She giggled. "I expect they are quite used to summer lovers from Cheyne Spa."

Patrick swallowed and cleared his throat. "Budolph? Ah, well, that requires some thought, doesn't it? I mean, the company plays there, you know. I am not exactly a stranger in Budolph." By the light from the ballroom, he could see that she was looking at him oddly.

"You do want to marry me, do you not?"

Patrick swallowed again and nodded.

"Then you must slip away and see to our transportation while I go back inside and continue dancing to keep them from suspecting anything."

"But, Barbara—"

"Hurry, my darling. I shall be waiting. You must slip away down the terrace steps while I go back inside."

She kissed him again and the heady sensation quite drove off any practicality from his thoughts. His brain was in a whirl, his mouth was dry; but his heart was racing. This lovely girl, this prize of all prizes, was to be his own.

At the doorway she turned back. "And Patrick, darling . . ."

"Yes, my dearest?"

"For heaven's sake, change out of those ridiculous kilts."

"Severn. I want you!"

The manservant eyed his lordship with resigned patience. "Right here, my lord. There is no need to shout."

"This shaving water is tepid. How the blazes do you expect me to shave without hot water?"

"Well, sir, we are all rather at sixes and sevens, aren't we? We did not expect to be outfitting your lordship at such a late time of day, did we, sir? When you take a sudden notion into your head, you must allow for one or two trifling inconveniences."

The old earl glowered. "Are you being impertinent, rascal?"

"I hope I am not, sir. Would you like me to finish shaving you?"

"No, thank you. I expect I should end up with a scarlet throat. Is my coat laid out?"

"Yes, your honour."

"And you informed Griggs that he would be needed?"

"Yes, sir, though that was not accomplished without a certain amount of grumbling since he has only just made the same trip to Cheyne with her ladyship."

"My sister? That sly minx. She said nothing to me of going to Cheyne. What the devil is she up to?" He waved the razor in the air.

"Do be careful, sir. I really wish you would allow me to—"

"I can shave meself, bedad. What does she want in the town? This is an Assembly night. She never goes to the balls."

"Has your lordship forgotten that this is rather a special ball? The annual fancy-dress masquerade?"

"Well, what of that? What is your point?"

"Her ladyship always attends the masquerades, sir. Every year."

"Humph, really? I was not aware of that."

"That is because you so rarely attend them yourself, I expect sir," said Severn imperturbably. "Are you certain you shall only want your evening clothes, after all? There are one or two rather handsome costumes which I found in the attics."

"No, I shall merely wear a domino mask and be demmed to them. Silly lot of folderol, dressing up as kings and queens if you are of no family and as beggars and orange girls if you are." He looked at Severn suspiciously. "Costumes from the attics? What were you doing up there, if I may ask?"

Severn did not flinch in the slightest from this interrogation. "Well, sir, once I had settled you in for the evening, I had rather thought I might ride into Cheyne myself."

"Ha! To mix with the gentry, eh? You'll find them not worth your while, my man. A lot of parvenus and social climbers. Cheyne ain't what it was in the days of Beau Carlisle. He never would have allowed this rackety crowd they have these days, what?"

"I am sure you are right, your lordship," Severn answered. "Nevertheless, with your lordship's permission—"

"Permission? When did you ever bother about my permission? You shall ride in the carriage with me, if you like, though after we arrive I shall take no responsibility for you. You have a ticket, I suppose?"

"Oh yes, sir."

"Then you had better snap about and change, hadn't you?" He picked up the domino and tied it awkwardly about his head. "How is that? Will they recognise me?"

The manservant rolled his eyes to the ceiling. "Never in a thousand years, I am sure, my lord." His look was so droll that the earl laughed out loud.

"Never mind, old fellow. They all know each other at these affairs. The costumes don't hide much. Now off with you. Don't keep me waiting while you fuss and primp in front of the mirror."

The valet fairly flew out of the chamber, exhibiting surprising lightness for one of his age and girth, while the earl shrugged himself into his coat. He drew his cloak about his shoulders and adjusted his domino, peering into the looking glass with cynical wariness.

"What if the gel don't like me?" he asked aloud. "What if she won't have anything to do with me after all these years?"

His reflection had no answer.

═ 23 ═

THE EARL'S SISTER had been much pleased and gratified by her conversation with the dear duchess. They sat together now and gazed with benevolent dignity upon the dancers, whirling about in an energetic Scottish reel.

"And who is that young man with whom she is dancing now?" Lady Elspeth asked Lady Augusta from behind her fan. "Someone suitable, I hope?"

"My dear Lady Elspeth, it is only a dance," the duchess protested with a reassuring smile. "He is of quite an ancient lineage, I believe, and quite charming, as I know from experience. Unfortunately, he has scarcely two shillings to rub together and a vast family to think about. He will need an undoubted heiress to survive, I fear. Only an alliance with one of the great fortunes of England can help him."

Lady Elspeth pulled a sad face. "We cannot be certain of Elinor's future to that extent, I fear. I shall be leaving my niece a little, but I cannot speak for her grandfather. He is as unpredictable as the wind."

The duchess leaned closer. "What about her cousin Cecil?" she asked with a curious look in her eye.

Lady Elspeth drew back as if faced with an adder, and her eyes fairly snapped. "I am certain your grace is merely testing me. There is no way in the world that I would promote such an alliance. Are you at all acquainted with Cecil's mother?"

The duchess nodded.

"Then you take my point, I am sure. Nothing would

persuade me to put any young girl in the power of such a creature as Evangeline Partridge, who all but drove her poor husband to death with her constant spending and gambling. Now she lives upon a mere pittance which is all she retains, but should she ever come into ascendancy over great wealth with no one to curb her, I shudder to think of the consequences."

The duchess stared at her companion. "But, surely, when Cecil comes into possession of the title . . ."

Lady Elspeth's thin mouth reduced itself still further to a mere line across the lower half of her features. "I shall only say, madam, that it would be bad enough for the child to be linked to such a poor thing as her cousin, title or no, without condemning her to such a mother-in-law."

"I see you do not get on," the duchess chuckled archly, and Lady Elspeth recovered herself enough to smile a little in response.

"What a quiz you are, your grace. You have quite taken me in."

Lady Augusta now indicated another couple with her fan. "There is, of course, young Weymouth, who is dancing with that remarkably pretty milkmaid, although I have rather a different course marked out for him. Dear Elinor has been quite helpful in that regard."

"Who is the milkmaid?"

"An actress, I believe," the duchess answered.

That elicited a sharp intake of breath from the woman at her side. "At the Assembly Ball? How things have changed."

"The barriers have rather let down, you know, since the days of Beau Carlisle," the duchess commented. "I am not decided how I feel about it, but it is certain that society has become more interesting as a result. There is the famous Mrs. Mudge as well." She was surprised at the reaction of her new friend. "My dear, have I said something wrong?"

A look of what appeared to be remorse, almost guilt, crossed the older woman's face; and she stumbled as she spoke. "Surely that is quite different. Mrs. Mudge is a lady of great reputation as well as age."

"I daresay she was as young and pretty as that milkmaid once upon a time," Lady Augusta observed. It did not escape her that Lady Elspeth shifted uncomfortably in her chair.

Mrs. Mudge was, in fact, looking quite handsome in a striped gown and tall plumed hat which cleverly recalled Gainsborough's handsome portrait of Mrs. Siddons. It seemed to the earl's sister that she was far sprightlier than the age Lady Elspeth knew her to be and without a vestige of the sorrow Lady Elspeth expected. On a sudden impulse she rose and made her bob to the duchess.

"It has been such a pleasure, your grace," she said, "and most instructive."

As Lady Augusta watched, the tall woman moved purposefully through the crowded room until she stood directly beside the actress whom they had, only a moment ago, been discussing.

What a pity, thought the duchess, *that I cannot read their lips. It looks most amusing a situation.*

But, in fact, Lady Elspeth, now that she was here, found her courage beginning to ebb. "Mrs. Mudge, I believe?" she asked weakly.

"Yes, I am she. What may I do for you?" Mrs. Mudge was not at all one of those players who fawn upon their admirers, though she was quite willing to be cordial if the situation warranted.

Now that she had begun, her ladyship did not know how to go on, and she faltered badly. "I—I—That is, I merely wanted to say how fine a player you have become. I admire you a great deal."

The piercing eyes remained upon her as an expression of increased interest passed over the curiously ageless face. " 'Ere, I know you! You're Eddie's sister aincher?"

The common speech rolled out in that impressive voice gave Lady Elspeth a curious feeling, setting this encounter somehow near the far edge of reality. She screwed up her courage once more to make the apology she had waited all these years to articulate.

"I also want to say—That is, I want to make a confession. I am, you see, most awfully sorry for the harm I did all those years ago. I see now how wrong it was. I suppose I knew even then, but I was too blindly proud to admit it." Her eyes searched the actress's face. "Can you ever forgive me?"

Mrs. Mudge's countenance had gone completely slack in surprise. "Garn," she said. "Whatever d'yer mean?"

Lady Elspeth swallowed painfully and went on with her self-recrimination. She had always known it would be difficult, but that did not now lessen her discomfort. "It was I," she said in a small voice, then stopped for a fraction of a second before going on. "It was I who turned my brother away from marrying you, all those years ago. It was I who spoilt it, so that you had to remain in the state to which God had called you."

Mrs. Mudge looked at her even more blankly. "Eh?" she asked. "You done what?"

"I persuaded him not to propose marriage to you, and now—Now I am so sorry."

The other woman's face broke into a smile of comprehension. The lines and wrinkles were few, but the great good will was not. "Oh, you did, did you? And you've come to me after all this time to confess it? Yer wot I mean when I think of a real lydy, bless yer. Settles 'er debts no matter 'ow long it takes."

"Then you will not hate me for it?"

The actress took the lady's large hand in her own. "It sounds to me, luv, as if you 'ave been hating *yourself* for it for too long a time, m'dearie. The fact is that Eddie proposed to me not once but a good many times over the years. I turned him down regular, and I would turn him down tonight. His kind—yer own kind—and mine don't mix, y'see. I know Eddie. 'E'd no sooner 'ave a ring on my finger than 'e'd be demanding that I give up the stage to settle down wiv the two of you in that great, drafty old house of yers." She snorted. "Can you imagine me there? I'd die of boredom in a month." She recovered herself slightly. "No offence, you understand. I expect it is a fine life for them as can stand it, but I'd soon be off me noddle an' that's a fact. I was saying as much to yer brother only last week. No, I could never give up the profession to become a mere lydy. I'll continue to play 'em on stage as long as I'm able, but I'll allus put 'em off when the play is done and the curtain 'as come down."

"Do you mean to say . . .?" began Lady Elspeth, and the character woman nodded vigourously.

"I *do* mean to say, m'dear." She reddened slightly. "I 'ave been a friend of yer brother all these years. Not to put too fine a point on it, we 'as been rather *more* than friendly."

Lady Elspeth was not so sheltered that it took long for the import of the words to sink in. "What, all these years?"

Mrs. Mudge nodded. "I've always loved 'im, you see, but the profession was my life, wasn't it? I could do with seeing Eddie only once in a while, but I should 'ave died without the stage."

Those who were watching the two disparate women were treated to the sight of her ladyship throwing her arms about the other. "Oh, my dear soul, if I had only known." She paused and reconsidered. "No, perhaps it is just as well that I did not. But I am very glad to know it now!"

The dancers swirled about them and lightly tripped to the strains of a felicitous tune. "I do hope," Lady Elspeth continued, "that since the old secret is out, we can become friends. I daresay I am far too dull for you, but I should like to try."

For the first time, Mrs. Mudge looked rather wary, as if she anticipated some sort of trap. "Friends? Well, we could give it a whirl for a bit, I suppose, but I will be moving on at the end of the season. There are other theatres, even in winter, and other plays."

Across the room, Elinor, to her mixed delight and consternation, had become quite the rage of the evening. Whether it was her own substantial charm or the perverse humour of certain young guardsmen, every beau in the room found it imperative to have at least once dance with her.

"It indicates an enormous lack of breeding," sniffed the Duchess of Doddington to her old friend, the Marquess of Lorn.

The old roué, true to his code, laid one long finger aside of his nose and gave her a bold and rather bawdy wink. "Nevertheless, madam," he cajoled, "you and I have had a few ripe times of our own in years past, have we not? Such a famous beauty as you were always acknowledged to be could not have escaped at least one or two flings in those more liberal days. And you must admit that her uniform sets off a superb figger, eh? You don't see such a shape often in these days."

"Not so much of it, certainly," the old dowager snapped back at him. Still, his jest had put her back in temper, and she danced off with a smile upon the arm of her Malvolio.

Ben Weymouth, for his part, had scarcely taken his eyes from the young pseudo-cornet despite the fact that Lady Barbara Pentreath, with whom he was dancing, chided him in no uncertain terms.

"Sauce for the goose, sauce for the gander, old thing," Ben defended himself. "If you can spend all of your evening mooning over that actor fellah, I don't see why I should not look elsewhere as well. I believe my last partner is a friend of Tyrone."

"I suppose you mean that milkmaid creature. I am sure she is no better than she should be. But it is Elinor whom you seem to be ogling now."

"Even you must admit, she is something to see."

Barbara sneered. "Breeding will out, I am sure. But

what is it you mean about Patrick and that milkmaid creature?"

"Oh, it has become 'Patrick,' has it? Gone far beyond 'Mr. Tyrone,' I daresay. Well, for your information, it appears that Miss Monaghan and your 'Patrick' were once affianced or so she tells me. You appear to have set that all awry."

"What a dreadful thing to say. I have never cut out another woman in my life."

Ben could scarcely believe his ears. "My dear Barbara, you have done so scores of times. Why, I have seen you working your spell over three or four chaps at once."

Lady Barbara relaxed a little. "Oh, but that was only flirting. It meant nothing at all."

"Not to you, perhaps, but I always pitied those fellows who believed you had made a firm commitment to them. The chaps *and* the young ladies they deserted at the crooking of your finger."

Barbara flushed, then turned quite pale. "How dare you say such a thing to me?" she asked through clenched teeth. "You are quite insufferable. Please take me off the floor at once."

Ben merely tightened his grasp on her waist. "Nothing of the kind, old girl. Don't make a spectacle of us."

The Pentreath temper was running high, and the tide could not be stemmed. Drawing back her free arm in a long gesture, Barbara struck her partner full force across the mouth with the edge of her fan then swung furiously about and strode from the dance floor. Everyone was staring, of course. Ben laughed uncomfortably and lifted a chary finger to his lips, drawing it away with a few drops of blood. Trevor and Elinor came to him at once.

"I say, old fellah, what in the world . . .?"

Ben would have none of Trev's solicitousness. "Lady Elinor, may I have the honour of this dance? You don't mind, Quenton, do you?"

Elinor's eyes widened, but she acquiesced gracefully at

Trevor's nodding agreement. "Mr. Quenton, I hope we will dance again later?"

Trev bowed. "That is a promise, your ladyship."

Weymouth swept her off, and Elinor felt the burden of conversation fall quite heavily upon her shoulders. Though she had witnessed the scene along with everyone else, she felt it impossibly tactless to allude to it. Instead, she found herself babbling aimlessly, about whatever passed through her mind.

"The costumes lend so much to the evening, do you not agree, Mr. Weymouth? How amusing it is to see Anne Boleyn dancing so gaily with one of those Indian potentates. What is it they are called? Maharajahs?"

Ben smiled down at her and even laid a finger gently across her lips. "There is no need for conversation, is there, Elinor? I thought you and I knew each other better than that?"

As if she had been freed of a heavy burden, the girl relaxed in his arms and returned to her normal mode of speech. "I daresay I had forgotten it, sir."

He gave her a curiously deep look, almost as if he were seeing her for the first time. "What a marvellously sensible girl you are," he said appreciatively. "Have you made up your mind which of all these chaps you are going to marry? I expect you will make a most excellent mother and wife."

Elinor giggled in amused surprise. "To whom, sir? The doors have not exactly been beaten down in Regent's Crescent."

Then Ben said something which quite shocked her breath away. "Actually, I was thinking of myself, you know."

"Yourself? Married to me? Ben, do be serious."

"Well, why not?" he asked truculently. "We get on very well, you must admit. We have many of the same tastes. I think we would suit admirably."

Elinor kissed his cheek, oblivious to anyone who might

be looking. "Not when you are so desperate for Barbara. You love her very much, I think."

Weymouth's rueful look was a full admission. "But she won't have me, and you aren't promised to someone else, are you? I am certain we could make a good thing of it."

Elinor knew that such marriages of convenience were looked upon with favour by society, infatuation tending to quail at the rigours of daily life, but she knew that she could not bear such an arrangement with Ben. With someone else perhaps, someone she knew to be emotionally unattached; but not with Ben. She would see Barbara in his eyes forever. As they swept past the entrance, they spied Trevor striding purposefully toward them with a look of alarm upon his face.

"What is it, old man? Has something happened?" asked Ben.

"It is Barbara," Trev answered in a low voice. "When you swept her ladyship away from me, I went out on the balcony for a breath of air." He gulped before he could continue, as if he were breathless even now. "I saw Barbara getting into a phaeton with that actor fellah. What is more, there was a small leather trunk strapped on behind."

"Good Lord," Ben hissed. "Eloping?"

"It looked like it to me. They seemed to be heading out toward the Budolph Road, though, of course, they could have turned at any corner."

Ben swung about, vainly searching for a particular face amongst the costumed dancers. "Miss Monaghan," he called out loudly. "Where are you?"

"Ben, for heaven's sake!" Trevor expostulated, and Elinor caught at his arm.

"Mr. Weymouth, what on earth?"

"If Barbara has truly eloped with Mr. Tyrone," he told her tersely, "Miss Monaghan has as much a stake in it as anyone."

"Miss Monaghan!" he called out again over the music.

"Trevor, my friend, see if you can get us a phaeton or a carriage—even a pony cart. We must follow them at once."

The young Irishwoman thrust herself through the dancers. "Here I am, yer honour. What is it?"

The duchess, too, had made her way to them. "Ben, what in the world is going on? Can you see that you are disrupting the ball?"

"It is Barbara, your grace. She seems to have run off with Tyrone, and they may be on their way to Budolph where it is not required that banns be posted."

"Do you mean the actor?" wailed Lady Augusta. "But he hasn't a penny, so far as I know. What are we to do?"

"I am going after them," Weymouth declared. "Lady Elinor, could you come as chaperone to Miss Monaghan and myself?"

"Of course I will, if the duchess approves. May I, madam?"

"Yes, go, my dear. I will find Jack and Lavinia, and we will follow immediately."

The trio hurried out of the Assembly to find Trevor standing by a gig which had only a tender young filly between the shafts. "It was all I could manage on such short notice. It only accommodates three, so I shall hurry to the stables and follow on horseback.

"My mount should catch up with you in short order. A pity I didn't bring the hunter into town. She fairly eats up the miles."

He clambered down and handed the reins to Ben. "On your way, my friend. It is up to you to stop Barbara from making the greatest mistake of her life."

= 24 =

THE EARL OF GLASTONIA rode less sedately in his coach than he was wont to do and even watched with amusement as Severn bounded about under the rigours of the journey. Griggs, the old man knew, was very much put out at making the trip a second time this day. Like the valet, the coachman had been with his lordship a great many years and considered that he was due certain recognised perks: one of which being the occasional huff when he believed himself put upon. Fortunately, since he was on the box and the others inside, they did not rub together as rawly as they might have done. Griggs was allowed only the luxury of a long and continuous grumble. Some of these importunate words were uttered so loudly they drifted back to assault his lordship, but the old man did not take them much to heart. He had to live with the servants, after all, being too settled to change them. They had been a part of the household much too long to be discharged.

He was, however, quite unprepared for the violent jostling he and Severn received as the coachman pulled drastically aside to avoid collision with a pretty, little phaeton which appeared suddenly out of the evening mists, speeding hell-for-leather toward Budolph. The earl thrust his head out of the window and thought he perceived a man in company with a remarkably beautiful young woman, but since his eyesight had become limited over the years, he was not altogether certain of this until Griggs was presently heard shouting at still another equipage emerging out of the shadows.

To some question which the old man did not hear but could easily surmise, the coachman replied in a surly tone of voice, "And what if we did, sir? I suppose it may be *your* business whom we pass on a public highway?"

The earl leaned again from the window to ameliorate, if he could, his servant's ingrained brusqueness. "Can I be of any assistance?"

He saw that beside them was a pony cart, the poor beast already frothing and heaving at such unaccustomed exercise. He perceived two more young women and a man in his early twenties, but in the near dark he was not aware that one of those women was his granddaughter until he heard a voice so like that of his long-departed mother he could not mistake the resemblance.

Exactly as if they were intimate in their relationship and in the habit of speaking every day, his lordship called out to her in familiar tones: "Where are you headed, my dear? I hope you are not doing anything foolish."

The girl answered him in the same easygoing spirit and laughed slightly as she answered. "Do you mean to enquire if I am eloping, Grandfather?"

"Something like that. You will vastly disappoint your aunt, you know, if such is the case. I believe she means to make something of an occasion of it when you marry."

"No one has asked me yet, sir." There was the most brief of pauses before she amended her statement. "At least no one I felt free to accept."

The earl detected a certain chagrin as her companion asked again about the previous equipage and received answer from his lordship.

"Thank you, sir, and good-bye. I fear we must be on our way."

"Drive carefully, my boy. You are carrying a cargo very precious to me. Good-bye, my dear. I shall present your respects to your aunt, if I may?"

The flash of a white handkerchief waved through the gloaming as an answer, and he sank back into his seat with a satisfied expression. Severn took the liberty of leaning out to urge the carriage on. Despite what he knew of the lad's family and background, the old man had found it a great relief that his granddaughter was not to be married before he had done more than make her acquaintance. He stared reflectively into the darkness as Griggs drove on toward Cheyne Spa.

Given a choice, he wondered, *who would I match the gel up with?*

He had a strong suspicion that it mattered little how he might answer that. He did not doubt that the chit would make her own selection rather than defer to a grandsire she hardly knew, yet it was an amusing game of speculation with which to pass the time. There was no great hurry to reach the Assembly Rooms since the object of his attendance had just ridden off in the opposite direction. Had he the stomach for a further bout with Griggs, he might even have reversed the carriage and returned home; but, since his sister had also to be fetched home, he feared the notion might prove to be the proverbial back-backing straw. He chuckled quietly to himself and, though the coachman was unlikely to have heard him, a voice came from the box above.

"Everything all right, milord?"

The earl answered, "Only an old man's vagaries, Griggs. Turn about and follow them, if you please."

Severn gasped in pique that he would be missing the masquerade, but the coachman merely smiled and tapped his hat deferentially. "Right you are, milord."

The earl settled back into his seat, his mind a swirling confusion of new ideas and old intermixed. He expected to retain his title for some years to come. Yet, now it was possible, just possible, that it might pass on to someone worthy when he had done with it.

* * *

Lady Augusta hurried from the Assembly Rooms, trying to conceal her agitation, and found her way blocked by the splendid figure of Tyger Dobyn in the garb of an eastern mameluke.

"I beg your grace's pardon, but it is urgent that I have a word with you."

The duchess gave him barely a glance. "Not just now, sir, if you please. I fear I have a crisis in hand." Then to her niece's husband, "Jack, is the coach ready?"

"In the square, madam."

Dobyn was not to be denied. "It is about Miss—Lady Elinor."

She thrust him aside impatiently. "Not *now*, Dobyn. I fear there has been a rather hasty elopement which may yet be foiled. Certainly I must do my best to stop it."

The Tyger fairly reeled at the juxtaposition of Elinor with elopement, and his rational processes came quite unhinged. He caught at the duchess's arm.

"But, madam . . ."

She, however, had already brushed by and was hurrying out of the Assembly Rooms. "Sir, now is not the time!"

Thrown into a sudden sweat, the pugilist turned his attention to the tall, elderly woman who followed in the duchess's wake. It was the old earl's sister, known to him by sight. He accosted her roughly. "Miss Hardy, your ladyship. Where has she gone?"

The woman stared back at him with a cool, shrewd expression. "My niece, I believe, sir, is at this moment on her way to Budolph with young Ben Weymouth."

She explained nothing of the circumstances, but it is unlikely he would have heard if she had. Despite the relative brevity of his costume, Dobyn dashed out of the building and raced toward the stable yard where his mount was quartered. The old woman stared after him with a benign expression as though a puzzle piece had just clicked into place.

As Tyger approached the horse shed, there was the

sound of pounding hooves and another hasty rider burst from the passage, nearly riding the fighter down. Dobyn uttered a pungent oath and hurled himself against the wall long enough for Trevor Quenton to pass. Tyger dashed into the stable and demanded urgent service from the proprietor, a bandy-legged old fellow who seemed unperturbed by the series of fancy-dress apparitions which had recently passed before him.

"If you'll take my advice, sir, you'll throw that there horse blanket about you. Begging yer honour's pardon, but you don't appear too warmly dressed for a night's outing. It do get chill hereabouts, you see. Especially on the highroad."

"Don't bother about me, man. Just ready the horse. I'm heading toward Budolph, and I'll stop by my lodging for a cloak and breeches."

He paced impatiently while the horse coper led out the mount and saddled it with maddening lassitude. "Come on, man. Come on."

A tall, spare outline appeared against the light of the lantern, and Lady Elspeth Hardy's voice spoke. "Mr. Dobyn, a word before you go."

The Tyger grimaced. "I have little time to spare, your ladyship, if I am to prevent your niece from making a grave error of judgement."

"I appreciate your haste, sir, but I am not certain I understand it. Why should you concern yourself with Elinor's plans, whatever they might be?"

He stared at her as if she had lost her senses. "Because it appears her intention to marry young Weymouth, and she would regret it for the rest of her life."

"Regret marrying into the Weymouth family? I doubt that. It is my understanding that they are a most amiable lot and certainly well set up. She would never want for material comforts, I believe."

The pugilist looked quite outraged. "Material comforts? Oh, I daresay she would have them, but I tell you, madam," and here he shook his finger pedagogically, "there are more comforts in this world than mere wealth and ease."

"Indeed?" the old woman said doubtfully. "And supposing that you *do* catch up with them—I suppose you have something to say to her? May I ask what it would be?"

The Tyger hesitated, then spoke forcefully. "That I love her, madam, and that if she will trust her life to my care, I will do my utmost to requite it."

"By returning her to the uncertain life she led with my nevvy, I suppose?" Lady Elspeth sneered disdainfully. Her response made the Tyger stare. Then he answered seriously enough to allay her fears.

"I mean no offence, your ladyship, but the situation is different in one important respect. With Elinor's father, gambling was an obsession. For me it is a profession to which I am uniquely suited. I believe less in the phenomenon of luck than in my own skill. I allow myself the pleasure of excitement to be sure, but I hope I do not tempt the gods when I say that never once have I succumbed to the fever. Like any professional, I know when the tide is running against me and have enough control to withdraw from the play until a better time."

"In the case of my niece? Will you gamble on?"

The horse, saddled and lively, was brought out into the stable yard. As he mounted, Tyger Dobyn grinned down at the angular spinster. "Yes, madam, I *will*, simply because, if I arrive in time, I have every chance of winning."

"Begging yer pardon, yer honour," said the stable man, tugging at his forelock deferentially, "but did I here 'ee say Budolph, sir? There's a quicker way than the highroad, you know. Take the river road and skirt the fen. You'll save a good bit o' time. It is nought but a track and ye must be careful, but it may be worth it to ye."

Tyger acknowledged the information thankfully as the horse stamped, as impatient to be stretching its legs as its master was to be on his way. Dobyn saluted the earl's sister gallantly, waved at the stable man and cantered smartly out into the street. In a moment he had turned the corner and was lost to sight.

"Is there aught I can do for you, ma'am?"

Lady Elspeth shook herself from her reverie and pressed a coin into the man's hand.

"What's this for, then?"

"For the horse, when Mr. Dobyn returns. An extra portion of oats and bran mash. I have a feeling the beast will have earned it."

=== 25 ===

HAD ONE THE eye of a bird flying high above the Budolph Road, one might with some justice marvel at the string of travellers drawn out along it. There was first, of course, Lady Barbara and her captive fiancé. A mile or so behind them came Ben and his two companions in the pony cart with the brave, chestnut roan straining between the shafts. The caution of the earl's coachman guided his lordship's equipage another measured space behind, followed by Trevor at a gallop, and our dear duchess and company after him.

Lady Barbara urged her lover on impatiently. "Really, Patrick, for an Irishman you seem to have little touch for the reins. Can you not use the whip? At this rate we shall see the sun come up on Budolph."

The thespian turned his head to her sadly. "I never pretended to be a horseman, dearest. We did not run to that sort of thing in our level of society, you know. That was why I left County Mayo to seek my fortune on the stage."

"Well enough, but every man should be able to handle the ribbons. I thought it was a part of that masculine instinct one hears so much about. My cousin Jack would have us spanking along at a great rate, I do assure you, and my sister Lavinia would do even better."

"Your sister is not with us, my love," Tyrone reminded her reproachfully.

As his mistress pulled an impatient face, the actor began

devoutly to wish the Countess Lavinia *was* at the reins with he himself snug in his own lodging accompanied only by a pipe and a new role to study. It was all very well to be dazzled by the condescension of the gentry, but had he made a grave mistake? How was Lady Barbara likely to fit into such a cosy picture once they were married? He stole a glance sideward and saw that her mouth was set in a petulant pout.

For a brief moment it seemed to him that the face of Mary Monaghan superimposed itself over that of the duchess's niece. However, Mary would not be pouting. This would be a great adventure to her. In the past it would have been an adventure to Patrick as well. Why was it not an adventure now? He was not even altogether certain that he had made the decision to embark upon this flight. Lady Barbara had spoken and he had obeyed. Was that how their married life would be conducted? As if to verify his apprehensions, her ladyship reached abruptly across him and snatched the whip from its bracket, touching the horses lightly along their flanks.

"Hi-yah!" The animals picked up the pace admirably at the command, and Barbara smiled toward her companion with indulgent patronage. "You see? It is only a bit of urging that is required."

Patrick Tyrone scowled. "Would you care to take the ribbons as well, milady? I had no idea you were such a Bonducca. It is no wonder you were after chiding me for my lack of skill."

Barbara shot him a look of puzzlement. She was quite unused to hearing such a tone from those handsomely cut lips, or from anyone for that matter. People did not often question what she said; but, since she loved him, she was prepared to overlook it this once.

"I certainly am capable of doing so, if that is what you mean," she said lightly. "I come from a horse-loving family, even though I am least of them."

Patrick passed the reins to her with an obviously ironic flourish. "At your pleasure, my dear girl."

He was chagrined to find her boast had been no idle one. In only a few moments they were proceeding along the highway at a smart clip, the phaeton rocking gently from side to side as they traversed the miles toward matrimonial bliss. It was difficult to feed his state of pique when his bride was so capable and the vehicle swayed so restfully from side to side. It was, in fact, extremely pleasant to be so cradled; and Patrick's eyes soon grew heavy. His jaw relaxed, and his chin dropped. In a moment he had begun to snore gently with his head upon Lady Barbara's shoulder.

Trevor Quenton had passed the earl's coach by now, caught up to the pony cart and was racing along with it at an even neck, shouting out to the driver.

"What the devil will you say to her when you get there?"

Ben scowled. "I shall insist she stop such foolishness at once and come back to Cheyne Spa like a sensible girl."

The two young men exchanged glances while Trevor, playing devil's advocate, pursued his own line of thought. "Why should she do that? If she wants to marry this actor chap, why should that stop her?"

"Be serious," Ben shouted back as the car careered wildly around a curve, and the women squealed in remonstration. "What woman in her right mind would marry an actor if she had any option?"

"I would," shouted Miss Mary Monaghan. "If we catch up to them in time, I guarantee that Patrick Tyrone will not be marrying himself off to Miss Money-breeches. Like to like is what I say."

"What?" called Trevor. "What did she say?"

"Like to like," Ben repeated.

Trevor nodded emphatically. "There, you see? Even Miss Monaghan understands. Like to like."

"No!" Elinor entered the discussion emphatically. "That

is what is wrong with the world. Why shouldn't Barbara marry Mr. Tyrone, if she chooses?"

"Because she'd be deuced unhappy." Ben coughed as a cloud of dust caught in his throat. "She ought to be marrying someone who will know how to deal with her." He laughed and waved gaily to his friend. "And not you, old chap, but me!"

Elinor tugged at his sleeve. "Not good enough. Why should she marry you particularly?"

The question seemed to set Ben back on his heels, but only for the briefest moment. "She should marry me . . . because I love her!" He shouted it out triumphantly, laughing at his own admission. "And because I have no intention of letting her get away from me."

Elinor squeezed his arm affectionately. "There, you see? Now you must tell *her*. I doubt that you have ever bothered."

"No," Weymouth agreed, "I never have. I only just found it out myself, you see."

"What does she say?" asked Trevor, leaning toward them.

"She says that I never bothered to tell Barbara that I cared for her."

"No more you did," Trev answered as his mount pulled ahead of them. "Neither did I. Perhaps that is what has been wrong all along."

He looked back along the road behind them. "Hello, who is that coming up on us? I passed them a while since, but they seem to be making deuced good time."

Elinor, too, looked back across her shoulder. "It is my grandfather. I thought he was headed in the other direction toward Cheyne."

"Sure an' he was doing just that when last we saw him," Mary Monaghan agreed. "What a fine-looking old gentleman he is to be sure," she said with a twinkle, "and what a fine-looking equipage he drives. I expect he is very rich. Is he a lonely old widower, then?"

Her words were carried away on the wind, and Elinor leaned closer to catch them. "What did you say?"

Eyes sparkling, the actress cupped her hands against Elinor's ear. "Is the old gentleman married?"

Elinor wrinkled her forehead in surprise. "I thought you were set on wedding Patrick Tyrone? Isn't that why you are bent on preventing his marriage to Barbara?"

"What, marry Patrick? Not under heaven. Why would I be doing such a foolish thing as that? Just because I know it would be a mistake for him to marry that hoighty-toity quean doesn't mean I would make the same mistake meself. Patrick hasn't enough in him to give to two mistresses, and the stage will be enough of a wife for him."

Meanwhile, from behind the coach of the old earl, still another vehicle could be discerned.

The party in the lead was making quite good time under the whip hand of Lady Barbara, and she was well satisfied by that. "I see I shall have to take you in hand, my dear," she said smugly to her fiancé as she jiggled the reins and he listened sleepily. "There are a thousand things a gentleman knows from instinct that I daresay you must set yourself to learn. Since you are beginning so late in life, we shall have to make a drill of it, but I shall be patient and help you as much as ever I can." She patted his knee rather maternally. "There is that habit you have of sucking your teeth, you know, which is really most annoying."

"Do I suck my teeth?" asked Tyrone in surprise. "I never knew I did such a thing. I shall have to be careful not to allow it onstage."

Barbara chuckled. "You forget that you will not have to worry about *that* any longer."

"What do you mean?"

"My uncle, the duke, will be certain to settle a handsome allowance on me now that I am to be a married lady." She smiled contentedly.

Patrick was as contented as she. "Oh, I am forgetting

nothing, and that least of all. I love you, my adored, but the prospect of a dowry is an appealing one. Do you suppose it will be enough to inaugurate a company of my own? I am certain I can persuade Mrs. Mudge to join with us. She will be a great drawing card."

He did not notice that her ladyship was staring in disbelief. He went on enthusiastically. "Oh, my dearest, when you see the list of roles I have chosen for you, you will be delighted. Rosalind, for one. I know you will say you are still inexperienced, but your great beauty will carry whatever deficiencies there may be in your technique just at first. I am sure Mrs. Mudge will prove an admirable coach. She's played all the roles, you know. As to that, in Shakespeare it is the rhythm, you see. If you master the meter, the speeches all but play themselves."

Lady Barbara gaped at him dumbfounded. "Roles? Patrick, whatever do you mean?"

Tyrone coughed uneasily. "Mean, my dear? Why, I thought it was understood that your dowry would provide our step up in life. They love married acting partners, you know. I daresay they feel safe in finding respectability on the boards. Your family connexions will go a long way in that direction."

"Upon the boards? I am not going to exhibit myself on the stage, Patrick, dear."

It made him blink. "Not to act? But, my darling, of course you are. What else would you be doing? I do not think you would care to sit backstage and knit whilst I am onstage, Barbara. Much better to be sharing the plaudits of the crowd. So much less envy that way," he added shrewdly.

"Envy? Envy of what, pray?"

Patrick came close to blushing. "They *are* rather importunate, you know, my admirers. Sometimes they become quite carried away. Why are we stopping?" The horses champed the bit at the sudden halt. "We have no time to waste, if we are to have a good sleep before tomorrow's performance."

"There will be no performance tomorrow, Patrick," said Lady Barbara.

"Oh yes. You have forgotten that I play a matinee."

"There will be no matinee, dearest," she said firmly.

He all but laughed in her face. "Of course there will be a matinee. Did you think that just because I will be a new husband I can forget my duty? Edgar is a good chap, you see, but as an understudy—"

"You will not be acting again, Patrick. You must give up that queer notion. The nephew of the Duke of Towans upon the stage? How absurd. What would people think?"

"What would they think of a man who gave up his profession to live upon the gifts of his wife's family?" Patrick replied. "What they should really be thinking is that the duke's niece is demmed lucky to have such a clever and talented husband as her partner."

"We shall not exactly be partners, my dearest," Barbara said. There was evidence of a steely thread creeping into her tone. "Except in the conjugal sense, of course."

Tyrone's mouth all but dropped to his chest. "Bless my soul, girl, I believe you mean what you say."

"I always mean what I say. It makes life so much simpler, do you not agree, if one is straightforward? You must give up your profession."

He tried, against all reason, to placate her. "But, Barbara, what did you imagine marrying an actor would mean?"

"I never intended to marry 'an actor.' I meant to marry *you*." She did not even hear the implied insult to his ability. "I expect that you will sensibly give up the stage and become a gentleman as others have done. You cannot have seriously believed that I would jog about with you from town to town?"

The horses, feeling the laxness of the reins, had come to a complete halt as the two in the phaeton stared blankly at each another. Finally, Tyrone took the ribbons from the young woman's hands and turned the horses and equipage about to face again toward Cheyne Spa.

"As a matter of fact, that is exactly what I thought. Marrying an actor means becoming an actor's wife, Lady Barbara."

With his reversion to the formal mode of address a great chasm between them was acknowledged. Tyrone jiggled the reins, and the ears of the horses pricked up so that the bits of brass on their bridles rang merrily. Turning in this direction meant going home to a rubdown and careful currying by the stable man who loved them. Meanwhile, the two passengers carefully looked everywhere but at each other.

The time for unmasking had come, and Lady Elspeth cringed when the removal of a nearby Columbine mask revealed the person she particularly did not want to see. The animosity between herself and Evangeline Partridge was of no new inception and unchanged from when they were young. Even now, glancing furtively at one another, the old dislike flared. Yet, they were drawn to one another. Perhaps the ancient rivalry which had always kept them apart also lashed them inexorably together; through inconspicuous movements which seemed to have no purpose, they eventually found themselves face-to-face, each inspecting the other's countenance with minute care as if searching out and marking the inevitable inroads of time and weather.

Lady Elspeth would not be the first to speak. Considering herself the injured party of the pair, she felt that silence was her prerogative, although she was prepared to acknowledge any overture of the other woman. Because Mrs. Partridge did not at once see fit to make such a start, there was a long moment of stillness between them made more evident by the surrounding gaiety. Cecil's mother languidly waved her fan to and fro until it was clear that Lady

Elspeth would follow her usual custom. Even then Mrs. Partridge saw fit only to mention the atmosphere.

"It is very close. Between the crush and the candles, I expect the temperature has raised alarmingly," she said as if to no one in particular. Still, it needed more than this to draw out her ladyship; and at length Evangeline rolled her eyes ceilingward and pursed her lips into a beesting of annoyance. "I see, Elspeth, that nothing on God's earth will alter you." She looked her opponent up and down insolently.

Her ladyship was an old hand at this game and did not rise to such a lure, though it was difficult. She was well aware that beneath Evangeline's fluffy feminity dwelt a will of steel and complete self-devotion which placed any other consideration in the shade. The assumed air of helplessness, the clinging-vine approach to dealing with the world were invariably successful, even long after the victims had become aware they were being manipulated. This was not Lady Elspeth's way of doing things—she had not the necessary arsenal for such manoeuvres, but she recognised its effectiveness. Now she merely gazed back at Evangeline, who gave a disdainful little twist to her lips.

"I seem to remember that gown. I wish I had your talent for economy." She shrugged prettily. "And you are going to continue this silly feud, are you? Really, Elspeth, after all these years I should think you might have had time to reflect on your narrow escape." She inclined her head to indicate Gully a little distance away. "I cannot believe you still pine for that weasely creature. Think what it would have been like to be married to him instead of merely seeing him run off to help spend your nephew's inheritance."

"I was not alone in my infatuation, as I recall," Lady Elspeth said at last. "You also found him rather taking, I believe."

Evangeline Partridge laughed sharply. "All too taking. The night he disappeared, the pearls my father gave me vanished as well. If it is any comfort to you, I never cared a whit for him."

Lady Elspeth shook her head, watching as Gully and Cecil Partridge made their way toward her and Cecil's mother. "It is no comfort whatsoever," she said.

Cecil's expression changed to a fatuous smile of congratulation. "How fine it is to see the two of you in conversation at last." He indicated his companion. "Mother, you remember Mr. Gully, the M.P. from the duke's district?"

"Of course," said Mrs. Partridge with a perfectly calm demeanour. "Lady Elspeth, I daresay you remember him as well?"

Her ladyship could scarcely keep from smiling. Here was the lover who had betrayed her so long ago, now presented to her by the very woman with whom the betrayal had been accomplished, all with the surface of elegant manner which society required. How well Evangeline accomplished that, though it was all Elspeth could do to keep from laughing. Her former rival had been quite right about one thing, Gully *was* quite a weasely little man and Evangeline, quite lucky to have married Mr. Partridge after all. Certainly she had done so very quickly. The wretch had hardly run off to London before her betrothal was announced.

Something clicked within Lady Elspeth's brain. She could hardly believe that such a possibility had never occurred to her before. She looked from Gully's face to that of Cecil and back again. The same eyes. The same ugly nose. It was all there quite clearly before her.

Evangeline Partridge was staring at her now with something very like fear—or was it hate? Lady Elspeth needed no more confirmation to be assured that her conjecture was not mere imagining. Cecil was not a Hardy at all, not Partridge's son. He was, she was convinced, the son of the man who stood next to him: a tedious little politician who had never been any better than he should be. A number of explanations fell into place along with this assumption:

why Gully had so abruptly dropped his courtship of her when it would have stood him in excellent stead to be the brother-in-law of an earl; why Evangeline had always displayed such unvoiced hostility; perhaps even why her own brother had for so long dallied in the matter of acknowledging Cecil as his heir.

Lady Elspeth chuckled aloud as the others stared at her in confusion. "Never mind," she told them, "it is a jest not readily explained." Then, to the astonishment of all three, she leaned forward and placed a generous buss upon the cheek of her old opponent. "Bless you, Evangeline," she said, "for being exactly what you are."

How bright the music seemed now; how fresh the laughter.

The pair in the phaeton met the remainder of the procession only a mile or two after turning back toward Cheyne Spa. "What shall we do?" Lady Barbara asked, rather nervously for her. "What shall we tell them?"

Tyrone answered quite calmly. Since the stop mark had been put to their romance, he felt quite in command of himself again. "We shall merely say the truth, that we have made ourselves aware that we are, after all, unsuited for marriage. At least to each other," he added after a moment's reflection for he had spied the bright tresses of Mary Monaghan in the approaching cart.

His tone was so easy and held so little shadow of regret that her position was quickly brought home to Lady Barbara. Had she done the unforgivable thing at last in running away with this man who was at her side? Had she crossed the pale? Despite her former infatuation, she now saw that he was so little a gentleman as to profess no melancholy at their parting.

Good Lord, what had she done? Could she profess a touch of momentary madness? They had ridden off unchaperoned, it is true; but they had turned back. They were, on the other hand, being met by at least one and perhaps two young women who might find it to their own advantage to dim the lustre of Barbara's reputation. As the pony cart drew abreast of them and stopped, she could see that the look on Ben's face as well boded anything but good.

He handed the reins to Elinor Hardy and stepped purposefully from the cart, crossing the few feet to where Tyrone had drawn up. "Barbara," he said, "get down from there at once."

Her ladyship tossed her head. "Don't be absurd, Ben. Why should I? And who are these people? Why is Trevor with you and Miss Hardy?" She saw no reason now for continuing the fiction of a title for Elinor. "We are only out for a little drive in the evening air. As you can see, we are already on our way back to Cheyne."

"You are lucky, Barbara, to have friends who think of your reputation and welfare even if you do not. Now, if you please, get down from that phaeton and into the pony cart."

"I shall do no such thing. There is not enough room in there, and I do not like to be crowded."

Hearing this, Mary Monaghan rose from her seat and scrambled to the roadway. "I will gladly yield my place to your ladyship." Her eyes sought those of her fellow Hibernian. "Perhaps, indeed, we may exchange places."

Barbara regardly her coldly. "How very kind," she said in a chilly voice which implied that the young Irishwoman had no conceivable business putting her under obligation. Then Barbara looked hard at Elinor. "I suppose you felt compelled to save my reputation as well?"

"In a way," replied that young lady. "You see, Mr. Weymouth has done me the honour of asking me to marry him, and I felt it my duty to come along."

Few of those present knew of the existence of such a proposal, let alone its refusal. There was a concerted gasp of astonishment. All had come to think of Ben as Lady Barbara's personal property to be disposed of in whatever way she might see fit. This notion to the contrary left Barbara especially aghast.

"He cannot marry *you*," she blurted before she had leisure to consider the words. "Is this true, Ben?"

Mr. Weymouth did not hesitate to take advantage of the confusion. "It is true," he said. "I proposed marriage to Lady Elinor earlier this evening." He did not expand upon his statement; and, even as Lady Barbara glared speechlessly at him, two more vehicles could be seen rolling steadily along the road toward them. There were, it seemed, to be further witnesses to the lovely creature's downfall.

Barbara gazed from one to another of the group surrounding her and rubbed her eyes as might a small child awakening confused from a particularly vivid dream. "But Benjamin," she asked quite reasonably, "why did you follow us if you did not wish to save me for yourself? It does not make a great deal of sense to me."

"Trevor followed you as well," Weymouth pointed out, then stopped dead as if aware that he might be putting a dangerous thought into her head. He need not have worried about that, for Lady Barbara merely smiled kindly at their friend.

"Trev has always known it was impossible that he and I should marry," she said. "The question, dear Ben, was always whether it would be you or someone else." She gazed out into the starlit night along the highway, and her face brightened. "Aunt Augusta," she said thankfully. "She will know what is to be done." Barbara waved her arms in the air and called out, "Aunt! Here, here!" as if her brother-in-law, who was guiding the coach, could have missed the knot of people, animals and conveyances which quite blocked the road.

The coach drew alongside. Mawson leapt down to open the door and help his wife and her aunt to descend. The duchess glanced about with something very like wry amusement. "Will someone explain to me what is going on?"

Nearly everyone began to speak at once. Elinor alone was silent. "My dear," said the duchess to her unofficial ward, "will you not help make sense of all this?"

The others fell silent as Elinor laughed uneasily. "It is quite simple, duchess. Mr. Weymouth, Miss Monaghan and I started forth to save Lady Barbara from what we perceived to be the fruit of her folly. Mr. Quenton soon joined us, and we travelled as a perfectly respectable party upon a perfectly respectable errand. However, presumably Lady Barbara and Mr. Tyrone came to their own realization of their error with no assistance, for we encountered them here on their way back to Cheyne Spa."

The duchess seemed not entirely disapproving. "A perfectly respectable direction to be taking all in all," she remarked, then gazed with surprise at her niece who had dissolved in uncharacteristic tears.

"Ben has gone and foolishly affianced himself to—that creature!" Barbara wailed and pointed accusingly at Elinor.

"Is that true, granddaughter?" asked a booming masculine voice from the fourth vehicle which had drawn up quietly beside them. The earl stepped down. "I admit that I have little right to ask, but I am doing so in any case. Have you truly affianced yourself to young Weymouth there?"

Elinor found herself suddenly engulfed by a wave of love or kinship for the distinguished old man who walked toward her through the starlight. "No, Grandfather, I have not."

"Oh, what a howler!" cried Barbara incredulously. "Why, Ben, himself has just told me—"

"I merely told you," said Weymouth, "that I had proposed to Lady Elinor. I did not say that she was foolish enough to accept me."

"Not accept you? Who in the world does she think she

is?" Barbara bounded down from the phaeton and laid her hand on Ben's arm consolingly.

"Elinor is the granddaughter of the Earl of Glastonia," Barbara's aunt retorted sharply, "and consequently of a lineage which puts all of us in the position of mere children, hereditarily speaking. Remember yourself, Barbara, if you please."

The young woman so addressed pulled a face and pointed her lips coquettishly at the man beside her. "I think she is a very silly creature not to have accepted you, Ben. I see that I shall have to accept you myself if only to preserve you from such narrow escapes in future."

"I do not believe you have recently been asked, have you?" enquired the Countess Lavinia. She loved her younger sister but sometimes found her a great trial.

Lady Barbara searched Ben's face for sign of refusal. "I hope he will," she said quietly.

Ben smiled down at her as if the outcome were already an understood fact—as, indeed, perhaps it was.

=== 26 ===

LADY BASSINGBROOK LOOKED smugly around the gambling room. The crowd was heavy tonight, scarcely allowing enough room to move between the tables; and the clink of gold and silver falling into her coffers was a lovely sound. She was well aware that it had been a stroke of pure luck which made Tyger Dobyn a welcome addition to the staff. He was personable and popular and enjoyed a reputation for honesty rare among those in the profession. Lady Bassingbrook, clever though she was at operating close to the line, understood that honour is everything in a gambling house. Should a patron feel cheated, an illusion is destroyed; and the gamester will move on to other scenes of play.

The pugilist had been a fixture here for some three weeks now, and the flow of business had increased dramatically in the meantime. Lady Bassingbrook, who was not so ancient a lady as to be invulnerable to a personable man, congratulated herself on bringing off quite a coup in acquiring him. Unfortunately, their connexion was in the business realm alone. Try as she would, her flirtatiousness with him seemed to go unnoticed. He did his job. He was popular with the patrons, and the house showed a comfortable profit since his arrival. Yet, he seemed somehow aloof, at one remove from the business of living.

Lady Bassingbrook threaded her way across the room and ran appreciative fingers along the sleeve of the Tyger's beautifully tailored coat. "Shall I expect you for our usual small glass together, Tyger?"

"Certainly, your ladyship," said the boxer almost indifferently, "although I have an appointment later in the evening."

His employer bristled. "An appointment? With whom?" Several nearby players looked up in curiosity at her hostile tone, and the Tyger shot a sideways glance in her direction.

"It is a private appointment, madam, with a pair of young gentlemen."

The proprietress tossed her head disdainfully. "Ah, those *boys?* I fear they are becoming rather too much of a fixture here. It seems to me I cannot take a step without falling over one or the other of them."

Dobyn smiled sardonically. "I do not remember you refusing their money, madam. I am certain that would be an admirably effective way of discouraging them."

She laughed edgily. "Fie, sir. You are forever making jokes at my expense. The lads are always welcome, of course, so long as they pay their wagers." Her voice took on the shadow of a whine. "Only, need you spend so much time with them outside the club as well as in?"

It was obvious to the Tyger that their conversation was becoming of more interest to his fellow players than the game itself. He raised a hand to snap fingers at a subordinate a few feet away.

"Ransome, will you be good enough to take my place?"

"Certainly, sir."

The exchange was made, and Dobyn placed an imperative arm beneath her ladyship's elbow, leading her unobtrusively toward the counting room at one end of the floor. Once inside with the door closed behind them, he eyed her sourly.

"If you please, madam, there will be no more of that sort of thing where others can hear. I am neither your plaything nor your lapdog. I shall go where I like and at what hours and with whom I please. If such is unsatisfactory to you, I shall be happy to seek other employment since I have had one or two rather good offers in the last few days."

"Tyger!" she said reproachfully. "You wouldn't!"

"You may drive me to it."

Lady Bassingbrook fairly cringed, even though she knew such behaviour was the last thing in the world to win him. "But, dearest, I see so little of you."

The Tyger stared at her in disbelief. "Egad, woman, I spend twelve hours a day in this establishment. That should be enough to satisfy any employer's requirements."

"I never see you privately, I mean to say." She pouted. "I have so much, dear man. Is it so dreadful that I wish to share it with you?"

The hardness left Dobyn's eyes. Ever since the night he had so foolishly set off on a false trail toward Budolph—the night Elinor Hardy, though not marrying young Weymouth, had been restored to the bosom of her family and a position in the world far above any to which he could aspire—he had tried to put the lass out of his mind. Some in society might have chuckled at his scruple. When Elinor had been poor he would not have hesitated in the least to ask her to join forces with him. Now, as an eligible young heiress, she had drifted far beyond his reach. He was no miser, and he needed a rich helpmeet to live comfortably beyond his means. That helpmeet, however, would not be Elinor Hardy. He cared too much for her to allow such a state of things. Luckily, there would always be Lady Bassingbrooks in the world; and when this one or that had tired of him, or he of her, there would be another to fall back upon in times of adversity.

He smiled down at the woman beside him. "I am grateful, your ladyship, but I cannot be bound. Do you understand me?"

The gamestress sighed profoundly. "All too well, dear man. What you are saying is that we suit, but not perfectly."

"No," he agreed, "not perfectly."

Later, after their small glass and a shared bit of supper, as he once more cast a supervisory glance about the gambling rooms, his eye was caught by the appearance of a most unlikely trio of patrons. The old woman was strikingly familiar, but he could not put a name to her until she waved imperiously and called him by name. The pair of young bucks with her grinned broadly as well, and Dobyn made his way through the crowded room to join them.

"Acorn, Marston, how are you? I have just been having a chat about you. Are we still on for a bit of a carouse after closing?"

He bent over the hand of the elderly woman. "You will forgive me, madam. My eyes recall you, but my memory has let me down, I fear."

"I am Lady Elspeth Hardy, Mr. Dobyn, Elinor's great-aunt. You may remember our brief meeting a few months ago in Cheyne Spa."

The night of his pitiful ride to Budolph flashed painfully to mind. "Ah yes," he acknowledged. "A bit chilly for such an errand as I was upon." He indicated her two companions. "But what puts you into the way of two such scapegraces as these?"

She laughed. "I have decided that, even at my time of life, it is not too late to venture out of my shell. Who better to squire me around the hells of London than a pair of energetic young fellows? They know all the fashionable places and tire of hypocrisy as quickly as I do. We make an admirable trio in my view. What do you say, boys?"

"She has more energy than both of us," admitted Marston, "and she is insatiable for novelty. Would you mind, Tyger, if her ladyship came along to the mill? She has never witnessed boxing."

Tyger would have demurred. "I cannot believe that Lady Elspeth has come up to town to see two men batter each other about."

"No," said the earl's sister, "I am here for rather a different reason. My niece is being presented, you know.

Her comeout has been arranged under the patronage of the Duchess of Towans."

"I can imagine that will be a grand affair," Dobyn observed. "Lady Elinor will cut a swathe, I expect."

Lady Elspeth shooed the two young fellows off, then tucked her arm through Dobyn's. "You don't mind showing me around, do you? I know very little of such places as this."

"I will be happy to instruct you, your ladyship." He made an ironic half bow. "This is my own milieu after all. I fare better in it than in yours."

She nodded. "I hope you are a more proficient man at the tables than in love, sir. The evening I saw you last, you made some foolish moves."

They were strolling the room's perimeter quite like old confidantes.

"I remember that evening all too well, madam. Following the advice of a stable man, I gambled upon a shortcut and lost."

She allowed him an indulgent smile. "I believe there is said to be a reverse correlation between love and gambling. Perhaps that is why you are not a ruined man like most players."

"I was not aware that your ladyship knew so much of my world," he observed with a smile.

"Out of character, do you think?" she asked. "I would have suspected it might be said to run in the family, considering the infatuation of my late nephew with the cards and that Elinor herself later made it her way of living." Elspeth peered about her curiously. "What is that fascinating wheel which spins over there?"

"That is called *rouge et noir*, madam. There are also games of hazard, French hazard, macao, *dux bellorum*, E.O. and faro."

"Faro sounds a familiar ring in my head. An antique sort of name to suit an old lady such as myself."

The gambler in him warmed at the thought of a goose so

223

ready for the plucking, but the humanitarian side of his nature attempted dissuasion. "It is the sort of game which appears simpler than it is, my lady. The danger of addiction, I believe, is rather high because it is so deceptive."

"It seems to me that I recognise various of the faces there. It must be a popular pastime, this game."

"Oh, it is," he answered dryly.

"And that gentleman at that other table . . . ?"

"The hazard table, madam?"

"Do I not know him?"

When Tyger saw who it was she meant, his face grew very still. "Would I had the power to put him out of the club. Although Mr. Gully lost his seat in the election, Lady Bassingbrook allows him to retain it here. It is my belief that he clings to the skirts of Lady Luck only by the most scrabbling of fingers."

He noticed Lady Elspeth's nostrils flare oddly. "I think I should like to try my hand at this hazard," she said.

"It is not a game for beginners, I fear. You will do better to play at something safer," the Tyger warned. "You would be duelling with a notorious man and very likely to lose."

"Very likely I shall," she said cheerfully, "but I have a taste for settling an old score if I can."

He saw that she was determined. "Then let us be partners, and I shall stand ready at the rescue should you sink too deep."

She preceded Dobyn to the table and stood watching till she believed she had the way of it, being careful not to indicate by so much as a glance that she recognised Mr. Gully. In fact, he looked quite dreadful, as if his fall from political grace had taken a heavy toll. His eyes were sunken, his face had a sickly off-white pallour; and, worst of all in that place, his linen was none too clean and his coat stained with careless droppings of food and tobacco. He had not stirred from his place at the table in some time, and he did not even glance up when Lady Elspeth took her place.

Gully's eyes followed only the bounce of the dice as they fell from the casting-box.

That box went from player to player. Each who took it named a sum as his stake and placed it on the table. The others of the company, any who wished to join in the wager, then matched the caster's sum before he tossed. The winning or loss, of course, was dependent upon the luck of the throw.

When the casting-box reached Gully, the former parliamentarian hesitated for a long moment before laying out his stake upon the table before him. One by one, the others withdrew. Perhaps they were disinclined to test their own luck by betting against what they guessed to be the last of his capital.

When he realised what was taking place, Gully darted fierce glances about and snarled. "Are all of you such poor sports that you will not cover me? What is it? Do you fear the curse of the losing player?" The others of the company either looked away or guiltily studied their well-manicured hands.

"Will no one wager?" Gully demanded again in an unsteady voice which said much of his condition.

"I will play against you, sir."

The calm voice was in direct contrast to his own. Lady Elspeth Hardy sat down at the table, her face expressionless. Despite her professed ignorance of gambling, her movements exhibited that economy which speaks of long acquaintance with a craft. Opening her reticule, she removed a sum of money, called for a rouleau and covered Gully's wager. Tyger, who only a few moments since might have advised that she stick to her petit point, now held his tongue.

At length, Gully recognised her. He sneered into the aged face. "Getting your own back are you, Lady Elspeth? Twenty years is a long while to cherish revenge."

"You trouble yourself unduly, sir," her ladyship replied. "It has been a welcome period of retirement. Setting aside any personal differences between us, I have another score to settle."

Gully laughed harshly, his discoloured teeth more closely resembling the canines of an animal than those of a man. There was, indeed, something very wolfish about him in his hour of near desperation.

"Some fancied wrong, I imagine?"

Her ladyship smiled, but it was a cold and wintery gaze she cast upon him. "You wagered against my dear nevvy when he was too foxed with drink to know what he was doing or to judge how best to go about it. You ruined him, although you professed to be his friend."

Gully's bloodshot eyes widened with bitter amusement. "And now you propose to ruin me, madam?"

"Ruin you? No, for we know that hazard is a game of pure chance. I would not be so proud. Make your cast, sir, if you please."

Gully hesitated a moment, then steeled himself and called his main, the point he would go for. "Seven," he said, "with a nick of eleven."

If either number appeared he would gather up his stake and that of his adversary. Then the casting-box would pass to Lady Elspeth.

"I say, Tyger, what is the old gel up to?" asked John Acorn in Dobyn's ear.

"I am not certain. If it be revenge, I can only fear for her. Gully is a demmed lucky chap sometimes. I have seen him wriggle out of worse scrapes than this."

"Well, she will have lost only money," said Marston in his other ear. "She can afford it."

"No," the Tyger murmured. "I do not think that the money is important. She wishes merely to see his defeat, and he would hate such a thing before her as before no other."

"Point," called the resplendently uniformed usher. "Take your stake, sir, if you please. Madam, will you wager?"

226

"I will," said the old woman in a clear, ringing voice and laid out five golden guineas.

Gully sneered and matched them from the hoard he had just won. "Conservative to the end, eh? It is your cross, Elspeth."

Lady Elspeth rattled the box professionally and made her call. "Six," she said, which gave her a nick of twelve.

Double sixes tumbled out upon the baize.

"Gad, she throws well," marvelled Marston. "She has taken our lessons splendidly, Corny." Young Acorn watched in fascination. "One would think she had been playing every day for years."

"Perhaps she has done just that," said a softer, more feminine voice. "I expect we all have our secret vices."

The Tyger did not turn around for a moment, though he recognised the voice instantly. He did not, in fact, trust himself. He was too much tempted to sweep the speaker into his arms, which might easily prove embarrassing if she had by now allied herself with another. Instead he turned slowly, being careful not to betray his feelings.

"Good evening, Miss Hardy," he greeted her. "What a pleasant and unexpected surprise it is to see you."

"Unexpected?" she asked. "Well, perhaps so. However, truly, if you would not come to me, sir, I had no option but to beard you in your den." She looked about appraisingly. "It seems to have changed very little here except to become more crowded. You must have proved a great attraction."

Jenks, the serving man, edged forward a tray. "Will you have wine, miss?" He peered at her more closely. "Bless me. Is it Miss Elinor?"

"It is," she agreed. "How have you been?"

Jenks shrugged. "Oh, much the same, but I hear tell you have prospered all out of mind. Come into a fortune, they say."

"I have been reunited with my family," she replied. "That is a very great thing to me."

The Tyger was careful to say nothing at all, knowing that Jenks would relay any word of his to the counting room where Lady Bassingbrook without doubt still lay in wait. A screaming scene would undoubtedly ensue, and Dobyn preferred to avoid that if possible.

"Take your stake, sir, if you please," said the usher to Mr. Gully. "Will you cast, madam?"

Jenks slid away to drift with apparent nonchalance toward the counting room. The Tyger could wait no longer. The implications of what Elinor had said to Jenks were too strong.

"I daresay that now your grandfather has settled on you, you may marry any one of those young sparks, even though you decided against young Weymouth."

"Yes, I hope to do just that," she answered.

"Will you cast, sir?" asked the usher of Gully.

Tyger Dobyn found himself fairly forcing out the next, shamefully obvious question. "Whom have you decided upon, may I ask? Young Quenton, perhaps?"

Meanwhile, Gully's voice trembled with triumph and not a little bravado. He had taken away Lady Elspeth's full rouleau and proposed to make the most of his moment. "I will wager all of it," he answered.

The usher's face remained impassive, and her ladyship motioned for another roll of coins to cover Gully.

"No," Elinor answered Tyger as if oblivious to the drama before them, as the gasping, avaricious crowd thrust forward to be as close as possible to this savage ritual. "I came to London for my comeout, you know, but also looking for you. I fancy there is unfinished business between us. Am I wrong?"

"Between us?" Dobyn asked rather stupidly. "I cannot say anything to you now. You know that. You have moved too far away from me."

"I thought you always meant to marry advantageously?" Elinor asked mischievously. "Will I not do as well as any other?"

The gamester's jaw clenched, and he spoke tersely. "Anyone else. Not you."

"Why not? Because the world would say that you loved my money, not me?"

"Yes," said the Tyger. "They would be at our backs, and you would never know how much attention to pay them."

"But do you love me, sir?"

He looked at the young woman in amazement. Elinor was not being girlish or flirtatious. On the contrary, he could see she was quite serious.

"I know it is a monstrously forward question," she added. "But do you?"

He could feel his resistance melting away in the warmth of her regard. Dobyn lifted a finger to trace the soft line of her cheek. "Too much to want the world to ever doubt it."

The young woman nodded in satisfaction. "Well, then, we can be married on Monday week, if you like. Or we could run away to Gretna this very night."

At the hazard table came a long groan from the crowd. "You have not made your point, madam, you may cast again."

Dobyn flushed. "Do not toy with me." There was a sharp edge to his words. "Go off and buy some young lad your own age, not a washed-out creature such as I am. You may not love him, but you can grow into marriage with him. You and I cannot afford each other, for you have too much money and I have none at all. If we married, I would lose my pride, and that is all the capital I have left."

Elinor looked at him in disgust. "What fools you men are," she said with exasperation. "I have no great fortune if that is what prevents us."

A smattering of cheers arose from the hazard table.

"Do you mean to say the old man has given you no money?" he asked above the noise. "I had believed that you and your grandfather—"

"Oh, we are quite reconciled," she said. "He is a dear old fellow, but there are responsibilities beyond those he has toward me. The bulk of his estate will go with the title to Cousin Cecil, I suppose."

"And you?"

Elinor shrugged as if it were of little consequence. "Oh, I am comfortable, but far from rich. A long way from being an heiress."

The crowd about the hazard table parted to reveal Gully with his head on his hands and Lady Elspeth triumphant. "Tyger!" she cried. "We have won! Come take your tip." She proffered a double handful of golden guineas. Then she looked shrewdly from Elinor to Tyger.

"Well, has the gel convinced you?"

"Almost, madam," the gentleman fighter acknowledged. He turned to Elinor. "If I am to be a rich man at poor Gully's expense," he said indicating the gold before him in Lady Elspeth's hands, "I suppose I must take a wife to manage me."

"I am certain that it is the wisest course," the young woman said, "but are you wise enough to follow it?"

The Tyger bent toward her, and his voice grew husky. "I love you, you demmed beautiful little witch," he said. "And as far as the wisdom of it goes, I should be a demmed fool if I did not."

FIERY ROMANCE

CALIFORNIA CARESS (2771, $3.75)
by Rebecca Sinclair

Hope Bennett was determined to save her brother's life. And if that meant paying notorious gunslinger Drake Frazier to take his place in a fight, she'd barter her last gold nugget. But Hope soon discovered she'd have to give the handsome rattlesnake more than riches if she wanted his help. His improper demands infuriated her; even as she luxuriated in the tantalizing heat of his embrace, she refused to yield to her desires.

ARIZONA CAPTIVE (2718, $3.75)
by Laree Bryant

Logan Powers had always taken his role as a lady-killer very seriously and no woman was going to change that. Not even the breathtakingly beautiful Callie Nolan with her luxuriant black hair and startling blue eyes. Logan might have considered a lusty romp with her but it was apparent she was a lady, through and through. Hard as he tried, Logan couldn't resist wanting to take her warm slender body in his arms and hold her close to his heart forever.

DECEPTION'S EMBRACE (2720, $3.75)
by Jeanne Hansen

Terrified heiress Katrina Montgomery fled Memphis with what little she could carry and headed west, hiding in a freight car. By the time she reached Kansas City, she was feeling almost safe . . . until the handsomest man she'd ever seen entered the car and swept her into his embrace. She didn't know who he was or why he refused to let her go, but when she gazed into his eyes, she somehow knew she could trust him with her life . . . and her heart.

Available wherever paperbacks are sold, or order direct from the Publisher. Send cover price plus 50¢ per copy for mailing and handling to Zebra Books, Dept. 3247, 475 Park Avenue South, New York, N.Y. 10016. Residents of New York, New Jersey and Pennsylvania must include sales tax. DO NOT SEND CASH.

ROMANCE REIGNS
WITH ZEBRA BOOKS!

SILVER ROSE (2275, $3.95)
by Penelope Neri
Fleeing her lecherous boss, Silver Dupres disguised herself as a boy and joined an expedition to chart the wild Colorado River. But with one glance at Jesse Wilder, the explorers' rugged, towering scout, Silver knew she'd have to abandon her protective masquerade or else be consumed by her raging unfulfilled desire!

STARLIT ECSTASY (2134, $3.95)
by Phoebe Conn
Cold-hearted heiress Alicia Caldwell swore that Rafael Ramirez, San Francisco's most successful attorney, would never win her money . . . or her love. But before she could refuse him, she was shamelessly clasped against Rafael's muscular chest and hungrily matching his relentless ardor!

LOVING LIES (2034, $3.95)
by Penelope Neri
When she agreed to wed Joel McCaleb, Seraphina wanted nothing more than to gain her best friend's inheritance. But then she saw the virile stranger . . . and the green-eyed beauty knew she'd never be able to escape the rapture of his kiss and the sweet agony of his caress.

EMERALD FIRE (3193, $4.50)
by Phoebe Conn
When his brother died for loving gorgeous Bianca Antonelli, Evan Sinclair swore to find the killer by seducing the tempress who lured him to his death. But once the blond witch willingly surrendered all he sought, Evan's lust for revenge gave way to the desire for unrestrained rapture.

SEA JEWEL (3013, $4.50)
by Penelope Neri
Hot-tempered Alaric had long planned the humiliation of Freya, the daughter of the most hated foe. He'd make the wench from across the ocean his lowly bedchamber slave—but he never suspected she would become the mistress of his heart, his treasured SEA JEWEL.

Available wherever paperbacks are sold, or order direct from the Publisher. Send cover price plus 50¢ per copy for mailing and handling to Zebra Books, Dept. 3247, 475 Park Avenue South, New York, N.Y. 10016. Residents of New York, New Jersey and Pennsylvania must include sales tax. DO NOT SEND CASH.

CATCH UP ON THE BEST IN CONTEMPORARY FICTION FROM ZEBRA BOOKS!

LOVE AFFAIR   (2181, $4.50)
by Syrell Rogovin Leahy
A poignant, supremely romantic story of an innocent young woman with a tragic past on her own in New York, and the seasoned newspaper reporter who vows to protect her from the harsh truths of the big city with his experience — and his love.

ROOMMATES   (2156, $4.50)
by Katherine Stone
No one could have prepared Carrie for the monumental changes she would face when she met her new circle of friends at Stanford University. For once their lives intertwined and became woven into the tapestry of the times, they would never be the same.

MARITAL AFFAIRS   (2033, $4.50)
by Sharleen Cooper Cohen
Everything the golden couple Liza and Jason Greene touched was charmed — except their marriage. And when Jason's thirst for glory led him to infidelity, Liza struck back in the only way possible.

RICH IS BEST   (1924, $4.50)
by Julie Ellis
From Palm Springs to Paris, from Monte Carlo to New York City, wealthy and powerful Diane Carstairs plays a ruthless game, living a life on the edge between danger and decadence. But when caught in a battle for the unobtainable, she gambles with the only thing she owns that she cannot control — her heart.

THE FLOWER GARDEN   (1396, $3.95)
by Margaret Pemberton
Born and bred in the opulent world of political high society, Nancy Leigh flees from her politician husband to the exotic island of Madeira. Irresistibly drawn to the arms of Ramon Sanford, the son of her father's deadliest enemy, Nancy is forced to make a dangerous choice between her family's honor and her heart's most fervent desire!

Available wherever paperbacks are sold, or order direct from the Publisher. Send cover price plus 50¢ per copy for mailing and handling to Zebra Books, Dept. 3247, 475 Park Avenue South, New York, N.Y. 10016. Residents of New York, New Jersey and Pennsylvania must include sales tax. DO NOT SEND CASH.